# THE CON CASE

## ALICE WHITE INVESTIGATOR BOOK THREE

## MARC HIRSCH

Copyright © 2018 by Marc Hirsch
All rights reserved. This book or any portion thereof
may not be reproduced or used in any manner whatsoever
without the express written permission of the publisher
except for the use of brief quotations in a book review.

Printed in the United States of America

First Printing, 2018

ISBN 978-1982091989

www.marchirsch.com

# TABLE OF CONTENTS

CHAPTER 1: Laundry Day......................Page 1

CHAPTER 2: Lovely Lady.....................Page 10

CHAPTER 3: Security.........…..….……...Page 24

CHAPTER 4: Eddy………..….………...Page 36

CHAPTER 5: The Interview…...….………Page 53

CHAPTER 6: Ride in the Country..…….....Page 69

CHAPTER 7: Massage….....…….....……..Page 81

CHAPTER 8: Bouncer..………......….……..Page 98

CHAPTER 9: Setting the Hook…….……...Page 115

CHAPTER 10: Awakening…....…..……..Page 126

CHAPTER 11: Family Reunion..…..……..Page 152

CHAPTER 12: On Advice of Council..…….Page 172

CHAPTER 13: Two Lions…………..…......Page 185

CHAPTER 14: On the Range….…..……...Page 198

CHAPTER 15: At the Post.....................Page 208

CHAPTER 16: Funeral……...………......Page 221

CHAPTER 17: Bachelorette…..……..…..Page 227

CHAPTER 18: Bags…………….…….…..Page 239

CHAPTER 19: Vice Cop……...…….…....Page 253

CHAPTER 20: Windows..……..…….…....Page 265

CHAPTER 21: About Adam……….…....Page 274

CHAPTER 22: Ground Rush……….…...Page 285

CHAPTER 23: Snitch....…….….…….…..Page 295

CHAPTER 24: At the Track……….……..Page 305

CHAPTER 25: And They're Off....….…...Page 319

CHAPTER 26: Captivity.....….….……...Page 332

CHAPTER 27: Freedom....….………..…..Page 344

CHAPTER 28: Island in the Pacific..….…..Page 365

CHAPTER 29: Luigi's Italian Restaurant & Bar....Page 374

CHAPTER 30: Bedtime…………....…....Page 389

# CHAPTER 1

## LAUNDRY DAY

Alice balled her hands into fists, brought her right knee to her chest, pivoted, and shot the heel of her sneakered foot into the struggling washing machine, just below the coin slide, a perfect shot. The blow resounded through the otherwise silent basement but did nothing to abate the grind of failing gears. Toshiro Mifune used that kick in a movie she had seen last month at the Japanese film festival in Manhattan. His kick broke the man's chest and knocked him out. Hers, on the other hand, was an exercise in futility. The machine paused briefly, then transitioned to a worse rattle, threatening to quit altogether, thumbing its nose at her. She kicked it again with no form at all, and it begrudgingly settled into a sort of steady hum.

It was Monday night, the only time Alice had to do her sheets, towels, and assorted laundry.

"What?" Henry Jones, the building superintendent, entered the laundry room. "That machine on the fritz again?"

He had popped in to investigate the noise of her assault on one of his precious washers.

"What do you mean 'again'?" Alice asked him. "It's been hanging on by a thread for the entire past year. I expect soon you'll rig up a bicycle for us to generate the electricity to run it. What's your next move, stealing parts from up the block?"

"Sorry, Miss White. Really. I have been trying to get the owner to turn loose with some cash for new ones. I think it's safe to say they got their money's worth out of these. I'll keep at it. Meantime, here's some change to take the sting out." He handed her a fistful of change he had removed earlier from the metal boxes under the coin slides.

"Gosh, thanks, Mr. J. You sure know how to treat a lady. Mrs. J. is one lucky woman."

"I like to think so, Miss White, but I'm not sure she sees it that way. Thanks for understanding my situation. Who knows? One of these days, you might be surprised by a couple of new machines. Of course, they'll probably take more money. The owner's a real humanitarian. Take it easy now."

Alice took her cleaned and dried laundry back to her one-bedroom apartment. She and Jim Peters were still in negotiation about whose place to cohabit, but the odds were stacked against her humble abode here in the North Bronx. It made far more sense for them to live in Jim's fortress on the tenth floor of a commercial structure near Broadway, where he worked constructing stage sets. Not to mention, she worked in Manhattan also. She wondered what made it so hard for her to give up this little Italian neighborhood, such a long commute to her office.

She was ambivalent about graduating from NYU Law because she had gotten used to the routine of nights at school and days working as a secretary and the sole investigator for a law firm in a seedy part of Nassau Street in Manhattan. Aside from disrupting her schedule, graduation marked the beginning of intense study for the New York State Bar.

After her recent depressing experience trying, and failing, to save the life of her neighbor Harry Applewood, Alice had considered changing her focus from criminal law to one of the less violent specialties, like taxes, copyrights, or estate planning. Thus, she could avoid lectures from her protector, Antonio Vargas, about surrendering to her darker side in an inevitable future of dealing with violent criminals. This last year had been loaded with electives. There were courses in trusts, taxes, and domestic relations, and, to satisfy herself that she did not want to join a large firm, she had studied securities regulation and antitrust law. At times she wondered if she was even cut out for the law, let alone working for a big-time law firm with dozens of other lawyers. She could just quit and get a job at a beauty parlor or in construction. But seriously? No. She was not giving up on her dream.

She sat down at the table in her kitchen and cracked a textbook. The radiator pipes made a reassuring series of hisses and bangs, adjusting to mystical variations in the flow of steam from the boiler in the basement. Henry Jones must have just shoveled a load of coal into the firebox. A pie tin half-filled with water sat on the radiator, humidifying the air. Winter in New York City took a degree of effort she did not miss in the spring and summer, but she loved the change of seasons and rejected the idea of full-time residence in the tropics, where the heat never let up, and the cockroaches needed saddles.

In a matter of months she would graduate. Showing her boyfriend off at special events hosted by the school for her and her classmates had posed the question: Did Jim even own a jacket and tie? She would have to help him pick them out and supervise him ironing a collared shirt. As she'd told him when they met, she ironed shirts for no man, but she was willing to kibitz from the sideline to make sure he didn't burn the shirt or himself.

# 5 | The Con Case

Stanley Kramer tramped down the snow-laden street. He wore mittens. His hands were curled inside to keep them from freezing in the biting cold. A sheepskin hat covered his head, flaps down over his ears. His brown leather jacket's fur collar was turned up and wrapped with a scarf that covered his nose and mouth. He wore black rubber galoshes over his shoes that allowed snow over their tops, which numbed his feet. He hated winter in this northernmost borough of New York City called the Bronx. It depressed him every year, and he figured it always would.

The curly haired young man turned into an alley, lined on one side by a row of dented metal trash cans, and emerged into the even more depressing, soot-blackened courtyard behind where Susan lived. She was Catholic, twenty-one, a year younger than him. Her father was never home. Daddy spent his time after work on a construction site in bars with women who were not Susan's mother. Susan's mother took the subway before dawn to a factory in the garment district of Manhattan, where she operated a sewing machine for long hours, at low pay, in unsafe conditions. The owners had learned nothing from the Triangle Shirtwaist Factory fire of 1911, in which 146 garment workers lost their lives.

Susan kept house for herself and her parents when she got home from working all morning and afternoon as a diner waitress. She made the beds, washed the floors, did the laundry, and put dinner on the table for herself and her mother, with leftovers for her father if he returned home on a given night.

There was plenty of time before her mother returned from the factory. Whenever Stanley yearned for Susan's company, he took the train to the Bronx from his studies at St. John's College and knocked on her door. He hoped he'd be in time to catch her before she changed out of her waitress outfit.

She worked a bus ride away. Her boss, the lascivious Greek owner Demetrius Geonopolis, had dreamed up this demeaning uniform for his female staff, consisting of a white blouse, a short plaid skirt, and knee socks, in an attempt to make them look like Catholic schoolgirls, but it succeeded only in making them look like hookers dressed like Catholic schoolgirls. Susan would glance in the mirror behind the counter while she cleared dishes and often caught customers staring at her from behind. She had to find a job where she got more respect.

Susan thought the uniform was sick, but she needed the money, so she put it on. Stanley seemed incapable of resisting the sight of her in that getup, so she wore it as long as she could when she got home, in the hope that he would show up. She made the beds and stuffed dirty clothes into pillowcases to take to the building's laundry room. She looked over her shoulder and checked herself out in a full-length mirror to see what it looked like when she bent forward. She could see why the sight so took Stanley. It was gross but effective. She did not like being alone, especially in this grim basement apartment.

The diner drew a massive, mostly male crowd seven days a week. It closed early on Sundays. Only the most hardened women felt comfortable in the leering Greek's place. She herself usually walked a few blocks to a sandwich shop for something to eat after work. On the days Stanley didn't appear, Susan took care of the preliminaries of cleaning her family's squalid two-bedroom apartment, then changed out of her uniform into more comfortable denim and a sweatshirt.

*Knock. Knock.* Susan opened the front door, trying not to appear overanxious. She was particularly hungry for human contact today.

"Susan, you are a sight for sore eyes," Stanley told her. He took in the sight of her eager face, the curve of her body, her adorable knee socks.

"You too, Stanley. Get in here."

She grabbed the front of his jacket, pulled him in, and shut the door behind him.

He had waited too many days to see her—just

too lazy to get on the train, he guessed. She was an oasis in his otherwise depressing existence. They were made for each other. She never knew when to expect him. She chalked it up to the selfishness of his youth. Men took longer to grow up, she decided.

He put his hand on her shoulder to balance himself while he peeled the wet rubbers off his shoes and dropped them in the hallway. He hung his hat and jacket on a peg on the wall. She took his hand and led him to the dining and living room, where she sat him down on one of the chairs at the dark wooden table and put a glass of water in front of him.

She had spotted him in a neighborhood candy store one afternoon, a year ago, and brazenly taken him home. Now he looked at her with those sad, hungry brown eyes. She needed to be wanted, and, from the moment they'd met, she could tell he wanted her.

She began their usual ritual by fetching a mop and bucket. Aside from the old rectangular dining table, the apartment's central room had six spindle-backed chairs surrounding it and a couch in poor repair. A lone ceiling fixture cast insufficient light over the room. Stanley relaxed and warmed himself in the steam heat after his long subway ride and frigid walk while Susan took her empty bucket to the kitchen alcove to fill it. She shook scouring powder into the pail, then ran water into it. She carried the vessel back into the room, plunged the mop into its soapy water, wrung it out with her strong hands, then went to work on the floor.

She guessed he would never take her out on a real date, let alone ask her to marry him. That was a laugh, but she didn't care. He seemed to respect her and was willing to take steps not to get her pregnant. He derived such obvious pleasure from her company that she was compelled to sell herself short to please him. When she was done with the floor, she left the mop in the bucket leaning against the wall, took his hand, and led him to her bedroom.

They hardly spoke during these encounters. He would show up unannounced a few times a week if she was lucky. Afterward, she would put on her less formal clothes, and he would leave. She knew what he wanted from her was only physical, but, sadly, it was better than nothing.

He had to get back to his mysterious existence as a college student. Neither of them knew when it would end. Before that happened, they were determined to wrest whatever animal warmth they could from each other.

He was gone. It was time for her to get serious about finishing the cleaning and putting supper on the table.

# CHAPTER 2

## LOVELY LADY

Helen Parker was a vision of loveliness. Her skin was pale, unblemished, and smooth as a baby's bottom, the result of ongoing care by the most expensive dermatologists and plastic surgeons. Her blond hair was pinned away from her ears, revealing diamond stud earrings attached by posts through pierced lobes. Her striking blue eyes, turned blue by contact lenses designed for the purpose, were framed by lashes thickened with mascara perfectly applied. She wore a short black-silk dress with a matching jacket. The full-length mink coat he had given her hung on a special rack in the manager's office. A northeasterly January wind was blowing down 53rd Street. The coat had shielded her from it as they crossed the sidewalk from the limousine. A strand of pearls circled her neck. The black seams of her stockings rose out of expensive black leather high-heeled pumps over perfectly shaped legs. Patrons and staff of the luxurious restaurant tried not to stare.

The Stork Club was established in New York City in the 1920s by a bootlegger from Oklahoma named Sherman Billingsley. After several moves, it had settled on 53rd Street, east of Fifth Avenue.

Before leaving the hotel for dinner, Nadine had showered with her sixty-year-old companion. She shaved her legs while he looked on. She soaped his back and had him soap hers. After they dried off, she had him pour them each a glass of champagne. She controlled the speed of his lovemaking, maintaining the illusion that he was in complete charge. Then, with the impeccable timing of a paid professional, she turned the tables on him and cleaned his clock, just as she had done with dozens of other men at the direction of her employer.

Nadine Byrkowski was not a prostitute in the conventional sense of the word. She had been trained by the man she worked for to do his bidding with any man, or woman, he set her upon.

In exchange for absolute obedience, Nadine's desperate life as a street-walking junkie, living hand to mouth one step ahead of the law, had been transformed into one of apparent wealth and luxury. She rode in the back of chauffeur-driven limousines. She was assisted regularly by Rivka, a mature older woman, in picking out appropriate attire for day- and nightwear. Her hair was professionally colored every few weeks, more often if necessary. When possible, a cosmetologist made her up, but she had been trained to do it herself when the situation required, as it had tonight. After her daily workout and steam on most days, she was massaged by Maurice. She loved Maurice like a brother and completely trusted him with her naked body. He had no interest in women and was kept satisfied by a series of male escorts provided by their mutual employer.

"Helen, may I say, you look sensational tonight," Abraham Schumann told his date. He used the name Helen Parker, which she had given him when they first met by apparent accident at a Carnegie Hall concert. Mozart. They now shared a booth in the VIP room of this famous East Side establishment. Before them on a white linen cloth stood a flute of champagne for her and a bourbon on the rocks for him. Caviar and its fixings were arrayed on a platter with gold hardware. The discarded shells of eleven raw oysters were piled on a plate. Nadine dropped the last shell on the pile, and a busboy promptly whisked them away.

She smiled and gazed at her mark with feigned satisfaction, theoretically resulting from his masterful behavior in the bedroom earlier. She had practiced the look in a mirror with Rivka many times.

Abraham's face radiated the pride she was hoping to elicit. Men were all alike, especially married men stepping out on their wives. They were so easy to manipulate. A touch of the hand. A little flattery. She was getting bored with this life. Several times in these situations, things had turned wrong, absolutely not her fault. Her boss paid her hospital bills. Once a target had shot her. Once she had been stabbed by a wife nobody knew existed. There were major scenes in fancy restaurants when the mark had caught wise because of Nadine's sloppiness—from too much alcohol, she admitted. She had paid dearly for those, and her boss covered the medical expenses for the damage he himself had inflicted. Now, the two couples at the next table looked like they were just in from out of town with their spouses and friends for a good time. They were, in fact, her protection against the mayhem these kinds of situations sometimes incited. Whenever she was on assignment, people were kept close at hand to protect her, if they could, so she could concentrate on the part she was supposed to play. She had so much to remember, especially with this guy.

"You take my breath away, Abraham," she said. "No man has ever handled me the way you do." She smiled at him through the nausea. "You make me feel safe. I can, at least for a while, forget my troubles. I feel like a princess in your company."

"I don't know what to say to you, Helen. A woman with your looks must have many suitors knocking on her door. You seem so comfortable with me. I naturally assumed you felt that way with any man you've been close to."

"That's not true, Abraham. You are the first man I've allowed into my bed in years. I haven't felt safe since my father attacked me when I was a teenager." She resisted the urge to burst into laughter. Men just ate that story up—the pretty blond teenager at home, alone with her lascivious father.

"Helen. You don't have to say another word. I'm sorry for my suggestion that you dated many men. Please forgive me."

Abraham had assembled a portfolio on Miss Helen Parker. For a price paid by her employer, his investigator had passed him the carefully crafted biography that had been painstakingly memorized by Nadine Byrkowski. It told of a single, independently wealthy young woman who had been left a fortune by her late father, the completely fictitious Douglas Parker. It documented travel around the world looking for distraction and—the report implied— of a sadly, unsuccessful search for love. He now reversed his assumption that she had been serially promiscuous. An honest mistake. It heightened his appreciation of her receptivity to his advances. How wrong could he have been? The file alluded to a childhood trauma, possibly at the hands of her father. No further details were available or necessary. A sexual attack by a parent certainly qualified as a trauma that someone with Helen Parker's looks and means would go to great lengths to conceal. Schumann was ashamed at his supposition.

"Abraham, we've only just met. I hardly know you, but I feel I can trust you. I'm so glad."

"I didn't mean to pry, Helen. Accept my apologies. I will always be there to listen if you feel the need to talk."

"Well, Abraham," she told him coquettishly, "I will forgive you if you feed me, ply me with a glass of suitable vintage wine, and take me back to the hotel. We have unfinished business to attend."

---

Michael Pope opened his eyes inside his sleeping mask. He took inventory and grasped the unfortunate reality that, although he ruled an empire, he was just as unhappy as when he had gone to bed. Wealth and power were not what he thought they would be. Neither could he find satisfaction in the company of sycophants or the beautiful women who depended on him for their survival. He could not scratch the itch of discontent driving him to distraction. More and more, he turned to the whiskey bottle and the opium pipe for relief, but even they no longer worked. They only succeeded in fogging his brain and leaving him victim to frequent hangovers and bouts of melancholy. He was concerned he might take his own life.

He surveyed his body. Nausea, muscle aches, and a splitting headache were this morning's punishment for last night's overindulgence.

"Mr. P.," came an overly enthusiastic voice from the other side of the mask. "Time to get up and get it together." This was Leonard Sabrinkoff, his personal trainer.

The scrape of the curtains being drawn got Pope's pained attention. He imagined the view of the Upper East Side from the top floor of his two-story penthouse. He did not want to get up.

The trainer lifted the edge of his mask.

"God, Len, that's extremely bright. Why don't you just shoot me and get it over with? Better yet, close the curtains and let me go back to sleep."

"I have just the thing for you, my good man." Leonard ignored his boss's plea. "Sit up," he ordered Pope, who did as he was told.

Pope accepted a tumbler of vodka, tomato juice, Tabasco, and Worcestershire, topped with a pinch of salt—the perfect Bloody Mary—along with a handful of aspirin. He tossed back the aspirin and washed them down with the entire contents of the glass in a few large gulps. He handed the empty vessel to his trainer.

"Lenny, you are a prince among men. I need to drive these blues away, and physical exertion is just the ticket on a dreary winter morning like this. I don't know what it is, man. I just can't generate enthusiasm for anything. Hungover every morning is not how I envisioned success."

"Quit your bellyaching. That's the problem with having everything you could ever want," Leonard retorted. "You've got to shut your mind down, turn it off for a while. Take a few minutes to stop scheming and manipulating. Understand, paisano?"

"You are so lucky I let you talk to me that way," Pope told his steroid-enhanced, artificially tanned trainer and bodyguard. Leonard usually rode shotgun in the front of Pope's limo. The tinted divider window often went up to give the boss privacy with whomever he brought along for company, and sometimes intimacy.

In truth, Pope's heart belonged to only one woman. Her name was Darlene. He could not be with her now, not yet. She was stashed away. No one knew where. They conversed briefly, on a regular schedule, by covert means they'd arranged before they had separated. In the meantime, he would have to settle for the company of women half Darlene's age on his payroll.

"What are you gonna do about it?" Lenny broke into his boss's fantasy. "You gonna fire me? I don't think so. Someone's gotta keep you in line, or you're gonna lose your mind entirely. Who else is there to trust but me?"

"My bookie, Vin."

"Okay, one other guy, but I don't envy you being surrounded by people afraid to tell you the truth … about anything. Are you gonna stop paying the mortgage on my father's house? No. You love him more than you are irritated by me. Would it change my behavior anyway? No. My only value to you is a sharp wit and a straight tongue. If I stop telling you the truth, fire me."

"Don't tempt me, Len."

"Sure, I'm afraid of you, but if you get rid of me, you'll be completely alone. So, get the hell out of bed and follow me down that fancy staircase of yours to your very expensive gymnasium."

"Okay. Okay. Geez, man. The easy part is getting down there. The hard part is actually working out."

"Look. I told you, boss. Stop thinking about

later. Concentrate on now. Sit in the chair for a while before we go down."

Pope was wearing dark blue silk pajamas with white piping. He moved to the oversized leather chair and sat.

"Close your eyes and feel the aspirin and the booze kicking in. And don't fall asleep. You have to learn to quiet your mind. Start small."

"You calling my mind small?"

"Just do it, for God sakes?"

Pope put his hands on the arms of the chair, straightened his back, and closed his eyes. After ten seconds, he opened his eyes, grabbed a pack of cigarettes, and pressed a button on the side of the lampstand.

"It's a beginning," his disapproving trainer said, grabbing the table lighter to ignite Pope's cigarette.

A young man in a black vest and bow tie appeared. "Sir?"

"Coffee." Pope turned to Lenny. "You want some?" Leonard nodded. "Two," he told the servant. "Lenny takes cream and sugar."

The kid disappeared.

"Sit, Lenny. I gotta take a quick schvitz to change my mood before we go."

With that, Pope tossed his cigarette into the oversized ashtray and disappeared into the bathroom. Lenny heard the knobs of the shower squeak open and the sound of running water. This was followed by Pope relieving himself into the toilet. A pajama top flew out the bathroom door. Then the bottoms. Humming ensued.

While Pope was in the shower, shorts and a T-shirt were laid out by a maid in a very short skirt. Leonard wanted to jump her. Unhappily, he understood this was neither the time nor the place to take even the slightest attention off his erratic and dangerous employer. Pope was demanding, selfish, and self-centered in the extreme. Instead, Len distracted himself by watching the girl lay the togs out on the bed then place tennis shoes and socks on the floor. She knew exactly the effect she was having on him. Of that, he was positive. She also knew that neither of them would dare act on their impulses while their boss was so close at hand, so she gave him an extra wiggle, raised her eyebrows, and smiled at him. *Maybe later.* The thought wafted in the air between them. She exited through the door.

The water turned off, and Pope emerged naked, soaking wet, drying himself with a large terry cloth towel. He didn't look bad for his age. In his forties, he had only a modest swelling around his midsection. Unattended, both knew, it would become grotesque.

"I'm almost ready to ride." Pope retrieved a bottle of Bacardi from a bookshelf just as the coffee arrived. "Coffee Royale?" he asked. He spiked his black coffee generously with the rum and looked at Lenny, who shook his head in the negative and rolled his eyes.

Pope finished drying off and donned the outfit laid out for him. Then he sat on the bed and put on the socks and sneakers.

"All set. Take your coffee, Len. Let's go."

They went down a hallway and descended a wrought iron spiral staircase to the floor below. At the bottom of the stairs was a spacious carpeted room with a bench, a rack of weights, a stationary bicycle, a rowing machine, and some old-fashioned exercise pins he never used, which hung decoratively on the wall.

While Leonard orchestrated his employer's workout, starting with the bicycle, a middle-aged man in an open-collared shirt and sports jacket and a woman in business attire entered the room and stood quietly in a corner, awaiting an invitation to speak.

A very pretty young girl with another one of those skimpy black skirts and a white blouse sat down against the wall with a steno pad and appeared ready to take notes.

Pope took a seat on the end of the weight bench. Lenny placed manhole-sized black metal plates on each end of the bar. The same young man who had brought the coffee put an open can of beer and a lit cigarette in an ashtray next to the bench.

"Boss," the man in the sports jacket said, "the subject you're currently engaged with is primed and ready to go. Your agent only awaits instruction."

"Tell Nadine to hold her horses until she hears from me," Pope replied, "and tell her I'm proud of her work, and when we succeed, she will be handsomely rewarded. I want her to continue to entertain the victim—I mean client—to his heart's content. Naturally at his own expense, until I tell her otherwise. I want him completely relaxed when I'm ready to raise the curtain. Understood?"

"Understood." The man left.

The older woman in the business suit spoke. "Sir. The market tanked yesterday. If now is a good time, I have some trades I want to make I should go over with you."

"Martha, please. You have my complete confidence. I give you permission to attend to this with your usual finesse. Keep up the good work."

She made for the door.

"Next," Pope said to the girl against the wall. She looked down at the pad and twirled her pencil.

"That's it for now," she informed him. "Is there anything more I can do for you, Mr. Pope?" she asked with a look.

He looked back at her. "Not right now, honey. This man you see ordering me around has other plans."

She walked over to him and planted a kiss on his cheek, then turned her back on him and headed toward the door.

He took a puff off the smoke, threw it back in the ashtray, and took a couple of swallows of beer. "Okay, my man. Let's get this done." He lay back on the bench and gripped the bar with more excitement than he'd thought he possessed, pressed it up off its stand, and began pumping it up and down from his chest.

# CHAPTER 3

## SECURITY

Antonio sat listening, his motorcycle boots planted on the edge of his desk.

"So, let me tell you about the man you're thinking of hiring, Mr. Vargas," Stewart Johnson informed him. "He has not been entirely honest with you. To his credit, he admitted to the two stretches in Joliet, but he wisely did not offer up the names of his current associates, who I have listed here." Stewart handed Vargas a typewritten page for his perusal. "I think he's more of a security liability than an asset."

Stewart Johnson, aka Pluto, was a high school buddy of Alice White's former office boy, Eddie Williams. Like Eddie, he was a genius, but more importantly, he was a born intelligence gatherer. Too bad he was too young to have served in the last world war. Alice was concerned about the several near-fatal mistakes Vargas had made in personnel and client selection since she'd known him. So she sent Johnson to help screen them for Antonio's security organization.

"Alice was right," Vargas told the youngster. "You are the real deal. You got brains and street smarts. You know, with all respect, you are rather scrawny. I could fix you up with a membership in a gym I do security for, put you on a diet, and beef you up—steak, potatoes, beer, just like a sumo wrestler, only way less fat. The chicks won't be able to keep their hands off you. I could train you in some simple fighting styles. You have an instinct for security work. With some help, you could be a menace to society like me. I'd hire you in a minute. What do you say?"

"Uh, thanks, Mr. Vargas. I appreciate the offer, I really do. I don't think I'm cut out for your line of work, with all gratitude to you. It involves bloodshed, maybe even my own. Besides, I can't spare the circulation from my brain. I would also humbly point out, one man to another, that many beautiful women in New York City are irresistibly drawn to a weakling like myself. Maybe it's their maternal instinct. I don't know, and I don't care, but I do all right in that department just as I am. Thank you, though, for your kind offer. I consider it high praise coming from a man like you."

"Okay. Thank you, Stewart, for enlightening me."

"You're welcome. Let me know when you've got another potential employee or a client you want me to look into. I'm trying to keep up with my studies at City College. There's new technology developing in the computing industry that started during the war. A crude computing machine called Enigma helped decipher German code, but that was just a beginning. It's gonna explode in function and application. It'll save amazing amounts of time making calculations and searching for information. I'm excited to get in on the ground floor. Maybe I can help make it happen."

"I'm glad to know you are not hurting for female companionship. I appreciate what you have done for me. Here is a little something for your time. Please do not argue that it is too much. I'm sure you know the story about the horseshoe falling off and losing the battle because a nail was rotten or something like that. I read the classic comic book when I was a small boy. Say hello to your father for me. You told me he rides the back of a garbage truck. He must be very proud of you. Anytime you want, I'll tell him what a credit you are to him and your mother."

"Thanks, Mr. Vargas. I might take you up on that. It's confusing for him, here in America, to understand what exactly I do to feed myself while I'm going to school. He and my mom have been as good to me as they could. Thanks for the cash. It is way too much, but I won't argue. See you around."

Stewart headed over to a soda fountain on Amsterdam Avenue, near City College, CCNY, to meet his friend Stanley. He sat down on a stool at the counter and ordered two chocolate malteds.

"Hey, Pluto, how's it going?" Stanley sat down on the stool next to his buddy.

"I'm doing fine, Stan. I just made some pocket change doing a security check for a friend of Alice White's. You remember her. She's a secretary at the law office Eddie used to work at, the older woman he had the hots for. We used to tease him about it all the time."

"Yeah, vaguely."

"So, what have you been doing with yourself, Stan? I haven't seen you around in a dog's age. You still going up to the Bronx to visit your girlfriend?"

"Yes, as a matter of fact, I am. I try to stay away, but I can't seem to stop taking the subway up to see her. I don't know what it is exactly that I feel for her. We don't talk much about anything meaningful. In fact, we hardly talk at all. We, you know, fool around. It's strange. She seems like a very nice person, but we're both kind of shy. I guess it's only a physical thing between us. I'm too screwed up to know how to treat her."

"Give it time, Stan. A physical relationship could be the beginning of something special."

"I don't know, Pluto. I keep thinking there's something out there for me that I'm missing. I need a purpose besides trying to get into medical school and visiting Susan. I don't want my feelings for her to make me miss out on something better."

"I hope you know, Stan, you might already have what you're looking for. You're getting an education. You have a girl who, from what you tell me, sounds terrific. You have a future. It hurts me to watch you struggle, man, but what do I know?"

The malteds arrived, and they put down a quarter each.

Stu asked his friend, "What is it you think you're missing? We're simple guys, made to be happy with simple lives. I don't know what it is you're looking for, but whatever it is, I hope you find it. Let me know. I'm always open to suggestions."

"Okay, Stu. I'll try to stay in better touch."

"Do me a favor, Stanley. Be careful. There are predators out there who would love to take advantage of a good-looking, desperate young fellow like yourself. They could steal your soul before you even notice it's gone."

"I hear you, Stu. I'll be careful."

"Yeah, and don't keep to yourself so much, Stan. It makes me nervous. I think you're a little depressed."

---

Stanley decided to skip seeing Susan. He stayed downtown to study. She was probably hoping he would come, but he couldn't worry about what she wanted right now. She'd still be there tomorrow. His biggest fear was that life was passing him by. He wanted to be there when whatever was in store for him finally arrived. The reason he was premed at St. John's, he thought, was because he couldn't think of anything else to do with his life, not because he was so interested in becoming a doctor. He felt too sorry for himself right now to worry about helping other people, day and night, as a doctor. His boozer parents had led him to a dead end. It was all their fault that he felt so empty. Susan was only temporary relief from the storm of his uncontrolled emotions. In the scheme of things, she really didn't matter. Their pathetic excuse for a relationship was going nowhere. When they were together, he wasn't really present. He was busy thinking about better things to come.

He walked and walked the cold city streets until he came upon a small delicatessen on 126th Street and Broadway. It was the perfect time to grab a bite. The place was not too busy. He could hide out and get some studying done. If he was gonna become a doctor, he had better keep his grades up.

He took an empty table toward the back and opened the chemistry text he had brought along. A too-happy waitress brought him pastrami on rye, a sour pickle, a potato knish, and a bottle of celery soda.

Stanley spread mustard on the bread from the crockery mustard jar leaning against the napkin holder. One bite told him he had made the right decision—a little bit of heaven in the quiet isolation of a New York City deli. Life was temporarily good. He could relax, enjoy his dinner, and concentrate on chemistry. He was into the periodic table of elements, hoping to avoid blowing himself up in the lab next week.

Two young women came in the front door and attracted Stanley's peripheral attention. They noticed him studying and walked down the aisle to take the table next to him, mainly to annoy yet another cute boy trying to focus on something other than them. He tried to keep his attention on his chemistry text. He took another bite of his sandwich. They looked like trouble. They were not ordinary women. One was blond, and one was brunette, and they were gorgeous. He could smell them. It was like a field of flowers. He began to sweat. He forced himself not to look directly at them, like at the sun. He had to leave very soon. He could not sit here, wanting what he could never have. He had planned to study. Anyway, who among their kind would give him a second look? They were expensively dressed. He had on a ratty jacket. They wore expensive jewelry. He had on a cheap watch. He tried to concentrate on the book rather than on them, but he was trapped. If he left now, he would have to pass them on his way out. He might stumble and even fall. He would look like a complete fool. He was frozen in indecision.

*Clang.* A piece of silverware from their table hit the floor. He tried to ignore it. They were young and perfectly capable of picking it up themselves.

"Excuse me. Sir?" One of them intruded on his racing thoughts. "Would you be so kind as to retrieve my fork from the floor? I'm terribly sorry for disturbing your concentration on that book."

His mouth went dry. "Not at all," he answered. His tongue sticking to the roof of his mouth made him sound like an idiot. He would give her the fork and get the heck out of there.

He bent down and grabbed the utensil off the floor. He banged his head on the table on the way up and almost knocked himself out. He was sure he had cut his scalp.

"Oh my God," the blond said. "You're bleeding. Let me help you."

He couldn't look at her. He'd been around a lot of girls, but none like this.

"Bend your head down to me," she instructed him.

She dipped a napkin in a glass of water and blotted Stanley's head where the blood was coming from.

"There. It stopped. It was only a surface wound."

Stanley pulled himself together and handed her the fork. He looked into her blue eyes.

"Thank you so much," she said. "How nice of you to pick it up for me. I'm just so terribly clumsy."

The brunette giggled at her friend.

"Not at all," Stanley replied.

His response was exactly what she'd expected when she pushed the fork off the table. It was like pulling the wings off a fly. Imagine the nerve of him trying to ignore them. She would have been insulted if it wasn't so funny.

She spoke, "If you don't mind me asking, what is that awfully thick book you're reading?"

He turned his head to look back at his table. "Uh, that's chemistry. I was trying to find a quiet place to study when I came in here."

"Well, don't let us distract you. Please, return to what you were doing," she said, acting hurt and embarrassed.

"No," he said. "I didn't mean to put you off. Actually, I was just finished. What're your names?"

"I'm Janet. She's Paula. How about you?"

"Me? I'm Stanley."

His eyes moved to the second woman, Paula. She was another knockout.

*God, I'm never going to make it talking to these women. They're gonna get bored and tell me to take a hike.*

He needed to make an excuse and leave. He would walk over to a friend's apartment where he'd ask to sleep on the couch, get under the covers, and assume the fetal position.

"I've gotta go," he blurted.

"Not so fast," the brunette spoke. She saw him glance at her and watched him flush. There was no place he could look without turning red. It was adorable.

"Sit back down. You haven't finished your food. Didn't your mother ever tell you children are starving in Europe?"

He could not remember his mother saying any such thing. He did remember her blacking out at dinner one night, and her face falling into her food. Every fiber of his being told him that these girls were trouble. They were no good—beautiful, but rotten to the core. He sat down again at his table with his sandwich and his book.

The girls exchanged conspiratorial glances and reached a silent decision about what to do with their victim.

"May we join you?" said the spiders to the fly.

"No. I really have to go. I've got things to do."

They ignored what he said, took their silverware and water, and sat down at his table.

"What do you have to do that's more important than dinner with the two of us?" asked the blond, Janet.

Her smell was intoxicating.

"Things that would bore you."

They leaned in close.

"You're wrong. Nothing about you bores us. We want to get to know you, Stanley."

"No, you don't. Please. Do not do this. Let me go."

"We can't," said the brunette decisively.

"You've got to be kidding," he said. "What would you want with a man like me? You could have anybody."

"That's true," the blond answered. "We could have any man, and we want you. You are better looking than you think, young fellow. Maybe no one's ever told you that. I'm not saying you don't need a haircut and a new set of clothes, but we'll see about that later."

"Later than what?" he asked her.

Paula slid out, without ordering, and stood up.

"Pay the waitress," she told him.

The blond stood up and said, "Bring the book. I want to read it."

Stanley left the rest of his sandwich, his untouched knish, and the celery soda. He put cash on the table with a generous tip, took his textbook, and followed them out.

# CHAPTER 4

## EDDIE

"Bryce, Adams, and Eaton, Attorneys at Law. How may I help you?"

"Good morning. My name is Eddie Williams. I once worked at your firm. Can you tell me if Miss White is there and, if she is, does she have time to speak to me? What's your name?"

"Brenda Fox. Yes, she's here. I'll see if she can talk to you, Eddie."

Silence.

"She'd love to speak with you. She must really be fond of you because she's got a pile of work a mile high on her desk, and she usually won't talk to anyone under those circumstances. I should warn you, though, she has a serious boyfriend."

"You don't have to worry about me on that

account, Brenda. As she told me many times, I'm way too young for her. I tried to win her over when I worked there but only succeeded in embarrassing myself. Is she still in her closet-sized work space?"

"Yes, she is. They offered her a bigger office, but she refused to move. It must be something like not wanting to leave the womb. I better put her on so she can say hello and get back to work."

"Hello, Eddie. How the heck are you?" Alice was excited to hear from her long-lost assistant. "I miss you so much. When I needed something, you always handed it to me before I asked—names, histories, financial statements . . . heck, remember when you got me a map of Stanton, up the river? Now I have friends up there, including the grumpy old sheriff who wasn't gonna help us when our client was accused of negligent homicide. Jim, the builder, and I are now an item. Good help is hard to find, Eddie. I felt spoiled rotten. Where are you?"

"It's nice to hear your voice too, Miss White. I'm in New York. In fact, I'm in Manhattan visiting friends at this very moment. I couldn't get this close to you and not say hello. I'm older now, not much, but I know the age thing continues to apply. That doesn't mean you don't still have a place in my heart. Your operator told me not to put the moves on you because you have a boyfriend. How's that going?"

"We're still struggling to work out a

relationship without crowding each other. After what happened upstate with that innocent doctor dying in the house Jim built, Jim quit constructing homes and moved to Manhattan to resume his original career building stage sets for Broadway shows. That's what he was doing before he enlisted in the army during the war. I still have my little apartment in the Bronx, ever the modern, independent woman, and I'm not giving it up without a fight."

"That is so much like you, Miss White. You'll be happy to know the girls in Boston keep me busy in the little time I have left over from going to classes and working to pay for my food and rent. My folks have done enough for me. It's time I supported myself. Speaking of which, how's law school going, uh, Miss White?"

"Eddie. You can drop the 'Miss White' and call me Alice. It's cute, though, but I have a feeling we're gonna be friends into our old age, so we might as well start calling each other by our first names. I don't consider it disrespectful. It's sweet that you're still fond of me. A girl can never get enough of that. Clearly, you have moved on, and I'll have to settle for being like your older sister. Jim Peters is my guy, I guess."

"That is so strange about him, Alice. You told me you hated him. I distinctly remember your face turning red whenever you talked about him, especially about not ironing his clothes. You told me never to expect a woman to do that for me. Who would have thought you guys would get together? I still have a lot to learn about women. You are a complex species."

"We're another species from another planet. You don't want to cross us, Eddie."

"Gosh, I miss you, Alice. No woman I ever met talked to me like you do. Things go from your head right out your mouth, with nothing to stop them in between. I wish I was older and that Mr. Peters had another girlfriend."

"Gosh, Eddie. I won't tell him you said that, but it's nice of you to say so and my face is actually turning red."

"Your secretary, Brenda, told me you had a lot of work on your desk, so I won't keep you. I just wanted you to know I was in town and thinking about you, in the platonic sense, of course. I was a late bloomer. You were my first serious crush. I suppose you were preparing me for the pain other women would inflict on me, what with that perfume you wore, you remember, Wind Song by Prince Matchabelli. I'll never forget it. You made sure I remembered the name. Cruel, very cruel, Alice. You almost killed me with it. You knew it too. Don't feel guilty, though. Some of the women I've met in Cambridge are tougher on me than you ever were."

"Gosh, Eddie, you certainly have grown up. Please don't write me off entirely. Remember, as you and I get older, we get closer in age. I may have to call you if things don't work out with Mr. Peters. You never know. So tell me, how's your mother? The last time we talked, you said she wasn't doing well. Don't worry about the time. This is my coffee break, and I've had enough coffee today already to last a week."

"Gee, Alice, you were always so thoughtful about my mom. I appreciated that very much. She never did stop smoking like the doctor told her. She passed away last year. I should have called you, I know. I'm sorry, but it was harder than I thought it would be, and I couldn't bring myself to tell you. I was afraid you would start crying, and I didn't know if I could take it. She was more okay about dying than I was about watching her die."

"I'm sorry for your loss, Eddie. Oh, for Pete's sake, now I am crying. Please forgive me."

"I knew you would, but enough time's gone by that I can handle it now."

"Maybe we could meet for lunch, Eddie, if you're gonna be in town." She blew her nose. "Just not today, for obvious reasons."

"That would be wonderful. How about tomorrow, noon? I'll pick you up, and we'll walk over to a lunch place near the office. Okay?"

"Fine. I'm writing it on my calendar. See you then. I'll tell you all about law school and Jim, and you can fill me in on life at MIT and the girls of Cambridge, Massachusetts."

---

The sun shone down on the city. Stanley's mind and body could not have taken much more abuse. He felt awful. He dared to open his eyes. The drapes were closed, but sunlight crept in around them and hurt his eyeballs. He was stark naked on a big bed. He lifted his head from a satin-covered pillow and set off a wave of throbbing pain in his temples. He turned to look for his clothes and spotted his shoes, socks, underwear, pants, shirt, and jacket in a pile on the floor. His chemistry book was open on the dresser next to his wristwatch. A wave of nausea almost caused him to empty his stomach.

He was afraid to look further, yet he knew he must. As he'd dreaded, the two women from the delicatessen lay next to him, sound asleep. The dark-haired one was snoring peacefully away. He wished he could fully appreciate them, but he had never been so hungover in his life.

He vaguely remembered the night before. He

was sure that his brain was permanently damaged by the sheer volume of alcohol he'd consumed and the things the girls did with him. He could never see these women again. He would enter a monastery and live the rest of his life as a monk, in quiet contemplation. He put his hand to the side of his head to keep it from falling off and slid his feet over the side of the bed to the floor. Unsteadily, he tiptoed toward his clothes.

"You up already?" Janet, the blond, spoke, her eyes still closed. "It's much too early. Lay down next to me and go back to sleep. Please don't make me have to come get you. Unless you want us to dish out more of the same, you'll do what I say. You know, Stanley, I tried to read your textbook after I thought you passed out, but you were only playing possum and wouldn't let me concentrate. Thank goodness you finally did pass out so we could get some sleep." She opened her eyes. "What're you doing? You thought you could sneak out of here and never see us again, huh? In your dreams, sonny."

"I'm sorry. I don't mean to be rude. It's just that I never experienced anything like you two before in my life."

"We get that a lot."

"I'll never forget you."

"My heavens," Janet exclaimed. "We really

messed you up, didn't we? You were so pathetically grateful. It was too flattering to resist."

"Paula, wake up." She shook her brunette friend's shoulder.

The snoring stopped. "What's up? Gosh, I must have conked out."

Paula lifted her head and opened her eyes. She caught sight of Stanley standing near his pile of clothes, like a thief in the night. "Are you okay, Stanley? Was he trying to escape? He looks like he was trying to escape. Shame on you, Stanley."

"I'm okay. I'm just fine," Stanley told them. "But I have to get back to my friend's apartment. He must be worried sick about me not coming home last night. I need to get showered and get to my morning classes. I'll never make it on time."

"When's your first class, Stan?"

"Nine."

"That ship has sailed, boyo," Janet told him. "Don't be in such a hurry. We can't let you go until we know you're all right."

"I'm fine. See." He made a feeble attempt at a hop and groaned in pain. "Believe me. I really have to go."

"Forget it, buddy," the dark-haired one told him. "You can't walk away yet. Can he, Janet?"

"Certainly not. You don't want to hurt our feelings, do you? Two poor, defenseless girls like us."

He could think of many words to describe them, but poor and defenseless were not among them. He couldn't stay.

"No sir, mister. Put that sock back down on the pile and back away," Janet told him.

Paula said, "Settle down. Let's have some coffee, and we'll discuss what to do with you. There aren't that many handsome young men wandering around Manhattan these days."

"You don't want to get involved with me," he said. "I'm not exactly the life of the party. You girls deserve someone who knows how to have a good time. I'm totally ignorant about women, and I'm often very depressed."

"I don't know about that, Stanley," Janet said. "You seemed to do pretty well. You nearly wore us out and that's not easy to do. With a little training, we could make you into a first-class ladies' man, turn you loose on some of the women our boss does business with. You would be a real asset to him. I have a feeling he could make you an offer of employment that you would find hard to refuse. Think about it. While you're thinking, I'm gonna start a pot of coffee and fetch you some vodka and aspirin for your headache. Don't you dare put your clothes on while I'm gone. Paula, watch him."

With that, the blond arose and left the room.

Paula began massaging Stanley's neck.

He put his hand out for the aspirins Janet brought him and washed them down with vodka.

"You are so tense," Paula told him as she worked his neck. "You wouldn't have been any good at school. Why don't you take a hot shower and get dressed and we'll have breakfast? There's a toothbrush and toothpaste in the medicine cabinet. If you want some music, turn on the radio built into the wall of the shower. Help yourself to a towel. There's a lot of them on the shelf."

Stanley stumbled into a luxurious bathroom.

He brushed his teeth.

"This apartment must cost a fortune," he yelled in to Paula. He turned the faucets on and when it was warm he stepped into the shower. "If you don't mind me asking," he shouted again, "how do the two of you afford a place like this?"

"That's easy," Paula yelled back. "We don't. Our boss pays the rent."

She came into the bathroom. "I think you'll enjoy meeting him, sweetheart. The booze, our clothing, this apartment, the limousines we ride around in, all of it belongs to him. He's a full-service employer. If you and he hit it off, he will make your dreams come true, and some things you've never even dreamed of. There's nothing he can't get you. When we're done with breakfast, we'll call his office and see if you can meet him sometime soon. I think he'll like you. There's a long line of women waiting for you to take care of them. We are just the tip of the iceberg."

He had no idea what she was talking about. All he could do was let go. His hangover slowly let up.

"Sweet Stanley. Let's get you dried off and dressed. Then we'll have a wonderful breakfast. Just leave everything to us."

---

"I shoulda thought it out better," Eddie said to Alice. "This place is packed."

Every table in the lunch joint was filled. Customers stood in the aisles. Manhattan on a workday is no place for the timid. You assert yourself or get trampled. It's nothing personal. New Yorkers aren't actually pushy. They just struggle for survival. A year in New England and Eddie had lost his edge in the city's dog-eat-dog competition. Real estate was at a premium here, so the restaurant had half the space it needed to feed the masses. People stood shoulder to shoulder, waiting for a seat, but they remained strangely detached from each other. An out-of-towner might think it psychotic behavior, but New Yorkers consider it finding tranquility in a crowd.

Alice and Eddie gratefully shared a table with two strangers in suits and ties. The men looked like middle-aged stockbrokers. They nodded briefly to the newcomers, then resumed shoveling food down at breakneck speed, clearly on a tight schedule, not uttering a word to each other or anyone else.

"Don't worry about the noise, Eddie. I can hear you fine and, believe me, nobody is listening to us talk. I love New York City. Don't you miss it?"

"Now that I'm here with you, sitting down, having lunch, I have to honestly say, NO, I do not miss New York City. I miss you, yes. I miss my friends too, but, with all due respect Alice, there's no room to breathe here. New England has spoiled me. Granted, there are times Cambridge is not much better than this, but often the streets are empty. I never paid much attention to the ocean of humanity in this city, particularly Manhattan."

"Gosh, Eddie. I don't think I'll ever be able to live without the hustle and bustle. When I get back from a visit to the country, I kiss the pavement. Maybe I don't want to be alone. I like crowds. I need cement under my feet and exhaust in my lungs. I need people bumping into me and being rude regularly, or I'll go nuts. It distracts me from my troubles. You have to pay attention to keep from being trampled by the crowds. Instant feedback. What a place."

"I'm glad you're happy here, Alice. Now, my favorite part of visiting New York is leaving. I feel like I've aged a century in Cambridge."

"Yes, you have, Eddie. You've grown up so much since I saw you last. I thought you were good-looking when you were a kid, but look at you now. You're a lady-killer. I really am jealous of the coeds in Cambridge. I might have to dump my boyfriend and move to Boston, become a waitress in a greasy spoon. So, tell me, how's it going at the Massachusetts Institute of Technology?"

"MIT is amazing. The professors are brilliant. Every one of them is a great speaker. They're incredibly gifted at explaining ideas I couldn't understand by just reading about them in books. I finally see why my uncle in Berkeley is so crazy about graduating from MIT. It's worth the work and long hours. I was intimidated when I first got there, but I got over it. What about you?"

"I guess I'll tell you the bad stuff first." Alice looked at him, serious. "First, I want to offer my sincere condolences on the death of your mother."

His eyes dampened. "Thanks."

"Now I'll share with you the realities of my life. I got shot six months ago. Don't get upset. It was in my arm and went through without hitting anything important. I tried, unsuccessfully, to get a neighbor of mine in the Bronx, a customs inspector, out of a jam on the docks. He's dead for my trouble. Maybe it was my fault. Maybe not. No one's blaming me, but I wish I could've stopped it. They shot him in the neck and chest.

"I was visiting him at his apartment one night, and that's when I got shot trying to stop men from kidnapping him. They knocked me out with a blow to my head and left me bleeding to death from my arm. Sometimes I'm not sure I'm cut out for this kind of work. I don't know if I have the nerve for it. My friend, Antonio, begs to differ with me on that point. He thinks I'm a born killer. Right? He's prejudiced because, as you know, I saved his life the first time we met—another accident of fate, I assure you."

"God, Alice. You do cut it close, but you must admit, you're good at getting to the bottom of things. Someone's got to stand up for people who're being pushed around."

"I suppose. I don't know. Why not somebody else? I would have died unconscious on that floor if it hadn't been for my window washer, if you can believe that, who didn't trust me to take care of myself that night and followed me. It was all for nothing, though, 'cause I lost the customs guy. I suppose it was inevitable. He waited a long time to ask for help. I keep saying that like it's an excuse. I only tell you this because it's affecting my decision about what to do after I graduate law school in the spring. I thought about just being an investigator, not using my law degree. We have a new criminal defense associate, a seasoned veteran named Clarence Eaton. He wants me to keep investigating, but he also wants me to practice criminal law with him as my mentor."

"It sounds like Mr. Eaton has faith in you."

"But Eddie, the bullet wounded more than my arm. I thought I was tough. I could have been killed. A couple of inches and I would have been killed. That makes three times in the last two years I've come close to buying the farm, pushing up daisies, cashing in at the big casino."

"You still have a sense of humor about it. I get your point, though, Alice."

"Once, my brakes were disabled. Once, someone tried to drown me in a boathouse. Then I got shot. So, you see, it's not so crazy, me thinking about quitting. I just don't know what else I would do."

"No, you're not crazy, but I'm glad you're still friends with the gangster, Antonio, from the garage. Mr. Vargas."

"Which reminds me, Eddie, I put him in touch with your pal Pluto, to help him screen new personnel and potential clients. People keep secrets when he interviews them, don't you know."

"There's something about him I like, Alice. You say he told you not to let fear rule your life. That sounds like good advice for me, too, but don't ask me. I'm still just a kid."

"A kid? Hardly. You are wise beyond your years, Eddie. Thanks for caring about what happens to me."

"I can't help it, Alice, but you're welcome."

"Antonio says your friend is saving him a lot of trouble and money."

"I guess he is. He told me Antonio's been more than generous with him for his work."

"Antonio is not stingy when he's grateful," Alice said.

"I'm headed back to the salt mines tomorrow, Alice. I'm so glad we had a chance to talk."

"Enjoy yourself while you can, Eddie. You'll settle down soon enough, get married, have children. Please stay in touch with me and let me know how you are. If you're in New York in June, I'd love for you to come to my graduation. Give me your address, and I'll send you an invitation. Please don't make a special trip just for that. Graduation ceremonies are boring for everybody, especially the guests. The party afterward, though, is a different story. It could be fun. Just come for that if you can, and feel free to bring a girlfriend."

"Okay, Alice, it's only a four-hour drive. I might just do that."

# CHAPTER 5

## THE INTERVIEW

Stanley sat between his two new girlfriends in a booth at the Stork Club. He had heard of it but never thought he'd see the legendary nightspot from the inside. It was the end of a busy day. He settled into the soft leather, grateful for a break. He was looking sharp in the black blazer and gray slacks the girls had picked out for him. They'd taken him to the Plaza Hotel, where his face had been wrapped in a hot towel, then lathered and shaved with a straight razor by the animated aged Italian barber. After the shave, the old gentleman whistled back and forth with his caged birds before cutting and styling Stanley's hair. Stanley's nails were clipped, filed, and buffed by a young girl sitting beside the barber chair on a stool. He felt and looked like a different man after all the attention.

Now, he needed a drink. The waiter placed a flute of champagne on the white linen cloth in front of him. The girls were served large glasses of gin, straight up, with a twist of lemon.

Shortly after Stanley and his escorts sat down, the same couples that had shadowed Nadine Byrkowski and Abraham Schumann were led by a hostess to the adjoining table, giggling and chatting amongst themselves as they filed in.

Tonight was a big night for Janet and Paula and their unacknowledged entourage. Tonight the boss would honor them with his presence. He wanted to meet and talk to the new guy. They hoped he liked what he saw. They were all on edge. Michael Pope's unpredictable mood swings had become a depressing reality of their lives. Without warning, any one of them could be publicly humiliated, even terminated without cause. Pope said he did it to keep them on their toes, but he was becoming more emotionally unstable every day, and they were being made to pay the price. He had them "locked in," as he liked to call it, completely dependent on him for survival. A few years earlier, when most of them were new, the prospect of him putting in an appearance would have elated them. They had relished his company and reveled in his attention. He would be interested in them, in their families, in their happiness, and in their well-being. Their delight had turned to resentment this past year. Now when he laughed, they all laughed with him, like in some B gangster movie where the boss tells a bad joke and they all burst into phony hysterics and slap their legs.

After Janet, Paula, and Stanley were settled in with drinks and had made some conversation about New York's current weather, Michael Pope was shown to their table. The girls quickly jumped up to make a fuss over him, hugging and kissing their boss on his cheeks.

"Please, dear ladies, really. I appreciate your excitement, but let's not be rude to our guest. Do introduce me."

Janet spoke up. "Michael Pope, meet Stanley Kramer, a premed student at St. John's College. Stanley, this is our beloved employer, Michael Pope."

To Janet's eye, Pope was pleased with the look they had achieved with Stanley. There was something about this young college boy that engaged Pope. Good. Stanley was handsome, especially in his new duds, manicured and coiffed. The girls were proud of themselves. Pope was looking at him like a new automobile. With care and maintenance, and training, their prey would have unsuspecting women eating out of the palm of his hand.

"Mr. Kramer." Pope shook hands with Stanley. "You remind me of myself at your age. That was when I discovered the true purpose of life."

"What is that?" Stanley asked innocently.

Pope took a seat. "Why, self-indulgence, of course, young man. Wine, women, fancy cars, diamonds, and, most importantly, getting other people to pay for it all. That, I believe, is what we were all born for. It's just that some of us are more successful at taking than others. If you stick around, I will teach you how. Just by looking at you, I can see that you have the right stuff to do the job. I could certainly use the distraction of supervising your training."

Paula noticed the effect Stanley was having on their boss. She figured it would be good for a couple of days, a week at most before the novelty wore off. *Eat, drink, and be merry, Stanley,* she thought, *for tomorrow you die*. Stanley was in for a rude awakening. He should have acted on his urge to flee when he woke up this morning. Now, it was too late. Too bad for him, but, Paula thought, misery loves company. So they'd walked him into Michael Pope's orbit like a lamb to the slaughter. The mind-altering roll in the hay they had given him last night would have to satisfy him the rest of his life.

She told her boss, "We met him last night in a deli. It was love at first sight. We couldn't help ourselves. We had to have him. So we took him home to your apartment and did what girls do."

Pope observed, "I'm sure you did. He's positively glowing. Then there's the outfit and the haircut. Who exactly paid for all that?" he queried. "I'm afraid to ask."

Paula answered, "Why, Mr. Pope, you know perfectly well who paid for it. You did, of course. You pay for everything any of us wants."

The group at the next table tried not to listen to Paula's obsequious drivel. It was too depressing.

Paula herself had to keep from getting sick.

She told Stanley, "We have Mr. Pope wrapped around our little fingers. He tells us all the time, that's the way he wants it. So"—she turned back to Pope—"don't complain."

Paula couldn't remember ever being so unhappy about her lot in life. She wished Michael Pope would have a heart attack and die. It had taken time in his gang for her to reach this sad state.

The happily ignorant young Stanley took it all at face value. He was as excited by the glitz and glamour as they all were when they'd first met Pope.

"Of course, Mr. Kramer," Pope told him, "whether you stick around or not, the clothing is yours. Consider it a gift in honor of our new friendship."

The couples at the adjacent table kept their

talk loud enough so the new man would not suspect they were there as guards. The deceptively soft women were as trained and vicious as the men. Overhearing the conversation between Pope and the new guy, their hearts sank as they witnessed a classic recruitment. Pope put a roof over their heads, clothing on their backs, food on their tables, gas in their cars, and cash in their pockets. He owned them body and soul. They could never leave his employ unless he fired them. There was no place to hide. If they ran away without being told to leave, they would be hunted down and brought back. He had demonstrated that fact by making examples of several disillusioned employees: they'd been framed for crimes, beaten, and humiliated severely enough to ensure future compliance. One such man had locked himself in a hotel room and drank himself to death. Stanley seemed like a nice guy, but, having reached this stage, there was nothing anyone could do to save him.

Michael Pope turned to his new buddy, "So, Stanley, what do you think?"

"I, er, don't know what to say, sir. Last night I was having a pastrami on rye, trying to study, and these girls descended on me like beautiful ravenous birds. I couldn't take my eyes off them. They told me I was coming home with them and didn't have anything to say about it. Nothing like this has ever happened to me. At the apartment, they nearly killed me with kindness and generosity until I finally passed out. Today they dressed me and cut my hair like I was a doll little girls play with. I've never looked so good. I could get used to this."

"Ladies," Michael asked, "what are we going to do with this young man?"

"We don't know, Michael," Paula said. "We haven't gotten around to asking him if he still wants to stay in school. That was quite a performance you gave last night, Stanley. I doubt that even the two of us would be able to keep up with you very long."

"A man after my own heart," Pope told him. "Let's talk about your dreams and mine sometime soon, Stanley. Tonight is no time for serious matters. This is a night for decadence, for the indulgence of the senses. After all, that's what life is all about. For starters, I'd like to introduce you to the caviar here. Waiter."

Pope raised a finger, and a well-tipped gentleman in a tuxedo sped to his side.

"Yes, sir?"

"Bring us a generous order of Beluga and surround it with chilled vodka shots, if you would."

"Very well, sir. I'll have that for you right away." The waiter disappeared.

"Now, girls, don't eat too much. And Stanley,

I would advise you to do the same. It appears you have more to learn from my two favorite employees, and I do not want any of you injured in the process. Let's get together again soon to see if I can make a place for you in my organization."

---

Jim Peters sat at the bar nursing a beer in a small downtown establishment. He wore dungarees and a collared sports shirt. He was tall and strong-looking, with sandy brown hair. A strikingly handsome man. He could have been a model for men's clothes if it weren't for the burn on the back of his wrinkled shirt from trying, unsuccessfully, to iron it. The adjacent stool was occupied by an imposing white-haired gentleman in a blue suit with a blue-and-red-diagonally-striped tie and pocket-handkerchief. The old guy sipped a martini with an olive on a toothpick soaking in it. He was heavily invested in Jim's current project.

He addressed the younger man, "Jim. I'm glad you're back on Broadway. I don't know what got into you leaving something you're so good at to build houses upstate. I hope you got that out of your system. I missed you. You are the most artistic and conscientious set builder I've ever worked with. I have never underestimated the value of your talent to the success of my shows, and I do not intend to start now. Because of you, man, I'll be able to help send my grandkids to college."

*Auntie Mame* had opened a few months earlier, on October 31, 1956, at the Broadhurst Theater, on West 44th.

"Thank you, Irving. It is good to be back in Manhattan. What got into me was that my wife and daughter wanted to move to the country. When I got back from the war, I took them up the river to what I thought would be the quiet of the Hudson Valley. It was anything but peaceful and quiet. I started building additions to existing homes, putting in fireplaces and decks. Then I began building entire houses. I didn't have to advertise. People found me by word of mouth. Even after my divorce, I stayed there to be near Ann and my daughter, Beth, and help them financially. It all fell apart when I got caught up in the shenanigans of the mob and some crazy doctor and his wife. I was building a home for them. I was blinded by my ambition to build this gigantic, embassy-like home for them, a big pillared entrance and a two-car garage on each end. Delusions of grandeur; them and me. The doctor was challenging to work with, but I was determined to succeed—what a mistake. The house turned out great, but, just before it was finished, an explosion in the bathroom killed an innocent man, a fellow doctor looking to partner up with the owner. The widow of the deceased and the townsfolk wanted to string me up, like the mob scene in *Frankenstein,* with torches, a rope, and a tree. They accused me of so-called negligent homicide, which I never heard of before, and all but convicted and hung me without a trial."

"My heavens, Jim," Irving exclaimed. "How did you escape from such a nightmare?"

"It was homicide all right, plain and simple. They got that right, only I didn't do it. It wasn't my fault. The nasty doctor I built the house for was supposed to die. They killed the wrong guy. I was just a convenient patsy. My now-girlfriend, Alice White, came up from this fair city with my childhood friend, one of the lawyers she works for, to rescue me. Before she figured out what really happened, they almost killed her . . . twice. How could I not fall in love with her? She was beautiful, opinionated, and she risked her life for me. She couldn't stand me at first, something about me not knowing how to iron my shirts. I ask you, did I not do a good job on this one? I know there's a slight burn on the back, but hey, I'm a guy. And my straight white teeth, for some reason, she said, they aggravated her too. You can see I haven't learned a thing about ironing, but there's nothing I can do about the teeth. My house up there was nicer than her apartment in the Bronx, something else I had no control over. Nothing was right about me. I think me taking an hour to iron a single shirt, and burning it in the process, is wearing her down. She's still resistant to the idea of us living together. I don't blame her. Let's get married first and then move in together. Don't you think, Irv? She saved my life. Isn't there a Chinese reverse thing about how I own her for that, or is it the other way around, that she owns me?"

"Jim, I'm no expert, are you kidding? I'm on my third wife. I haven't done so well in that department myself."

"This woman shows up for my client interview at my friend's office on Nassau Street. I can admit it now, she badly distracted me, and she knew it. After that, I could hardly concentrate on my own troubles, and she's not exactly easy to protect. She's headstrong and stubborn as a mule. All I'm saying is it's a good thing she kept her nerve, because without her persistence, I would have been convicted.

"She sounds like a keeper."

"She is, but I have to stay cool. Otherwise, I'll scare her off. At the end of our adventure up the river, I decided I should never have left Broadway to build houses. The grass is always greener, ya know. You're right. This is where I belong. I'm delighted to build sets for you and your friends. I'm not going anywhere."

"What a story, Jim. Maybe we could get someone to write it into a show. You better be taking good care of this woman."

"I'm doing the best I can. After my divorce, I was determined to spend the rest of my life as a bachelor. Alice was in exactly the same situation. She was divorced, living alone in the Bronx, working as a secretary. She is as much a victim as I am. It looks like she's gonna keep her little apartment and commute for the indefinite future."

"I'm glad you're happy, and I couldn't be more pleased with your work, Jim. I'm curious. Do you stay in touch with your daughter?"

"I don't mind you asking. Frankly, I'm glad you did, Irv. I still send money, but money's not enough. It's been a while since I've seen her. I think it's time."

---

Jim poured himself a cup of coffee and sat down opposite Alice at her kitchen table. She was taking notes on the law book lying open in front of her.

"I hate to interrupt you, Alice."

"No problem, honey. Something bothering you?"

"I'm feeling guilty about neglecting Beth. I had a beer with an investor in the show I'm working on. Out of nowhere, he asked me if I stay in touch with her. I've been too busy to see her much, if at all, this past year."

"Then drive up there, pronto. She's almost sixteen, 'sweet sixteen.' She needs contact with her daddy. I sometimes dream about the days my father brought me up on the subway from Queens, and we walked through the Botanical Gardens hand in hand and looked at the flowers and the plants inside the huge greenhouse. I love those memories. They make my heart ache. That's all I have left of him. Go see her."

"Alice, if you don't mind me saying so, not to make too big a thing about it, but I love you. You must've been a beautiful baby."

"Thank you, Jim. I feel the same way about you. Now go say hello to your daughter. A young woman can never get enough love from her dad. You can catch her up on your adventures. Tell her how you would have gone to prison for blowing that doctor up if I hadn't saved you."

"Alice, I did not blow that man up. Don't even joke about a thing like that. Next to the war, that might have been the most traumatic thing that ever happened to me. The widow wanted me dead. If I put myself in her place, I would have hated me too."

"Gosh, Jim. You've never talked to me about how much that hurt you. I'm glad I brought it up. Please talk to me about it whenever you feel like it, and I'll listen. I don't want you to hurt over what happened any more than you already have been hurt."

"Frankly, I was more worried about you than about being sent to jail myself. Later, I fell apart in private, in my big place outside Stanton. That's when I decided to come back to the city and resume working on Broadway. It's what I love."

"I'm glad you did, Jim. It put us closer together by an hour."

"And, Alice, I know Ann called you when the bad guys took out your brakes trying to kill you. When I found out she asked you to stay, I have to say, I was embarrassed and a little angry at her. Though, I was also impressed that she cared that much about me. You women are a tough bunch to figure out."

"Let me say, Jim, in all fairness to us, you men aren't that easy to understand either. You have this pride, which is sometimes a good thing, but sometimes not so much."

"Alice, I hope you know how grateful I am you didn't hang up on Ann. I want Beth, my daughter, to know how brave you are. I want her to have both of you in her life, even though Ann started dating another man."

"Really? I don't remember you telling me that, Jim. You've gotta be a little jealous."

"Me, jealous? Nah. I do not ever want to live with that woman again. I wish her new man all the luck in the world. He'll need it."

"Jim, there goes that pride I love so much. "You are such a liar. I don't care how you feel about her; you've gotta be jealous. In any case, though, I think it's good for Ann. As a fellow divorcée, I'll tell you: it does something to a woman's self-confidence when her marriage ends, no matter whose fault it is, even if it was only as short as mine and Andy's. I can't imagine how much worse it would have been if we had children."

"You're right. I want Ann to be happy again, just not too happy. Oh, and by the way, Alice, Beth's gonna want to know what our intentions are. What should I tell her?"

"Jim, do not use her as an excuse to push your luck with me. Get out of here right now. Let me get back to my studies. Tell Beth that formal negotiations are underway. Tell her that you're not willing to give up the splendor of your Manhattan residence, and I'm not willing to give up the squalor of mine. It's a

Mexican standoff."

"You know I'd give up my place in Manhattan in a second to be with you in a more traditional relationship."

"Geez, Jim. I'm under a lot of pressure here. How did we get on this topic anyway? Go see your daughter. I do really, really like you very much. I excruciatingly, painfully like you. Okay? I promise I'll give the matter serious consideration . . . very soon. I can't see either of us finding anyone who can stand us as much as we do."

"Well put, Alice."

"Make the call to Ann and Beth, then get out of here."

"I was just having fun with you, Alice. I'll let you know how it goes."

Jim took the phone out of the kitchen and closed the door behind him, gently, so as not to crush the cord.

# CHAPTER 6

## RIDE IN THE COUNTRY

It was a cold winter morning in the tenth-floor apartment of the commercial building that Jim Peters had made into his home. It was still dark outside.

"What happened?" Jim quietly asked the caller. He kept his voice down to not disturb Alice, who had apparently not awakened when the phone rang.

*Mame* had been running for more than two months.

"The ballroom chandelier is threatening to come loose and kill Auntie Mame. Please come over here sometime this morning and secure it so it doesn't fall during tonight's performance. Rosalind Russell's death is not in the script. Other than that, everything is fine. Ticket sales are up. Things couldn't be better.

Sorry to call so early in the morning, but I wanted to catch you before you went out and obliged me to spend the day hunting you down," the stage manager explained.

"I completely understand, Phil," Jim replied. "I'm thinking of swinging by with my honey for a matinee sometime soon. Maybe you could arrange for her to meet Miss Russell. I think that would be a riot. Two women like them meeting. I have to see that. Has our star noticed the chandelier coming loose? Maybe we should pass on introducing Alice to her."

"Hilarious, Jim. I'm sure she'd love to meet your girlfriend. Miss Russell is a trooper. If the lighting fell and didn't kill her, of course, she'd step over the mangled fixture and the broken glass and carry on as if it were written into the script."

"I'd bet you're right, but I'd rather not find out. I'll be down shortly to handle it."

Jim hung up and looked over at the still form of Miss Alice White next to him in bed—so beautiful, so peaceful, so quiet. She did not open her eyes but simply stated, "Coffee"—a tiger in sheep's clothing, but she was *his* tiger.

Jim kissed her exposed ear and rolled out of bed to do her bidding. She hardly ever stayed over on a weeknight, but she could not resist the convenience of Jim's heated premises on such cold and gloomy days as those of the past week. She had moved Jim's clothing over in his closet to make room for her own. She kept spare sets of her underwear scrunched in with his in his chest of drawers. She would have to rethink her daily commute to the Bronx after caffeine entered her bloodstream.

Jim brought Alice her coffee and the morning paper. This place was as nicely laid out as the house he had lived in, "up the river," when they first met, and she stayed in his guest room. In fact, if Alice didn't look out a window, she would never know they were in the middle of Manhattan. He even had potted plants scattered around the place for country charm. It was irritating that, even in the city, he lived better than she did. But she was not willing to trade her freedom in the Bronx for all the potted plants in China. Men were supposed to be slobs. Women were supposed to keep beautiful homes. With them, it was just the opposite. *I gotta remember to bring my laundry next time I come here to do it in Jim's washing machine, which does not require coins and which does not sound like it's about to quit every five minutes.*

"I have to shower and get to work," she told him. "What are you up to this frigid morning?"

"That call I just got was from the theater. I have some stage work to do on *Mame*. Then I'm going to meet with a producer looking to line me up for his next project. I think he heard I narrowly escaped disaster with this show and wants to get his bid in for my peculiar talent, wrangling unions and catching crew members falling from ladders. Frankly, I hope I never have an experience like that again. A person can age fast in this business."

"They're lucky to have you, and they know it."

"Are you coming back here tonight?" he asked her timidly. "I don't want to crowd you, but we could maybe hit a nice restaurant for dinner, or I could grill us some steaks on the veranda."

"Steak sounds good. Once I'm here, though, I'm not going out on your patio, in the cold, if I can avoid it. I wouldn't mind if you scampered in and out, freezing your tootsies off, to grill us some meat. Very caveman-ish. I would be much obliged. I wonder how someone like me who grew up in the northeast could be so intolerant of the cold. I'll pick up some vegetables on my way back here tonight. Those, I'll make on the stove, in the warmth of your ridiculously spacious kitchen, if you don't mind. There's wine in your pantry. I do not have one of those. I keep my wine in a broom closet."

"What can I say, Alice, sweetheart? All this could be yours. All you have to do is say the word. I'll shower after you. Please do not use up the hot water."

"No, Jim. If you want hot water, you're gonna

have to shower with me."

"Yes, ma'am," he said. "We'll have breakfast after."

---

Stanley Kramer had never felt so good in his life. He had arrived. What fools he and his friends were to have settled for lives of quiet desperation when they could have had all this. From now on, beautiful women, chauffeur-driven limousines, fancy clothes, and expensive jewelry were going to be his for the taking. This is what life was really all about. Thoughts of that girl in the Bronx faded as he assumed his rightful place in society.

Stanley sat in the back seat of a shiny black Cadillac limousine. Small purple flowers were sticking up from bud vases attached to the doorposts at either side of the back seat. He sipped his coffee and bit into a buttered roll. Michael Pope sat to his right so he could make eye contact with the chauffeur in the rearview mirror. He raised his brow, signaling the driver to flip on the recording equipment in the trunk. He never knew when he would collect incriminating statements to be used at a later date. They were cruising the countryside north of New

York City, through Westchester County, past tailored estates covered in snow. Pope told Stanley he preferred to conduct business in the privacy of his limo. He assured him the raised partition window separating them from the driver was soundproof.

"Are you enjoying the ride, Stanley?"

"Very much, Mr. Pope. Thank you for the coffee and the roll."

"You're welcome. Please call me Michael when we're alone like this. So, how are things going with the girls? Are they keeping you entertained?"

"Yes, sir, they are. I'm jealous of the way you have been living. All this time, I've been slaving away in school for lack of anything better to do with my life. If you can find a place for me, I'd love to be part of your business."

"Well, my new friend, you've impressed the girls. Why, just this morning, I spoke to Janet on the phone about you. She inclined me to offer you a position. I think we can work something out."

"Great."

"How important is it that you finish college and go to medical school?"

Stanley hesitated. "It's not as important as I thought. I'm not sure I was ever meant to be a doctor. Now that I've had a taste of the good life, I want in, if you'll have me. I want to live like you do."

Pope told him, "Perfect answer. I have one more important question for you. You don't have to answer, but I have to ask. Do you have any romantic entanglements? I mean, like a girlfriend?"

Stanley hesitated. "Not really, Mr.—I mean Michael." He pushed Susan's existence to the back of his mind. Where he was going, she could not come. There was no room for sentiment in this life. He knew that. It was just business. He might never get an opportunity like this again.

Pope saw the twinge in Stanley's expression when he answered. He was not being entirely truthful. There was someone Stanley cared for. He would find her.

"You have much to contribute, young man. Your good looks and boyish charm will come in handy, especially with my female clients. If you are willing to do whatever I say, you will do very well. It will take some training, but the girls tell me you're a natural. You'll have to give them up for a while. Other women will visit you. Tall, short, skinny, fat, old, young, pretty, and not so pretty. You must learn to please them all. I'll give you the apartment you're in now. The girls will have to move out. Say goodbye to them tonight."

Stanley missed them already, but he wasn't

about to blow this job before it began. He'd have to make some hard choices, cut some people out of his life as he had just done with Susan. His parents he would not miss. They were expendable.

"I won't let you down."

"No, Stanley. I believe you will not."

---

A week passed. Susan had not heard from Stanley. She was beginning to believe he had deserted her. She wondered what she had done to drive him away. She missed his company, their flirting, their furtive grappling. She missed him, but she had to let him go. She had to face the fact that their relationship was over.

Snow collected in drifts outside her door. Its height dwindled and the surface blackened with incinerator soot. Yellow lines in the snow, and brown clumps from neighborhood cats and dogs, had to be avoided. Fresh storms rendered everything white, and the cycle began again. Susan trudged back and forth from the bus stop every day. She suffered the insult of parading around in her skimpy uniform early in the day and the drudgery of housecleaning and preparing supper in the late afternoons and evenings.

Finally she had to face facts and determine whether Stanley was even still alive.

"Hello, Mrs. Kramer? My name is Susan Atkins. I'm a classmate of Stanley's," she lied.

"Yes, Miss Atkins. What can I do for you?"

"Miss Atkins." That told her Stanley's parents did not know she even existed. What a fool she had been.

"Stanley told me he stays with you when he comes up from school. I haven't seen him lately. I was concerned. He gave me this number once, so I thought I'd check and see if he's okay."

"Why, how thoughtful of you, dear. He's left us in the dark too. We haven't heard from him in a while. It's unusual for him not to call, but he's a grown man, and we don't want to butt into his affairs. Do you think we should do something?"

"I wouldn't go by my opinion, Mrs. Kramer. I hardly know him." Saying the words choked Susan up. Once again, she had allowed herself to become someone's doormat to wipe their shoes on. From now on, things were going to be different. "But, I promise, if I hear from him, I'll have him get in touch with you," she told the woman.

"Thank you, young lady. I'm happy Stanley has someone like you to worry about him. He's such a depressed boy. I can't imagine why. He's intelligent and charming. At least I think so, but then what does a mother really know about a child? He's always kept pretty much to himself. I don't think that's very healthy. Do you? Ask him to bring you around, dear. I'd love to meet you."

"That's nice of you, Mrs. Kramer. I'll do that if I see him. Meanwhile, if he gets in touch with you, please ask him to call me."

Susan hung up. She hadn't mentioned Stanley to her own parents, not that they'd care, so why should it bother her that Stanley's parents didn't know about her? There was no one to share her conflicted emotions with. She was alone in the world, just like Stanley was. No wonder they were so compatible. How could he drop her like this? Maybe he got hit by a car. If he were not lying unconscious in a hospital, then she would kill him herself if she ever saw him again.

Mrs. Kramer hung up. Her husband, Charlie, kept telling her to leave Stanley alone. They had been fading in and out of a bender this week. Whole days were lost to blackouts. She hardly knew where she was when she came to. They hadn't been sure where their son was for years. It wasn't the first time they'd lost track of him. Since his birth, whole periods of Stanley's life had gone by without him coming to their attention. Happily, he was a very independent child. He'd had an old two-wheel bicycle, with a

# The Con Case

basket for groceries, to get around the city. He managed quite well on his own. The refrigerator seemed to have something in it most of the time. They felt bad about it, but what could they do? Alcohol had them in its power, and that's all there was to it. They needed a drink to handle the day, and they could scarcely afford a rest cure at some fancy hospital, so alcohol was it. Once they started, they couldn't stop until they passed out. They would come to days later, either together or separately, with or without little Stanley. Charlie, her husband, could barely hold a job. He sobered up once in a while to make a few bucks for rent and electricity. They stole other people's newspapers and milk. They didn't have a television, just an old radio retrieved from the garbage somewhere, she couldn't remember. Stanley always managed to find his way home and sleep in his alcove. He was a good boy. They were proud of him and relieved he got along with so little attention from them.

*The kid's been depressed for a long time,* Mrs. Kramer told herself. Maybe he would finally hook up with that woman who called. Would that be so bad? *He needs to sow his wild oats. The girl and Stanley might even have a baby. I'll drink to that.* She took a slug of vodka—a grandchild.

She felt the alcohol and began to relax. It occurred to her she had no idea where her husband,

Charlie, was.

"Charlie," she shouted. "Are you there? I think we might be grandparents."

# CHAPTER 7

## MASSAGE

Nadine lay facedown on Maurice Kuzinski's massage table. He ran his eyes over the sweet perfection of her body. It was one of those rare moments when he bemoaned his lack of romantic interest in women. It was an opportunity best exploited by some other man, younger, and more compliant with society's norms, if only one of them could get past his martial arts skills. Why did everyone assume men who liked men were pacifists?

He removed the lit cigarette from his mouth and wondered what hot ash to her tush would do to her serenity. Instead, he opted to place it in the ashtray, specifically large enough to prevent it from rolling out onto the floor and catching the building on fire as he worked on Nadine. Of course, a fire would bring Sid, the doorman, up in a flash, and locking eyes with Sid was always a treat for Maurice. But nothing was worth incurring the wrath of Michael Pope by endangering one of his costly female operatives.

He dripped oil down her spine and up over her shoulder blades. "So, sweetheart, how's tricks?" He rubbed the oil into her muscles. She was another one of those deceptively soft-looking women who could rip your head off.

"Maurice, baby, do you ever tire of asking me that stupid question? I'm clean and sober now, trying to make a more or less honest living. Mostly, less. It always puzzles me how a man as good-looking as you can behold my luscious body and not want to jump me. Really. I've looked back there with a mirror. It makes me want to jump myself. It's every woman's fantasy to convert a homosexual. I wouldn't mind, you know, if you ever want to give me a test drive. It could be fun. Mr. Pope, on the other hand, would destroy your ass, and sue you on top of that for false advertising. He thinks of you as his court eunuch, but don't tell him I said that. I know you have cojones. I've seen you handle men twice your size trying to put the moves on me."

"Listen, honey," he replied. "I have no idea how I got this way, but I wouldn't trade places with any so-called normal man if you paid me a million dollars. Our boss keeps me in all the willing partners I need, although Sid and I are expressly forbidden from hooking up. Who knows why? Pope doesn't understand our kind of man. He probably thinks we'll be distracted on the job. I'm truly sorry, there's nothing left over for you in that department, but I do love rubbing your tuchus. That's Yiddish for backside."

"I can tell you love rubbing it. That's why I offered you my services. You are making me hot. You're good, Maury, really you are."

"Relax, will you please, Deen. Let the tension and worry work their way out of you. He's become a harsh taskmaster, our boss, hasn't he? He rides us hard and puts us away wet. Speaking of riding, how's 'Abe the babe' coming along?"

"Maurice, don't even joke about that man. Abraham is not a simple person to work on. He is sharper than he looks. He ran a security check on me like Pope said he would. I had to memorize the whole fake story of my life the boss fed to his investigator."

Maurice slid his hands down the backs of her thighs. Nadine's legs softened as the tightness and worry released. She let out a soft groan. He moved down her calves to her feet, one at a time.

"Oh, Maurice," she sighed, "that feels amazing. Those hands of yours are magic. Sex would be wasted on us."

"Yes, dear. I have always felt like your older brother. Just relax. No one will ever hurt you while I'm here."

"I know, Maurice. I do."

"I love dishing the dirt with you, Nade. Rubbing you down beats some of the sex I've been subjected to lately. Speaking of which, tell me, does Abraham have a big shvantz?"

"God, Maurice, you are so crude. Where did you get all these Jewish words from?"

"Honey, this is New York City, the Big Apple, the melting pot of America. The truth is, I had a Jewish boyfriend who taught me some of his favorite off-color Yiddish expressions."

"Okay then, I will say, yes, his 'shvantz' is pretty big, and you can bet that a man with all his money has had a lot of practice using it. For an old rich guy, he's not bad in the sack. He has moves, you know. He thinks I'm some wealthy abused heiress. I'll tell you this. I would enjoy sex with him a lot more if I weren't so distracted trying to remember my lines while it's happening. They had me memorize a pile of crap about my fictitious life. Mr. P.'s planning to fleece this boy badly, so he will kill me this time, for sure, if I screw it up. Last time he lost his temper he personally put me on life support, broke one of his knuckles, and blamed my battered condition on the mark I was working when the police came calling. I have to concentrate all my attention on fattening Schumann up for the kill."

"I'm sorry Pope hurt you, Nadine."

"That's all right, Maury. It had to be. We are all his slaves. Someday this will end, and we'll have to find real jobs. When and if that happens, I want to do what you do, maybe help train professional athletes, I don't really know. I'll cross that bridge when I come to it. Right now, Pope has me giving Abraham the VIP treatment—you know, the Stork Club, shaving my legs in front of him. Of course, Abraham is paying for it all. I will say this for Michael Pope: he knows how to cut down on overhead. Abraham is not a hard man to like. All that money, a society wife who occasionally steps out on him too. With all his wealth, he's not a very happy man. I think they love each other, but they just can't make it work in bed. Too bad. My whole life, they told me money could buy you happiness. I've never met a single rich man or woman who was all that thrilled by what they had in the bank."

---

Stanley paced the floor of his new apartment.

He was blessedly alone for the first time in days. He did not understand why he felt so trapped. Each time he passed the window, he lifted a slat and peeked through the venetian blinds at New York City's skyline. He felt like a caged animal. How could he have moved so quickly through wild excitement over his luxurious new life, to frustration and boredom? He'd thought pleasure and the trappings of wealth would keep him amused for the rest of his life. It felt like years since Janet and Paula had picked him up at the deli and taken him home with them. When he was given this place to live in, they were moved out. Other women had been sent in a blur to entertain and instruct him in the art of lovemaking and the judicious use of amphetamines and alcohol. He ought to have been thrilled, but with each passing day, happiness slipped further away from him. He never thought he would miss his booze-addled parents, and oh, how he missed the Catholic diner waitress he had taken so much for granted and turned his back on.

*Ding dong.* The chimes rang out.

Stanley opened the apartment door without looking through the peephole. He no longer cared who was on the other side. Who else could it be but another of Pope's minions? An attractive older woman, maybe in her sixties, wearing a business suit smiled and brushed past him into the apartment. Her attitude amused him. What was she here for? These women Pope sent were all so sure of themselves. Stanley had ceased resisting. He helped the woman off with her coat and hung it in the hall closet.

"Hi there," she said. "I'm Catherine. I've come to see how you're doing and answer any questions you may have. Our boss wants to make sure you're being well taken care of."

"Hello, Catherine. Of course, you know that I am Stanley Kramer. Everything is great, I guess. Are you going to tell Mr. Pope everything I say?"

"Not exactly, Stanley. All I need to do is give him the highlights. I take it you're not entirely happy."

"I am. I am. It's just that, for no reason, my mood has taken a turn. I'm feeling a little depressed by all this, instead of overjoyed like when I first got here. I thought my appetite for booze and pretty women was insatiable. After all, it's a dream come true—the clothes, the jewelry, the limo, the girls. I don't mean to be ungrateful."

"That's all right, Stanley. It happens to everybody when they first arrive in Mr. Pope's world. You are just a little ahead of schedule. We discover that self-indulgence is a pretty shallow basis on which to live. By the time we figure out that we've been conned, it's too late. This is when you start earning your keep."

"Maybe I'm just not cut out for this life."

"My dear boy, you talk as if you still have a choice."

"Don't I?"

"It may help you to hear my story. I felt the same way you did. My marriage had failed, as marriages do. I lost my job on Wall Street in 1929, at the beginning of the Depression. I started to drink. I drank all day, and I drank all night for more than a year. I blacked out frequently. I left bars with men I did not know, woke up alone or with people I couldn't remember meeting, sometimes badly beaten, but always with an empty purse. I did things I'm not proud of, shoplifted, wrote bad checks, committed acts of depravity with total strangers."

"I'm sorry to hear that. You don't have to tell me."

"Oh, but I do. I've been instructed to share every sordid detail with you. He wants you to understand just how deeply you are already committed to him. You and I both got here on a losing streak—just about everyone who works for Mr. Pope shares that in common. One afternoon I met a man, a somewhat older version of you, closer to my age. We drank together. He took me to his place. He was very respectful, very gentle, quite generous with me in bed, much like Janet and Paula were with you.

He made me feel loved and sexy as all heck. He bought me expensive gifts. I thought he genuinely cared for me."

"Yes, it was wonderful for me too," Stanley told her.

"Then, one morning, the man took me to a restaurant for breakfast, where I met Michael Pope. There were photographs of me in compromising situations, not just with this man, but with men I had been with in blackouts, stills of me stealing, of me performing disgusting acts in alleyways, sometimes receiving payment for them. He had been compiling a file on me. We were joined by a police detective who assured me there was enough evidence to put me away forever if I did not do what Mr. Pope told me to do. The man who brought me to the breakfast just went away, and I never saw him again. The policeman took me to a hotel room and subjected me to the kind of indignities and pain I hope I never experience again."

"My God," Stanley said. "That doesn't sound like the Michael Pope I know. He seems like such a decent man."

"He is a con artist, Stanley, and now you are one too. Looks can be deceiving, and in our business, they are meant to be. Welcome to the world of make-believe, my boy. As you can imagine, I was hurt and afraid. They turned me over to a woman who nursed my wounds. She took me to a plastic surgeon to repair my face. She got my hair styled and had me outfitted. A rather flamboyant man named Maurice began massaging me regularly to bring me back to life. Watch out for him. He likes good-looking men like you. I was visited in the apartment they put me up in by various men of all ages and sizes, who taught me how to please them. One night the police officer from that awful hotel room came to my apartment and once again did horrible things to me, only this time he did not touch my face. Evidently, he had been informed of the cost of the plastic surgery I required after our last encounter. He hurt me bad enough, even without leaving visible scars, and left me in a puddle of my own urine and feces. I'm sorry to disappoint you, sweetheart, but there is no free lunch, a lesson I learned that night. You play, you pay. This man does not fool around. You do what he says, and you will live a reasonably happy life. You don't, and he will hurt you, have you indicted for a crime you did not even commit, or worse. I came here to spare you further proof of your situation."

"I thought I was still auditioning for the job."

"I hate to break this to you, baby, but you passed the audition the moment those girls laid eyes on you. You just didn't know it. For that one night of pleasure, Mr. Pope bought you body and soul, from your eyeballs to your privates, and now, there is not a

# 91 | The Con Case

thing you can do about it. That's what I was sent to tell you."

"What if I want to leave?"

"That's not happening, my boy. He likes you. More importantly, he has plans for you. You are fresh meat. He has deals to make which require young men such as yourself to service women of various ages and sizes, like the ladies who've been sent to be with you since you arrived. They've reported that you're doing an excellent job and you're a quick study. There are wealthy women—daughters, sisters, wives, even mothers of wealthy and powerful men—that need to be taken care of to pull off certain deals. You need to entertain them while we relieve their families of cash and other assets. You'll remember that some of the women sent to be with you were quite a bit older than you. I bet you never thought women my age could be so appealing with their clothes off."

"Yes. I was amazed, but you're not saying anything to make me feel better. This morning I woke up wanting to leave."

"We all have. Mr. Pope knew it would happen with you sooner or later. My advice is to lose yourself in the work. Every woman you are sent will instruct you in different parts of life on the con. You can even love them, just don't actually fall in love with any of them. They're given to you on loan to teach you what you need to know. Don't you ever dare think you own them. They belong to the boss, just like you. They will love you in the same way. That's how we cope with our situation."

"I guess it's time for me to grow up. It doesn't seem like I have a choice."

"Now you're talking. It's just like real life, only we live in a parallel universe, hopefully invisible to the rest of the world. We've already begun to teach you how to use stimulants to keep you focused no matter how much alcohol you drink. You're going to have the pleasure of demonstrating that ability with me today and letting out your frustration and your fear. Once you completely surrender to your circumstances, you will feel a release like you've never felt before. It will be exhilarating, a spiritual experience even. I'm tough, but please be careful not to bruise me in your enthusiasm. We are going to become fast friends, Stanley. Mr. Pope doesn't care if you rage at your confinement, just as long as you don't act out on it. When you see him, if you know what's good for you, you will behave with the utmost respect, real or phony. He doesn't care. The penalty will be severe if you do not. If he presses me for details, I'll tell him what he already knows. You're gonna get quite good at lying. It's a tool of our trade. He knows how you feel and wants me to loosen you up, which I will gladly do. It won't altogether be business. We're gonna have fun, I promise."

# The Con Case

Stanley sat in silence. He wanted to mourn for the life he had so casually thrown away, but all he could feel was depression, fear, and self-pity.

"It's a lot to absorb, I know. You want to avoid negative thinking at all times. Think of it as being lucky to have a chance at a new life. It's just another job. Only this job has incredible benefits, sometimes out of this world—material, sexual, and social. Are you OK? Say something, Stanley."

"I don't know. All I can feel is panic. I've never been a very happy person. The few friends I have, I've taken for granted, and I hardly see them. My parents are blackout drunks. The sad thing is that, just like I feel about them, no one will miss me."

"That's the perfect attitude, Stanley. Forget about them. We are your new family. You owe your loyalty to us above everyone else."

"I didn't think my life could have gotten much worse," Stanley told Catherine. "I see now I was wrong. I don't like this. I want to go home."

"Put that thought out of your mind, Stanley. This is your home now. Get used to it, honey. It's not so bad."

"I want to tell you something else, Catherine. I think I hurt someone really bad, a girl I had a relationship with. I feel terribly guilty about it. I thought I was better than her. I didn't appreciate what a good person she was."

"What is her name, Stanley?"

"Susan Atkins."

"I heard you deny you had a girlfriend on the tape the boss made of you on your drive together."

"He recorded it? My God, he is a liar. It's too late to fix what I've done to Susan. She probably hates me."

"Yes, it is too late. You will want to forget you ever knew her. Mr. Pope demands complete allegiance. He will do whatever he must to secure it. He knew you were lying, anyway. Stay away from her. Don't call her. Your phone is tapped. Get used to it. You're gonna have to break quite a few hearts in this racket, beginning with mine if you're as good as they say you are. Try to have fun. I won't lie. Vodka helps. I know it's early, but let's have a drink, a tall one."

Stanley got glasses, put ice in them, and filled them to the top with the vodka chilling in the freezer.

Catherine told him, "Take a drink, then take your shirt off and sit in this chair so I can massage your neck."

Stanley drank half his glass and removed his shirt.

"You are a very handsome boy; you know

that, Stanley. You can have any woman you want. You're gonna have to forget everything else and give us both the comfort we deserve. Don't you dare hold out on me. That's it. Relax. Easy does it. Let that nasty tension go into my hands."

She rolled Stanley's head around then cradled him in her arms. His tears began spilling out in torrents. He broke into uncontrollable sobbing.

She laid his head on her breast.

"That's it. Let it out, baby. It's all right."

In the days that followed, Catherine stayed with him. She showed Stanley around town. They would have cocktails in one club and dinner in another. She became a mother, an older sister, a friend, and a lover to him. She instructed him on etiquette. Opening doors, dancing, silverware use, and tipping in advance for special service. She continued his education with amphetamines. On the rare occasion he let himself relax, he would unexpectedly come up short in a state of depression, guilt, and fear at his circumstances. Catherine told him it happened to everyone, that it would get better.

His appetite for self-indulgence, sexual and otherwise, disappeared entirely as if it had never existed. He felt increasingly hopeless. If self-indulgence was this empty, there was no reason to go on. He thought of taking his life.

He tried to stop thinking. He needed more alcohol and less stimulant, but he dared not get drunk lest he be summoned by the boss at any hour, day or night. Even with some degree of control, he drank too much. The hangovers were becoming horrible. He left four aspirin and a glass of vodka on the bedside table every night when he went to sleep.

The frightening thought crossed Stanley's mind that his parents might wake up in a stupor sometime and be worried about not hearing from him. The distraction of the past few weeks had diverted his attention from their pathetic existence. They could become a problem. They might even call the police if he didn't let them know he was okay. He could call them, but he needed to see them in person to make sure they registered his existence inside their thick skulls. His telephone was tapped. Theirs might be disconnected for lack of payment.

He dialed Pope's office.

"Hello, Sally? This is Stanley Kramer. I don't want to bother the boss, but I need to take the subway to the Bronx to stop my parents from calling the police about my disappearance. Do you think he would have any objections to that? Yes, okay, I promise I'll wait to hear from you before I go anywhere. Please tell him I'm sorry to bother him for something as trivial as this, but I didn't want to just disappear without letting him know where I was."

Pope sent a car to pick him up. They rode to the Bronx in a black Cadillac sedan. Ted, the driver, took Stanley to his parents' building and parked. He told him, "The boss said for me to wait with the car while you talk to your folks. His advice to you is to tell them nothing about your new work, just that you're doing good and you don't want them to worry. Anything more, and it could be bad for them and for you too."

Stanley followed instructions. He did not want anyone hurt.

# CHAPTER 8

## BOUNCER

Antonio Vargas stepped into the bar area of a fancy downtown watering hole. There were still plenty of vacant tables and stools. Customers were just beginning to trickle in from their offices. In an hour, the place would be standing room only, and the air would be filled with cigar and cigarette smoke and the noise of conversation.

"Hey, Charlie, how's it going?" Antonio asked the bartender.

"Good. Everything is good." Charlie wore a black bow tie and a rose-colored satin vest with a pen and a folded corkscrew sticking out of his breast pocket. His black hair, oiled and combed straight back, was thinned with age. He seemed remarkably like a paunchy older version of Antonio. He stood drying glasses and aligning them neatly on a shelf behind the bar.

"It's nice to see you, Antonio," he spoke over his shoulder. "Traffic's just beginning to pick up. The lawyers and the Wall Street people are on their first martinis, only some of them seem to have got started before they left their offices. They couldn't make it across the street without a snoot full. How're you doing, man? How's your lovely wife, Maria?"

"She's fine." Antonio grinned, remembering his wife's long goodbye before he left their apartment in Washington Heights. He could have made his rounds with a car and driver, but he hated wasting the workforce, so he took cabs and walked the city streets to check on his security crews spread throughout the restaurants and clubs of Manhattan. He needed the exercise and enjoyed the winter chill.

Two guys from a brokerage house entered the premises. They wore suits. Their ties were loosened. Poster boys for the hordes of brokers it takes to run the stock market. They stood for a while, scanning the bottles on the wall behind Charlie. They appeared to be well lubricated already and considerably hot under the collar.

"What were you thinking, Sammy?" One raised his voice to the other. "That lady was my customer, has been for years."

"I'm sorry, Rob. I lost my head. I'll never call

one of your people again. It was just that the stock started falling, and you were in the can. I didn't think it could wait."

"All right," the first man responded. "I'll accept your apology as long as I get the commission, Sammy."

"No way is that going to happen, man. I did the work."

The first man punched Sammy hard in the mouth without warning, causing a tooth to come loose and blood to drip from his split lip. Sammy raised his hand to his face, observed the blood on it, and clocked his colleague with his left fist to the nose, which made a cracking sound. The one called Rob almost went down with the blow.

Like a flamenco dancer, Antonio took two steps toward the men and brought his huge hands down on their suit collars, which he gripped tightly. As graceful as a gorilla with two clumps of bananas, he hefted them up, walked them out the front doors, and dropped them in a heap on the sidewalk.

The big Hispanic man turned and walked back into the establishment to a round of applause. A customer at the bar pivoted on his stool and said to him, "As long as I live, I will never forget what you just did. I have never seen anything so beautiful, so graceful, so elegant. I swear. You are one terrific bouncer. Please, let me buy you a drink. You have given me a story to tell at parties forever."

"Thank you. I'm glad you enjoyed it, but I must decline your offer of a drink. I never partake when I am working, which is more than I can say for those two gentlemen. Thank you anyway, and enjoy your evening."

At the bar, the man raised his glass to Antonio, took a big swallow in Antonio's honor, and returned to socializing with his colleagues.

"Thanks, Antonio," Charlie told him. "You are a class act. We are lucky to have you and your men taking care of us."

Antonio grinned and winked. "Sure thing. They won't be back. You take care, my friend. I see my employee, Ed, over there in the corner. He was watching, but, let me tell you, he is very fast on his feet and strong like an ox. If I wasn't here, he could easily have been here in one second and handled that mess himself. I'm just going to say hello to him before I leave."

---

Susan Atkins bundled herself up with everything she could find to protect her from the cold.

She layered on army surplus gear, a sweater, a wool cap stretched over her ears, and a thick woolen scarf to cover her nose and mouth. Her pants were rubber-banded at the ankles and stuffed into green rubber boots. Her coat was kept closed by buttons, a belt, and her crossed arms as she made her way south, down a path in the snow on the Grand Concourse's west side. On her way to the grocery store, around the corner at 205th Street, she walked down the hill toward Wilbert Avenue, the center of the densely populated Southern Italian neighborhood. While passing the basement entrance of the dirty white building, she recognized a heavily clad Alice White backing through the gate, her arms hugging two large, full grocery bags.

"Hello, Alice. It's me, Susan Atkins. You remember you got back my purse from that awful boy on Jerome Avenue last summer? His face must still be healing from hitting the sidewalk when you tripped him. It was in the paper. Did you see it?"

"Hello yourself, Susan. Of course, I remember, and, yes, I saw the piece about it in the *Post*. A friend of mine wrote it. It's framed on the wall of my office. My bosses never miss an opportunity to profit from me sticking my nose in other people's business. I'm so happy to see you this cold winter day. We said we were going to stay in touch, but we never did."

"I'm on my way to the grocery store down the hill, Alice. It looks like you just came from there. I can't tell you how happy I am to see you."

Alice asked, "Are we ever going to get together like we promised we would? In fact, are you in a rush right now, Susan?"

"Not really. I have some time before I have to get home and cook dinner for my family—well, for my mother and me at least. My father sometimes doesn't come home for days. Geez, I'm sorry. That was more than you needed to know. But, to answer your question, I'd love to take a few minutes and talk with you."

"Great. If you would, please open the basement door for me." Alice motioned her head toward the gray painted wooden door inside the small courtyard.

They took the elevator, an Otis, the first safety elevator in the world, invented not far north of the Bronx, in Yonkers. The name was imprinted on a brass plate on the elevator floor's front edge—to remind the residents, Alice supposed, of the monumental achievement in engineering achieved nearby. Upstairs she unpacked the groceries. She could barely squeeze the single box of frozen peas into the minuscule metal freezer compartment of her General Electric, made smaller by the perpetual layer of caked-on ice. She would have to defrost it sometime soon, but not now. The canned goods fit easily into the thinly populated cupboards. Beer mostly went on the floor of the broom-closet, but she put a few cans to share with her boyfriend on the bottom shelf of the fridge. More food and light bulbs had been stocked in the house since Jim Peters had begun staying over on weekends. However, the kitchen cabinets and refrigerator still had the unmistakable look of a Bohemian bachelorette pad.

"Susan, can I make you a cup of coffee? I'm having one."

"Yes, sure. I'd love one."

Alice put the smallest percolator she had on to boil and filled the basket with grounds. She refused to use instant.

"So what's new, Susan? Anybody special in your life?"

"Gee, Alice. You cut right to the painful chase, don't you?"

"I'm sorry. What can I say? I'm in law school. I cross-examine everyone I meet just for practice. I suppose I'll learn to tone it down."

"As a matter of fact, Alice, there is someone, or was someone, but I guess I'm not so special to him anymore."

"I see," Alice responded. "You want to tell me

about it? If you don't, I'll understand."

"I suppose it'll do me good to tell someone. I have nobody to speak to, quite frankly, and it's been driving me nuts. His name is Stanley Kramer."

"What's he like, Susan?"

"He's a very handsome boy. I suppose I was a bit forward when we first met in a soda fountain down the Concourse, and I just took him home with me. I feel a little ashamed considering how it turned out. Was I so wrong?"

"You're asking me? You've gotta be kidding. How should I know? I can't very well blame you for doing something I would do. I'm certainly no great authority on relationships. I have my own problems when it comes to men."

"That's not at all comforting, you know, Alice. Well, so, I guess I became attached to him, after months of taking advantage of him."

"You guess? Don't you know?"

"Yes, yes. Of course, I know. You're not making this any easier, fellow woman. I became attached to him. I couldn't stop myself. I was lonely, and he was helpless. I can't believe I was so stupid. I should've got to know him better before I, you know. Your cross-examination thing is making me nervous."

"Yes, well, if I do it right, it's supposed to make you nervous. Haven't you ever read Perry Mason? I'm trying to loosen you up like he does, so you'll crack and confess to a crime you didn't commit, to get me to stop badgering you like they do in Perry's books. It works for him. Only I think he's a lot smoother than me. I'll have to work on that."

"Yes, Alice, please work on it. I know it was shameless of me, a Catholic girl and all, to do such a dreadful thing, but I figured if thinking about it is a sin, I might as well do it. He was coming by my place when he felt like it, which was at least a few times a week. We didn't talk much. Does that make me a bad person?"

"Not at all. Actually, it makes me jealous of you. When it comes to men, I've always thought conversation is overrated anyway."

"Still, Alice, there was something intense between us, and I have trouble believing he didn't feel it as much as I did. Then he just stopped coming around. I haven't heard a word. I was worried something happened to him, so I called his mother. She told me he does this once in a while, but he eventually calls to keep her from worrying. She hasn't heard from him in a while, either."

"When did you speak to her, Susan?"

"A couple of days ago. Why?"

"You might want to call her again before you go jumping to conclusions. Do you have her number?"

"Yes. It's in my purse."

"Use my phone. I'll give you some privacy."

Alice showed Susan to the phone, then went into the kitchen to put the coffee basket in. She replaced the lid on the percolator and sat down to read the day's *New York Post*. Evidently, Stanley's parents were home. Alice heard Susan's animated voice questioning one of them about her boyfriend's whereabouts.

"So?" Alice asked Susan. "Have they heard from him?"

"You were right, Alice. He drove up from Manhattan to see his mother. He never even mentioned me. She told him I called, but he didn't seem all that interested."

When the coffee stopped perking, Alice poured two cups and took a bottle of cream out of the fridge and the sugar bowl off the counter.

They stirred their coffees in silence. Susan looked sad. "He told them he was fine. He said he dropped out of St. John's. He's not gonna be a doctor anymore. He's gonna start working for a wealthy man he met in Manhattan. Apparently, this person has a business with good possibilities for advancement.

Stanley's mother told me he was excited. She said she was glad because he's been unhappy for a very long time. I always suspected his life was a mess. That's probably why he went for a sad sack like me. Birds of a feather."

"Susan, you have got to be kidding. Have you looked in a mirror? You are a beautiful young lady. Someday I'm going to make you up with lipstick, mascara, rouge, a couple of earrings, and the right nail polish. You will be shocked by how beautiful you are. It is every young man's dream to be taken home by a woman like you."

"I don't feel beautiful right now, Alice. What kind of a man does that, disappears, without even having the courtesy to be hit by a bus?"

"A very young, inconsiderate man."

"His mother said he didn't react when she told him I called. What a bastard. That's it. If I ever see him again, I am gonna kill him."

"Susan, get used to it. Men are sometimes terribly thoughtless. Just don't take it personally."

"Alice, I feel like a jerk. I'm sorry I bothered you with this. He's just another awful man I invited to take advantage of me on his way to a better life with someone classier than I am. I can't really blame him, can I. I practically clubbed him over the head and dragged him back to my cave. What a failure I am as a woman and as a human being."

"Susan, I'm sorry this happened to you. I'm glad he's okay, so you can stop worrying about him and move on to despising him. Not all men are like that. You should wish him well because, with his attitude, he's almost certainly headed for disaster. You don't have to lift a finger against him for treating you like he did."

"Gee, Alice. You may be right. I'm just feeling sorry for myself."

"I hope I was some help."

"You were, Alice. I'm sorry I complained about your harsh interviewing technique. I'm sure you'll do very well as a lawyer. Witnesses will be confessing by the hundreds."

"My professors say that I'm 'rough around the edges,' that I attack like a vicious animal, but they say I have promise. Promise of what, they won't tell me."

"Thanks for the coffee and the company, and for encouraging me in yet another dark hour of my life. I gotta go now. That's twice you've saved me from situations of despair. Next time we meet, I hope we'll have something positive to talk about."

"Okay, Susan. Call me and let me know how you're doing. This time we will keep in touch. I don't trust you, so give me your phone number. Don't make me have to hunt you down."

"Oh, Alice. You are so sweet, and funny too. I'll write my number on this paper. Put it somewhere safe. If you don't mind, I'll copy yours off the phone dial."

"Fine, Susan."

"I promise I'll call you. I owe you a cup of coffee and maybe lunch too."


Later, Alice sat at her kitchen table, studying the appeals process. She put on another pot of coffee, the next size up.

She was on her fourth cup. Her bosses had given her the day off to catch up with her law studies. She had picked up the groceries, and Susan Atkins, and was now fulfilling her promise to buckle down.

The radiator hissed and banged in random fits, reflecting the conversion of water to steam inside the boiler in the building's basement and through the vast network of pipes and radiators heating the building's tenants.

*Ring. Ring.* Another interruption.

Abruptly, she answered the phone. "Yes?" she asked gruffly.

"It's me, Alice. It's Jim. Do you remember me? Are you all right? You sound tense."

"Sorry, Jim. I didn't mean to bite your head

off. I'm jacked up on coffee and trying to read the law. I know I need to understand it, but I wish there were a way to do so in my sleep."

"Stay with it, Alice. You are going to be one heck of a lawyer."

"It's very kind of you to say so, my dear. How is your day going, honey? Would you listen to me, talking like a middle-aged housewife."

"Alice, don't get upset. I've been called a lot worse than honey. We are two exceptionally good looking adults who have warm feelings for each other. It's nothing unusual—no need to panic. You're not gonna suddenly wake up married, in hair curlers, and pregnant. If that ever happens, at this stage of our lives, it will not have been an accident. Anyway, we have enough on our plates without having to be responsible for each other and a baby."

"That's very reassuring, I think."

"To answer your question, things are peaceful at the moment. I'm sitting at home in front of the fire. Alone, I might add, reading a book of beatnik poetry by a guy I never heard of named Allen Ginsberg. It just came out a few months ago. It's very 'cool.' I myself couldn't write my way out of a paper bag. I want you to know I have other things on my mind besides kidnapping you and impressing you into service in His Majesty's household. Although now that I've said that, I'm going to have trouble concentrating on reading poetry. So, what exactly are you studying in the law?"

"Appeals. I spoke with our criminal defense lawyer, Clarence Eaton. He talked me out of taxes, copyrights, estates, corporate law, everything I thought would be less dangerous than what he does for a living. He said I was avoiding the inevitable. Who was I kidding? If ever there was a lawyer made for crime, it was me. He told me my only choice was between prosecution and defense. He sounded like Antonio. They are standing in for my father, who I miss and wish he was alive to advise me himself."

"I'm sorry, Alice."

"Yeah, that's just the way it is. Clarence said I should face the fact that I would never be happy doing anything else. So, I'm taking electives in evidentiary issues, appeals, the death penalty, and ethical considerations of all of the above. I shouldn't find it as dull as I do. I mean, people's lives are going to be at stake. I may be a woman of action, but without these courses, I will be a woman of inappropriate and ineffectual action. Please save me."

"Patience, Alice, is a virtue we both have to cultivate. I didn't just start building Broadway sets right off the bat. I was an apprentice for a long time. It took you a while to find your calling. You are not that old to be entering the legal profession. Men and women older than you begin new careers all the time. Speaking of which, I could take the subway up to the Bronx and work on our patience together. What d'you say?"

"Smooth, Jim, very smooth. Oh, God, please, I beg of you, do not tempt me. I'll never get through this if I don't learn to practice some self-denial. I tell you what, you shower and show me that you know how to iron a collared shirt without burning it—that should take two or three hours. Be here in no sooner than four hours, and I will study diligently for another three and shower and, like you, iron my own shirt, and when you get here, we'll mosey down to Luigi's for spaghetti and meatballs, okay?"

"It's a deal. You are one tough negotiator. You gotta meet Rosalind Russell. I'm getting to know her, and you are so much alike. She's rather cute too, in her own way. Not as cute as you, believe me."

"I'm supposed to be distracting you, not the other way around, but I'm only a weak and frail woman."

"Alice, I wouldn't call you that, but I'm going to quit while I'm ahead. You've given me time to drop in at the theater and make sure things are set for tonight's performance. I told Miss Russell about you. She wants to meet you. You know *Auntie Mame* wouldn't be the smash hit it is without my considerable talents. She wants to make sure I'm with the right woman."

"Yes, Jim, you are an artist. I'll see if I can unswell your head when I get hold of it."

"I'm looking forward to that very much. See you after a while."

# CHAPTER 9

## SETTING THE HOOK

A group of well-groomed men and women gathered in Pope's gymnasium on the penthouse's lower level. Their boss sat on the end of his weight bench in shorts while the others sat on the few available chairs or cross-legged on the floor. Some stood against the wall.

"What is the latest on our new employee, Catherine? You've been spending quite a lot of time with him. Has he settled down to his life in captivity?"

Leonard loaded the weight bar, then nudged Pope onto his back. The side table was, as usual, close enough for Pope to roll to his left from his supine position and reach the lit cigarette laying in the ashtray and the open can of beer and take a pull on each before surrendering to the inevitable.

Leonard sighed. "Geez, would you cut that out?"

Catherine answered the question. "Young Stanley is doing very well. He has a natural desire to please women, and an appealing, rather boyish, need for approval. He made it past my sags and wrinkles with no problem and brought me back to the days of my youth with his enthusiasm. We've formed quite a bond of affection. You'll have no trouble from him. You can turn him loose with any woman you want, and he'll have her eating out of his hand in no time."

With Len spotting from above, Pope pressed the bar up off its cradle and dipped it down then away from his chest with an easy rhythm.

He spoke through the exertion, "Great. I have just the woman to try him out on. Our pretty young thing, Miss Sarah Truman, who requires special attention." Talking while pressing that much weight was an impressive demonstration of strength and intended to intimidate his troops. It was not lost on any of them, and they looked on with disgust, smiling thinly at their fearless leader, wishing him ill.

They were confused to learn that young Sarah was to be rewarded with the attentions of their handsome newcomer. All of them had heard that Sarah Truman was caught stealing money and jewelry, without permission, from her last assignment and had almost blown the show. Only quick thinking and intervention by her colleagues had saved the day. They were surprised Pope was not arranging some hideous punishment for her.

Pope moved on, undisturbed by the stir his announcement had caused among his troops. "Have you done background on Stanley—his family, social connections? It would be helpful to have some leverage when he decides to bolt. He's gotta try at least once."

After ten bench presses, he replaced the bar on its stand with Leonard's help. He reached for another puff on his cigarette and a swallow of beer.

A young man in a sweater spoke up. "His mother and father are blackout drunks. A neighbor says he's been a latchkey child since soon after he was born. He's been alone, fending for himself, easy pickings for Paula and Janet."

Paula popped her head up from an invisible position on the floor. "I beg your pardon. He was not that easy. We unleashed a fury of erotic intensity that would have killed a lesser man. He may be depressed, but he broke through it, and we blew the top off his head. He had the stamina of an Olympic marathon runner. We actually had to take turns so we could get some rest and hydration. There was a minute when I thought he had passed out, but it was Janet snoring. I don't think you have anything to worry about, boss, as far as Stanley going the distance. Even with two of us at a time, he held his own."

"Excellent," Pope remarked. "When I met him, I thought he had what it took. What about the love interest he tried to conceal? She someone we could use?"

"Yes, Mr. Pope," the young man piped back up. "He did lie about that. We took a snapshot of him the night you met him for dinner. I showed it around and found out he's been seeing a young waitress, visiting her at her parents' place, in the Bronx."

He continued, "It looks like a rather pathetic dalliance, only a couple of times a week for maybe an hour, but a guy as sensitive as he is has to be attached to her. We could use her for leverage if we need to. It doesn't look like anyone of consequence would miss her if she were to disappear. Her mother works in a sweatshop in the garment district, and her father's a construction worker, a philanderer, and a drunk. I think you could safely say we own Stanley—lock, stock, parents, and girlfriend. What do you think?"

"It's an excellent start, but, as you know, I'm a belt and suspenders kinda guy. I want insurance in every way possible. Set some young stud on the girl to catch her on the rebound. Stanley ought to be ashamed of himself dropping an innocent child like that. The thought of another man seducing her will drive him crazy."

Susan stood on her toes to retrieve a plate for a customer's sandwich. In the mirror, she caught him staring with hunger at her. She had his full attention. Another bad college boy, like the late Stanley Kramer. His shyness was evident. She was a sucker for lonely young men.

She used a knife to cut his sandwich and transfer it to the plate. She opened the stainless lid on the pickle compartment and put two pickle spears next to his sandwich instead of the usual one she was supposed to serve him.

"Are you from around here?" She smiled at him.

He stared back at her, looking a little frightened by her attention. "I er, I moved into an apartment not far from here a few months ago. I'm from Indiana."

"Well, hello, Indiana. Welcome to New York City. What's your name?"

"Adam Murphy. What's yours?"

"Susan Atkins. What brings you to our fair city, Adam? Don't let me hold you up. This must be your lunch hour. Can I get you a Coke?"

"I'd love a Coke. I'm a freshman at Columbia University, downtown, in Manhattan. I held off starting college to work with my folks on their farm."

Susan squirted Coke syrup into a glass and flooded it with seltzer. She figured he was just about her age. He had postponed his own ambitions to help his parents until they could spare him to go to school—what a guy.

The young fellow saw the look of sympathy and arousal on the waitress's face and made a note to include it in his report. She was cute in a plain sort of way. He was looking forward to getting to know her.

"What are you majoring in, Adam?" Susan shoveled ice into his soda, topped it with more seltzer, and stuck a paper-covered straw to the damp side of the glass. She put it down next to his sandwich.

Adam stripped the paper off his straw and took a sip. He answered her, "I haven't decided what I want to do when I graduate. It's all new to me, this going to school and planning my future thing. I've considered majoring in agriculture so I can help my parents out when I graduate, but Columbia is not big on farming, and there's a whole world out there I don't know anything about."

"It's none of my business, Adam, but have you made many friends since you got here?"

"I don't mind you asking. The truth is, no, I have not made a single friend, but sooner or later, I'm sure I will. It just takes me a little longer than most to get to know people."

He thought he detected a drop of saliva escape the corner of her mouth.

Susan noticed the distracted look on her new friend's face, which she mistook for desire.

"New York can be an intimidating place for a boy from the farm. Maybe I could show you around, help you figure out what to do with your life. I hope you don't think I'm being forward, but if I'm going to advise you, you're gonna have to show me where you live and tell me more about who you are. A farm boy, eh? I assume you possess a great deal of physical strength." She said it with a little flirt in her eyes. "How about tomorrow afternoon, when I get off work, you pick me up? Around three o'clock."

"That'd be wonderful. I got a place here in the Bronx to save on rent."

A sad recognition seized Susan: she had learned nothing from the heartbreak she had just experienced at the hands of Stanley Kramer. But she needed comforting, and so she just charged ahead with gay abandon.

"It's settled then," she spoke despite her better judgment. "I have to wait on some other customers, or my boss will yell at me. I'll leave you your check."

With that, Susan put his check on the counter, turned her back on what she thought was HER prey, and trotted off to serve someone else.

---

The first supermarket in Alice White's neighborhood had opened the year before, on the Grand Concourse at 204th Street, the year the building was completed. The market was at the opposite end of the same building the drugstore, on 205th Street, was in. The food emporium took up more space than any other business in the isolated block of commercial real estate. Between the market and the drugstore were a liquor store, a cleaner's, a beauty parlor, a luncheonette, and the entrance to the lobby of the apartment building upstairs. A twenty-four-hour uniformed doorman was stationed at the entrance, the only one who had worked there since the Japanese attack on Pearl Harbor had taken all the doormen on the Concourse to war sixteen years earlier.

For the provincial residents of the area, the market required getting used to. They were in the habit of hoofing it to the tiny, crowded grocery store down the hill where the owner personally retrieved each item on their lists, bagged it all in brown paper sacks, and made change.

Alice was curious to see what all the fuss was about and finally brought herself to give the supermarket a try. The owner was another one of the local Holocaust survivors, balding, with a gold tooth and a numbered tattoo on his forearm. He circulated through the place all day long, with that same wide grin and silly sense of humor that survivors all over New York City were unable to control.

Alice wheeled a brand-new silver shopping cart through the produce department. She picked out a head of lettuce and wondered if, by herself, she could eat it before it turned bad and had to be thrown out. Living alone was very inefficient. She decided to cut it down the middle and give half to Jim—the price of independence, but certainly not a good enough reason to move in together.

Down the aisle, she saw Susan Atkins breezing happily along, perusing the other end of the vegetable section.

"Susan," Alice called. "How nice to see you out and about." She moved toward the younger girl. "How do you like this place?"

"It's nice, Alice. The prices are right, and the floors are polished. I feel sad for the grocer down the hill, though. If everybody starts shopping up here, it's gonna put him out of business. Welcome to postwar America."

"It certainly is big, Susan. They sell fish, and they even have a meat department. But I am not abandoning Mr. Zabronski on Jerome Avenue in his butcher shop, or the fish market next to him. That's where you and I met when your purse was snatched. I walked out of Zabronski's with my lamb chops and just stuck my foot out in front of that creep. Gravity did the rest. He never knew what hit him. So how are you? You look like the cat that swallowed the canary, young woman. You're practically beaming. Come clean."

"You got me, Alice. I did swallow the canary. I have a new beau. His name is Adam Murphy. Running into you here will save me calling you on the phone and telling you. He's a freshman at Columbia. He's got a little apartment like yours here in the Bronx. It's his first time alone in a big city. He stayed on the family farm where he was born in Indiana to help out when he finished high school. He's a little older than most college boys. I'm helping him decide what to do with his life. He hangs on my every word. Can you imagine that, after my practically silent relationship with Stanley? And he's a good kisser too."

"I guess this means you're over Stanley."

"Stanley is history. I am so over that jerk."

Alice told her, "I'm glad you're finished mourning his loss."

"Darn it, Alice, I'm still a little depressed about it. I thought I was done with him forever. Now that I say the words, they feel like a lie. Good grief. I am such a pathetic failure as a grownup, but what happened with Stanley feels so wrong. Yes, it was painful for me, and God knows I'll never forgive him, but I can't help thinking he's in some trouble. It's been nagging at me. I've been trying to ignore it until now, here, seeing you. Am I crazy?"

"I don't know, Susan. I've never met Stanley, but, I must admit, I thought it was just me, but I had a similar thought. He just disappeared. I don't care what he told his parents about finding a new life. It is strange. Maybe you should move on and stay out of it."

# CHAPTER 10

## AWAKENING

Stanley regained consciousness in the leather chair beside his bed. The drapes were closed, but daylight streamed in around the edges. *It's morning,* he thought. He squinted through a throbbing headache. He had drunk quite a lot last night, he remembered, but the bennies, the amphetamines he took, were supposed to keep him wide awake and alert through anything. They had apparently failed. One thing was for sure, he was getting used to hangovers. He'd just take a handful of aspirin and pour himself a glass of vodka, as usual. Then a hot shower, and he'd be right as rain. He thought fondly of the pretty young woman, Sarah Truman, he'd been assigned to entertain last night. She'd turned out to be not only good-looking but smart as a whip too. It would be fun getting to know her. The short time he remembered being with her had taken his mind off the dire circumstances of his entrapment in the service of Michael Pope. He could not remember getting her into bed, and he was still fully dressed, so nothing must have happened in that department except, of course, that he had passed out because of defective stimulants. In the future, he would have to slow down on the booze. Mr. Pope would not be pleased when he found out what had happened.

He looked around the room. His heart nearly broke out of his chest at the scene he beheld. The body of Sarah Truman was spread out, nude, on the bed. Her beauty was marred by the deep gash cut across her throat, stretching from one ear to the other. Blood was everywhere. Her soft white skin was completely drained. The arteries must have been severed. The amount of blood was staggering.

He looked down at himself. His shirt was soaked in blood, as were his pants. On the floor lay a bloody knife with the imprint of a palm on the handle. His right hand was sticky with blood.

Tears of guilt, and fear, welled up and dripped down his face. His life was over. Before, he had thought there was still a chance of escape. Now he would have Sarah Truman's murder hanging over his head for all time. He had arrived, all right, only in hell.

He got out of the chair. He felt her wrist for a

pulse. Nothing. He was a dead man himself, dialing the phone.

"Hello, Sally. You're in early, good. Is the boss there?"

"Stanley, hi. How's my favorite fella? No, he's not. Mr. Pope is probably just getting out of bed. I can see if he's up if it's important. Are you okay?"

"No, I am not okay, Sally. Something bad has happened. I wouldn't disturb him, but it's an emergency. Could you see if he'll talk to me?"

"Sure, Stanley. I'll cut the chitchat and see if I can get him to call you back. Stay put."

Stanley hung up. His heart would not slow down. He sat on the edge of the bed, bent forward, his head in his hands. He couldn't bear to look at the dead body. He reflexively reached again for her pulse and again found none. He laid her arm back down on the bed.

*Ring, ring.*

Stanley almost vomited at the sound. "Hi, Stanley. It's me again, Sally. Mr. Pope says to sit tight right where you are. He'll have someone call you shortly. I told him it was urgent, and he said he was too busy right now to talk to you, but someone will get back to you, pronto. Are you okay with that?"

No help from Michael Pope. "I guess I'll have

to be. I'll wait for the call. Tell whoever it is to hurry, please."

He hung up.

In the silence, Stanley thought about running. He could leave the apartment and get out of the country. Without a passport or money of his own, though, where could he go? He longed for his old life. He knew now that he would never have it again.

*What's taking so long? Why doesn't someone call? I'm in trouble here.*

The telephone rang.

"Hello."

"Stanley, this is Pete Reynolds, one of Mr. Pope's assistants. What's up?"

"What's up is that I'm in terrible trouble here. Something truly awful has happened. I need to talk to Mr. Pope right away. Why can't he pick up the phone and speak to me? I thought I was his 'favorite son.'"

"Settle down, Stanley. You don't want to be talking that way about the boss. We try never to second-guess him. He heard you had some trouble and designated me to take care of it. Calm down and tell me what's going on."

"I'm sorry, but this is a catastrophe. The girl he had me take out last night, Sarah Truman, is dead. She is lying in a puddle of her own blood, on MY bed. Her throat has been cut. There's a bloody knife on the floor. Hold on a second."

Stanley dropped the receiver on the carpeted floor and launched himself into the bathroom to the toilet in time to empty his stomach into the bowl. He flushed and ran cold tap water into his cupped hands to gargle with.

"I'm back, Pete. I can't remember a thing that happened last night after I brought her back to the apartment. We had a few drinks, and I took some bennies. Then I must have passed out. What if the police show up? They'll think I did this. My God! They'll fry me for sure. You have to help me, Pete. Mr. Pope has to get me out of this. I don't want to die."

"Take a deep breath, Stanley. This is nothing we can't handle. There's no reason to get the boss involved."

"God forbid." Stanley failed to contain his anger.

"Shut up, man. Just shut up. Listen carefully. After you hang up, you're going to take off all your clothes, underwear and socks included, and leave them in a pile on the floor. Then you're going to take a shower. Do a good job. Shampoo. Soap and water. Use your hands, not a washcloth. Put on a whole new set of clothes. Don't touch anything and especially don't get any blood on the new clothes you put on. Stay in the apartment. Sit in the kitchen. Make yourself a cup of coffee and, for God's sake, don't call anyone. I'll be there with some people as soon as I can get them together. We'll take care of everything. Just don't let anybody in but me. I'll buzz you from the lobby, one long, two short. Sit tight. Try to calm down. You can spike your coffee with booze, but two shots only, no more."

Pete Reynolds rounded up the cleaners, who were available twenty-four hours a day, seven days a week, to handle just such an emergency as this. An hour later, they swooped in and fastidiously removed any trace of the life and death of Sarah Truman from Stanley Kramer's apartment. They steam cleaned the carpet, sprayed and wiped down the furniture and doorknobs, removed the bedding, and took away Stanley's bloody clothes.

Janet and Paula picked Stanley up as fast as they could get across town. One look at him, and they knew he was in shock. His face shined with nervous sweat. They felt guilt and sorrow for the pain they knew they had brought him. He had thrown away a promising future as a doctor for a roll in the hay with the two of them.

"Don't beat yourself up, Janet," Paula told her friend. "This is what Mr. Pope does to all his employees. We had our version of it, remember. The boss has to know he can depend on all of us when the going gets rough, that no matter how bad it gets, we won't bail out on him because we all know there's something worse facing us if we don't do exactly what he says. If it wasn't us that snatched this guy off the street, it would have been someone else. He was ripe for the picking. In New York City; are you kidding? Let's face it. Stanley Kramer was an accident waiting to happen."

No matter how many times they had seen it, the complete breakdown of a human being was a nightmare to witness, but, they tried to remind each other, it was strictly business. Nothing personal.

They guided Stanley out of the building into the back of a waiting limousine. The drive through Midtown was silent. Janet cradled Stanley in her arms and stroked his hair. He said nothing. His tears had dried up.

The limo came to a stop in front of a Greek restaurant. The driver opened the front passenger door and let Paula out. She, in turn, opened the back door, took Stanley by the hand, and pulled him out. Janet followed. They left the driver with the car and entered the establishment. They filed down the aisle to a table in the back with a checkered cloth. Already seated was a dark-complected, handsome young man who appeared to be in his late twenties. He rose to greet them.

"Stanley Kramer," Paula spoke with formality, "meet Sebastian Lupo, affectionately known as 'the Wolf.' Sebastian, this is Stanley Kramer."

Sebastian possessed the definition and strength of an acrobat. His black hair was held tightly in place with pomade. The two men shook hands. Sebastian could hardly miss Stanley's vacant stare.

"Nice to meet you, Stanley," Sebastian said with a distinct European accent. "I've heard a lot about you."

Sebastian did not expect an answer, but Stanley surprised him. "Nice to meet you too, Sebastian," he said with no enthusiasm. "I've heard absolutely nothing about you."

Janet spoke up, "Sebastian is one of Mr. Pope's most talented employees. He has certain skills Mr. Pope thought would come in handy in your service to him."

She bent toward Stanley and whispered firmly in his ear, "Lose the attitude."

"I'm all yours, I suppose, Mr. Lupo," Stanley said in surrender.

"We're not going anywhere," Janet told him. "We're going to help Sebastian with your training. Let's have lunch first."

"I'm aware of your recent difficulty, Stanley," Lupo told him. "My heart goes out to you."

"I appreciate that," Stanley offered. "Does this kind of thing happen often?"

"In our line of work, my friend, it's always a possibility. It's the price of doing our kind of business. We have had to discipline ourselves to recover quickly from such occurrences. Otherwise, one problem turns into two, or three, or even six. Do you understand, my new friend?"

"No, but I'll try to."

"Good answer. You can use things like this to become strong. You can learn to compartmentalize, so these things don't destroy you . . . or not," Sebastian added with his own touch of sarcasm.

"You think I'll ever get used to this?" Stanley asked. "A beautiful young girl bleeding to death in my bed?"

"Keep your voice down, Stanley," Paula told him.

"You're right." Stanley looked around to see if he had gotten anyone's attention. "I'm sorry."

Paula said, "What difference does it make? It's tragic, yes, but you're already up to your eyeballs in this business. You can blame Janet and me if you want, but you chose to come with us. You let your desires win out over your common sense. You're not alone. That's how we all got here. Now it's time to grow up or suffer the consequences, so watch your mouth. I'm sorry, but it's time you took some responsibility and woke up to the truth. Mr. Pope will go out of his way to give you a good life, but you have to get with the program. Okay?"

"I'm sorry." Stanley snapped out of it. "Sincerely. I'm gonna try. I promise."

"That's the spirit, old boy,," Sebastian told him, clapping Stanley on the shoulder. "Our session after lunch will take your total concentration, and I think you will be richly rewarded for your attention. Leave the big picture to the boss. Just follow your nose. That's how we do it. We have to trust each other to do our part even in tragic circumstances like those you now find yourself in. That's what separates successful professionals from rank amateurs. Amateurs end up in prison for lifting a few hundred dollars from the wrong people. We get away with hundreds of thousands."

"I'll try harder."

"It will be my pleasure to help you. I waited for you to order. Learn to eat through fear. You never know when you will get food again. Afterward, we will stroll over to my hotel for a talk and a little practical instruction in the tricks of my trade."

Stanley ordered a burger, fries, and a Coke. Amazingly, he had an appetite. Afterward, they bundled up and walked to Lupo's hotel. Their driver barely glanced up from his newspaper when they passed him parked at the curb.

"I am a Romanian gypsy, Mr. Kramer. When I was nineteen years old, I picked a man's pocket right here in Midtown. I got clean away with his wallet, and the Rolex watch off his wrist. I was in the zone when I bumped into him. I could have taken the suit off his back and left him standing there in just his underwear and socks. That man, unfortunately for me, was Michael Pope. After I stripped him of his watch and wallet, I passed them off to my sister. On her way to deliver the morning's haul to our uncle, she made an unforgivable detour to her drug dealer and got picked up. That's how fast Michael Pope moves. He gave his friends in vice a description of me. They found my sister, and within hours, she was nailed and jailed. The police returned the articles to Pope and asked him if he wanted to press charges. In exchange for my sister's freedom, we both entered his employ."

"You think he killed Sarah Truman?"

"Does it really matter, Mr. Kramer? Probably, yes, but you may never know. If he did, you would never be able to prove it. Anger will not help you. It will only weaken you. Please give it up. If fate means for you to find out who killed the girl, you will. For now, you focus on a new skill. I'm going to teach you how to pick pockets."

"What use would I have for picking a pocket?"

Paula answered him. "There will come a time, Stanley, when you will need access to someone's house. You may need to relieve them of assets, fine art, bonds, cash, or to make copies of documents. Let's say you and a lovely accomplice, such as myself, wearing a terribly low-cut dress, park across the street from their home and follow them to a restaurant for dinner. I accidentally bump into the man. All the blood rushes below his waist as he stares shamelessly down the front of my dress, all the way to my belly button. Before he recovers, you will have relieved him of his keys, maybe his wallet too. If his house is close enough, you can enter it and do your business. If it is too far away, you will make imprints of the keys. Another pretty woman, or even the same one, spills a drink down the front of his pants on his way to the bathroom and, while she's rubbing his crotch dry, so to speak, you replace the keys and the wallet. We do it all the time. It can be great fun. You'll see."

Lupo took over. "Let us start with the infamous gypsy tradition called the 'Seven Bells.'"

The Wolf took a sports jacket from a hanger in the closet. He let Stanley see the bells sewn into the lining. When he shook the jacket, they jingled. He held it out for Paula to step into.

"We will practice until you can take things from both side pockets, and the inside breast pocket, without making a sound. Then we'll move on to the trousers."

---

After the training session with Lupo, the girls and Stanley said goodbye to Sebastian and walked back to the limo.

"Where shall we dine?" Janet asked her companions.

"Please, count me out," Stanley said. "I've had enough for one day. I'd be much obliged if you would drop me off at my place. I want to turn in early."

"We understand," Paula told him. "You're tired and still upset. By now, your place is as good as new. You'll see."

Stanley told them, "I will get over this. I just need to be alone for a while and stop trying so hard not to think about it."

"You'll be all right." Janet hugged him. "Take a sleeping pill. It'll help. You'll wake up in the morning as good as new. Those pills are strong, so go easy on the booze you use to wash it down with."

"That sounds like just what I need. Thank you both for understanding."

Paula told him, "There's a roast beef sandwich in your fridge if you wake up in the middle of the night hungry. You didn't have much to eat today."

She doubted he would sleep even with the sleeping pill. Everyone knows there's no statute of limitation on murder. Michael Pope had him by his private parts, in permanent captivity. Just like he held everyone else who worked for him.

"Please don't report this to Mr. Pope," Stanley asked them. "I wouldn't want him to think I'm as disturbed as I am. I need to take a break."

"Believe me, he knows exactly how disturbed you are. As long as you don't do something stupid, he's okay with it," Janet told him. "You have been through an ordeal. As for me, I can think of nothing more relaxing to do tonight than to take a bath, make some popcorn, and lay out in front of the television set. That is, if I can find a channel without a lot of interference. I'm actually grateful you're giving us the night off. We'll check in with you tomorrow to see how you're doing. Don't worry about Mr. Pope."

Stanley got in the back of the limo with them. The driver let him off in front of his building.

"Good night, Stanley Kramer," Paula told him when he got out.

They left him standing there on the sidewalk.

Stanley did not want to return to the scene of the crime upstairs. Even if no trace of it were left, it would be too depressing. He raised his collar and pulled down the brim of his hat. The limo was out of sight. With each step down the street, once again, his panic rose. The pavement had been cleared of snow by the building's superintendent. He walked past the entrance. He ached for the lost companionship of Susan Atkins. He had put her out of his mind since this whole misadventure began. Tears of remorse welled up in his eyes. *What have I done?* He was afraid and very alone.

He found a pay phone and felt in his pants for change he no longer carried. He was driven everywhere by Pope's men. His food was bought by someone else. He found a single dollar bill in his wallet and walked on until he found a newsstand. He purchased a *Post* and returned to the phone booth with the change.

He sat on the seat and closed the door. *Dare I call her? How selfish could I possibly be? What can I say to get her to forgive me for abandoning her without a word? Even if she could help me, would she? Am I still so self-absorbed that I would dare to risk hurting her again?*

The answer, sadly, was yes. He was that selfish. He wanted to hear her voice again. He thought of her pain at the sound of his and forced it away. This was all about him, not her, wasn't it? He was rotten to his soul. He knew it now. He dropped a coin in the slot and dialed the number he had almost forgotten, hoping her parents would not answer.

"Susan?" he asked.

There was no response. Susan sat down at the telephone table near the front door, alone in the dark and dingy basement apartment. She was choked up, stunned, and saddened . . . and angered too. She had changed out of her work clothes and finished cleaning. She was about to start preparing dinner. It seemed a long time since she had stopped waiting for Stanley to appear.

"Uh, Stanley. How very nice, and strange, to hear from you. Why are you calling me?"

"Susan, oh Susan." He began sobbing. "How can I make up for the way I've treated you?"

"You can't, really, but it's quite all right. I've moved on."

Stanley felt like he'd been kicked in the stomach.

"I threw away our friendship. I can never forgive myself. I'm not asking you to forgive me, either. I just had to hear your voice."

"Well, you've heard my voice, Stanley. I hope it makes you happy." Susan's eyes filled with tears. She stifled a sob. "Think nothing of it. I'm fine. We never did much in the way of talking anyway. This was bound to happen. It's as much my fault as it is yours. I had so little self-respect that I settled for the pathetic little affair we had."

She was breaking his heart, and she knew it. She wanted to grind him into the ground. He was sorry he'd called. This was more painful than he could ever have imagined it would be.

"God, Susan. I'm so sorry. I was selfish. It was selfish of me to call you. I valued our friendship, and I just threw it away."

"That's fine, old man. Think nothing of it. So, to ask a stupid question, what possessed you to call me now? Things going well for you, and you wanted to gloat?"

"No, Susan, please. They are not. I don't think there's anything anyone can do to get me out of the trouble I've gotten myself into. I had to contact you and beg your forgiveness."

"Quite dramatic, Stan. You expect me to feel sorry for you? Regardless of how shallow our relationship was, I have feelings too. I wondered what I had done to drive you away. I thought we were at least friends. For God's sake, I gave myself to you—

repeatedly, if I recall correctly. What an idiot I was. I'd like to hate you."

"I understand, Susan. I was incredibly thoughtless of anyone but myself. These people, total strangers, took me off the street. Now they own me. They know where my parents live. I'm afraid they'll hurt them."

"My God, Stanley. You really have messed your life up. I've been praying something bad would happen to you. I never thought prayer worked. I guess I was wrong. I'm not sure I meant it to be quite this bad, but you hurt me, and I was outraged."

"I appreciate your honesty, Susan. I'd be angry too if I were you. I won't call you again."

"Wait a minute. That's it? You 'appreciate my honesty?' What is wrong with you, Stanley? You call me and make me feel bad about praying for your death, and now you're just going to drop back out of my life after inflicting another shot of pain? You hit the nail on the head, Stanley. You ARE incredibly selfish."

"What can I say, Susan? I apologized. I'm confused. I didn't think you'd want anything more to do with me. I just called to say I'm sorry and goodbye."

"I totally agree with you. You ARE sorry, Stanley. A sorry excuse for a human being. It's a good thing we're on the phone. Otherwise, I would beat you senseless with this receiver. You've done me a big favor calling me."

"I'm sorry."

"Stop saying that. Shut up about being sorry. Just shut up. I should hang up. I have no idea why I have not. I have a friend who has nerve, possibly insanity, that I've never seen in a woman before. I never thought I'd say this to any man, Stanley, but you are a horse's ass. That aside, however, this woman might be able to do something about your situation. She's reckless, she might even get you in worse trouble than you're already in, but beggars can't be choosers. The last person she helped was shot in the neck and chest and died, she says, if that's any comfort to you, which I hope it is not. But it sounds like you've done a spectacular job of endangering yourself and your family already, anyway, so she couldn't possibly make your problem any worse. If you live, you will owe me big, and I may never give you a chance to pay me back. You are a creep, Stanley."

"You're absolutely right, Susan. I am a creep. I wouldn't blame you if you hated me for the rest of your life. Why should you forgive me? Just do what you think is right. If nothing happens, I will still be grateful."

"Just be quiet about being grateful and tell me

something about what you are facing so I can decide whether just to let you rot . . . or not."

Stanley told her about Sarah Truman but left out the state of undress of her body. He also told her about Michael Pope. He knew the risk he was taking with Pope, but he had to tell someone, or he would go completely insane. He was facing the electric chair. He had nothing left to lose.

"I'll have to cancel my date with my new young man tonight," she told him, to inflict maximum pain. "Call me back tomorrow at the same time. If I don't hear from you again, good luck." She banged the receiver down and ended the call.

She made her excuses to Adam, told him something had come up. He was fine with not going out tonight. He was always so agreeable, so appreciative of the time he got to spend with her, unlike the miserable ingrate, Stanley Kramer, who had dumped her like a rotten tomato. Geez, what was she doing helping an inconsiderate pig like Stanley?

Adam was already bored with her. He welcomed the break.

Susan rolled what Stanley had said around in her head. She was angry with him. She thought of dropping the whole matter and not answering the phone when he called the next day. She wondered if Alice White would be at all interested in Stanley's problem or have time to do anything about it. One way or the other, as soon as this was over, Susan planned to forget Stanley even existed and go back to keeping company with sweet, adorable Adam, who wouldn't hurt a fly.

---

Alice waved the waitress over to take their order.

"Two coffees, please," Alice told her. "Susan, I'm buying. Do you want something with that?"

"Yes, please." She asked the woman, "Would you please bring me some cinnamon toast? I didn't have dinner."

"Coming right up." The woman ambled back behind the counter to pour their coffees. She told the cook through the pass-through, "Frank. Gimme a cinnamon toast, would'ja."

It was late. Susan didn't want to keep Alice out too long.

"I was supposed to have supper with Adam, but I canceled with him to talk to you about my creep ex-boyfriend who dropped me like a hot potato for a better life. Could I be this stupid?"

"It's all right, Susan. I've done worse things. I take it from your call he's in serious trouble. What's he got himself into?"

They were a half a block down the hill on 205th Street, between the basement entrance of Alice's building and Wilbert Ave.

"He's not doing so good in his new and beautiful life," Susan answered with irritation. "Big surprise, but I never thought he'd get himself into quite so spectacular a mess. He's actually quite miserable, which, if you ask me, he deserves to be. He made some lame apology for his behavior."

"How generous of him," Alice replied sympathetically. "What does he want from you?"

"That's why I asked you to meet me. I should be buying you coffee, not the other way around. Stanley's in big trouble. He needs help. I'm sure that's the reason he really called me. I shouldn't have even bothered you with this. Why should either of us lift a finger to help him? When you hear what kind of trouble he's in, you'll understand why I wanted to at least run this by you. I'm not exactly a model of the modern American woman. You're so much stronger than I am, Alice. I told Stanley I have a friend who might be able to help. That would be you, but I promised him nothing."

"Let's hear it."

"He might have killed someone. He doesn't know for sure. He blacked out. Somebody at least made it look like he did it. I can't believe I'm telling you this."

"Geez, Susan. He doesn't fool around, does he? He couldn't have just started with some petty crime? He moved right on to homicide."

"Alice, you don't have to do anything about this. Let him fry. Now that we're here talking about it, I don't think you should get involved. I'm sorry I called you."

"Let's not be hasty, Susan. Bullies and murder always pique my interest."

"It seems like Stanley, the ungrateful, inconsiderate brat, was looking for fame and fortune. I'll bet some woman had something to do with it. For his trouble, he got mixed up with a gang of cutthroats and thieves. This man, Michael Pope, managed to flatter Stanley into abandoning a college education, a career in medicine, and me, for a new and exciting life. He fell for it, hook, line, and sinker. A young girl was brutally murdered in the apartment he's living in. He thinks he might have been drugged. He's not sure. When he awoke, he found her dead body. Someone had cut her throat, maybe him. He doesn't know who. A bloody knife was on the floor. He was soaked in blood—hers, no doubt. He doesn't remember doing anything like that. They sent people to clean it up, but he's sure his fingerprints, at least, were all over the murder weapon. They probably kept the weapon along with his blood-soaked clothes. He's afraid they'll turn him in for the murder if he doesn't do exactly what they say from now on."

"Holy smoke." Alice paused to consider the young man's situation. "That is extreme. I've always wondered about gangs like this. It's amazing how quickly they can make an ordinary person do their bidding. By the time they know what happened, they're slaves, like Stanley. I can't believe this guy, Pope, maybe killed a woman to frame Stanley. She must have done something herself to anger Pope. I wonder how easy it would be to turn the tables on the boss man, Pope, beat him at his own game, con the con artist. Maybe it's time we found out."

"Alice, don't do this. These people sound dangerous. If they killed this girl, they won't take our meddling lying down. My God, where do you get the nerve to even think about doing something like that?"

"That really is the question, Susan, isn't it? I honestly don't know. I get so angry when I hear about a thing like this. Maybe it's because when I was a little girl, I hung out with my older brother, Phil, and his friends. I had to be rough and loud to keep up with them. In those days, I knew no fear. Phil died in Korea. I miss him. Now, sometimes, I do get afraid, but he toughened me up. I can't help myself. How hard could it be, anyway, to throw this man off balance? A guy like him is used to making people afraid. He would never expect to be double-crossed while he's double-crossing someone himself."

"You really think you can save Stanley?"

"Why not? I have friends, you know, Susan, and I carry a gun."

"A gun, Alice? You have to be kidding. You could hurt someone."

"That's the idea, Susan. Haven't you noticed? Your friend Stanley was practically kidnapped. The only question is, are you sure you want me to help him? We could just leave him to suffer the consequences of his actions and read about his fate in the funnies."

"I'm not sure of anything, Alice. Men are so infuriating. Half of me wants to choke the life out of him. The other half wants to take him home and cook him dinner. I wish I never met him, but if you're game, I am."

"Gosh, Susan, it's exhausting watching you talk yourself into helping him. Only understand one thing. If I am going to do this, you have to stay far out of my way. I don't want any civilian casualties. Do you agree?"

"I agree, Alice. I'll stay out of your way, but please promise me you will try not to get hurt yourself. I don't know what I would do if you suffered because of Stanley's poor choices."

# CHAPTER 11

## FAMILY REUNION

Ellen Davis called the Bronx from up north in the Hudson River Valley. "I'm going crazy, Alice. My little village is snowed in. The ground is frozen. The trees are pretty, though. They look sugar-coated, but the birds are gone."

Alice told her, "Calm down, Ellen. Winter can be grim. It's the same down here in the Bronx. There's no sunshine here either, and on top of that, there's dog and cat leavings on top of the snow, everywhere. It's what makes spring so much more wonderful."

"The last time we talked, Alice, was after the customs inspector was killed and that dreadful labor boss was locked up on death row in Sing Sing, waiting to be executed. We at least had the company of the inspector's lovely wife hiding out with us—that was, until he died. She was a wonderful guest. I miss her. It was so sad. Just when she finally gets pregnant by him after years of trying he gets shot and killed. She called us a few months ago to see how we were doing and to thank us again for our hospitality. What a sweetheart. She said she was well and that Detective Bennett was taking good care of her."

"Only the finest people live in my apartment building, Ellen," Alice told her.

"I believe that. She's a real lady. They say people in New York City are hard hearted. It's not true. After she called with season's greetings, though, the world turned white. Everything got quiet. Far too quiet if you ask me. Alice White, you have got to let us down more gently from your adventures. Going so fast from complete chaos to this much calm gives me the bends. These days I'm living in a tunnel between home and work at the hospital. On his way out to the garage in the morning, Milton grumbles about driving to a job site. Aren't you in any trouble we could help you out with?"

"Ellen. You are hysterical. Surely you can find something to entertain yourselves with in hibernation. You and your husband are inventive."

"Alice, dear, you are coming dangerously close to meddling in our conjugal affairs, which are quite healthy, if you want to know the truth. I suppose you're right, though. He's so bored around the house that sometimes he even comes with me to do the grocery shopping. We only have three television channels up here in the wilderness, and they only come in if we adjust the rabbit ears just right. I'm afraid he'll fall off the roof if I ask him to put an antenna up there to get another channel."

Alice asked Ellen, "You remember us taking you to see *My Fair Lady*? You and Milton asking Julie Andrews if she was getting enough sleep and was she eating her vegetables? Like she was your daughter? It was a riot. She was so grateful to be talking to normal people."

"Yes, dear, I remember. That was wonderful. Are we going to do that again sometime?"

"Well, yes. I think so. Jim was talking about how much fun it would be to put you two and me up against Rosalind Russell. I think she would out-mother all of us. She's not exactly a spring chicken like Julie Andrews. I'll ask him to line up some tickets for *Mame,* and the four of us will go together. I'll let you know when."

"Oh, how great. We will look forward to that."

"Besides the weather up there, Ellen, how are things going with you and Milton?"

"We are honestly doing very well, Alice. We have our health. Milt has plenty of work to keep him busy this time of year. Burst pipes, steam heat on the fritz. He's making a better living than our doctor. He tells people to let their faucets drip to keep their pipes from freezing, but do they listen? No. That's why he gets called at all hours of the day and night. Me, as I said, I'm working at the hospital and picking up extra shifts because of colds and flu, and icy driveways."

"That's one thing we don't have to stay home for, Ellen. Half the people in New York City don't own a car. If you can make it to a subway station, you can go anywhere, even to a Broadway show, even from the outlying boroughs. If you want to drive out of town to the country, you get a rental. That's what I do."

"This is not a complaint, Alice, dear, but the truth is that I won't be able to retire anytime soon. These young nurses are not all cut out for the work. It happens. Not every one of them, but some are more interested in coffee breaks than patient care. They drag their feet down the hallway to answer a bell as if it's an imposition. I don't blame them. It's not easy work. Let's face it: medicine is a calling, not a job. It's not as romantic as it looks in the movies. If it isn't in your blood, there are a million other ways to make a living. Look at you. You started as a shopgirl, then became a secretary, and now you're about to become a lawyer. You have a work ethic, for heaven's sake. Don't get me started. What's up with you and James? How's your mother?"

"Jim and I are fine. Mom's fine. I haven't been

getting together with my cousin Fran or my mother or my aunt as much as I used to. I have to give them a call. Thank you for asking. Fran works downtown, not too far from my office. There was a time when we met for lunch every single week. This weather is making me crazy too, Ellen. After work, all I want to do is run over to Jim's place and curl up in front of the fire, study law, or read Perry Mason mysteries. Can you believe he has a fireplace in the middle of New York City? Jim's so-called 'apartment' is the size of your entire house and garage put together. It takes up the entire tenth floor of a commercial building near Broadway. He's the only residential tenant in the whole building. It would be offensive if I didn't enjoy being there so much, especially in the winter."

"I hope you don't mind me sticking my nose into your business, Alice, but why don't you move in with him? I mean, you both work in Manhattan. Face it, you guys were meant for each other. You are adorable together. Take a look in the mirror. Hire a moviemaker to film the two of you sitting in a room together, trying to ignore each other."

"Please, Ellen. Please don't start with me. I'm trying not to think about such life-altering decisions at this juncture. I need room to study, which includes distance from temptation, okay? Jim and I are thrilled with this arrangement, just as it is. At least I am."

"Exactly, Alice. Jim is champing at the bit."

"Besides, how would I live without my Italian neighbors? Even when there's snow on the ground, it feels like home to me up here. The old guys are taking a break from bocce ball, but Luigi's is still open. Of course, half the clientele wear firearms under their jackets to dinner. They hire a troop of teenage gangsters-in-training to shovel the sidewalk in front of the restaurant, make it look like springtime in Miami for fifty feet. So many grown-up gangsters sit around the neighborhood in high-end cars, day and night, with their engines running for heat, that it's the safest neighborhood in New York, maybe even the country. The Italian housewives bring them hot coffee and bowls of soup. If the man in the car is cute and polite enough, they send their daughters with the soup. It's tough finding husbands for Italian mob-maidens in the new world. Sane men are afraid of them, no matter how pretty they are. Even in winter, everybody still goes to the Catholic church down the Concourse on Sundays. I turned out the lights in my apartment and looked out the window on Christmas Eve to watch them climb the hill for Midnight Mass. I'm not a God person, but I sometimes think of myself as an honorary Roman Catholic Italian, which I am neither of. The old guys told my friend the undertaker that they'd want to take me back to Sicily to meet their families and marry me off if it wasn't for Jim. They say time is wasting, and I'd better get married and start having babies. That's not happening anytime soon, maybe never."

"Oh, Alice. I love you like a daughter. Enjoy Jim in your own special way, and don't forget to call your family and tell your real mother I sent my regards."

"I will, Ellen. I promise. Thanks for calling. Give my love to your husband."

---

Just after sunrise, Susan Atkins's phone rang. The apartment was empty. Her mother was already riding the subway to the garment district. Her father had not come home last night. He was probably sleeping it off somewhere, with some strange woman.

Adam Murphy asked Susan with as much enthusiasm as he could muster, "How is my pretty lady this beautiful morning?"

"Well, hello, Adam. You're up early. I'm just getting ready to go to work. Is everything okay?"

"Yes, it is. Does something have to be wrong for me to call you? I just woke up thinking about you and couldn't get back to sleep. I missed you. Do you think maybe we could meet when you finish at the diner today? It's not just the sound of your voice I'm missing."

"Adam, you naughty boy. How about we go out for a hamburger?"

"That would be great. I'll meet you wherever you say."

Susan told him about a joint she liked and hung up. She picked the receiver back up and dialed Alice.

"Hi, Alice. I figured you'd be up. I hope I was right."

"Yes, Susan. I've been up for hours studying, listening to Arthur Godfrey on the radio, and straightening up. I'm always happy to hear from you. What can I do for you?"

"Alice, when and if, I grow up, I want to be just like you."

"Susan, I have had to fight social norms my whole life. I can't believe what the average woman puts up with. Sometime before my brother died, I got a great position at Strawbridge and Clothier, the department store in New Jersey. I was doing a brilliant job for them, even if I do say so myself. Then the men came back from overseas. I didn't begrudge them taking my job. They saved us from the Germans and the Japanese. It just meant I had to start over with a lower-paying position and work my way back up from there. I began at the law firm as a secretary. Now I'm finishing law school at night. I run up the Concourse to Jerome Avenue in the summer, wearing skimpy shorts, to the applause of men and the disapproval of the neighborhood women. I refuse to give in to circumstances forced on me because I'm a female."

"That's why you're my idol, Alice. I was about to flush myself down the toilet after Stanley disappeared. If he had asked me to marry him, give up my life to have his children, I would have. I thought so little of myself. I would have been cooking and cleaning and staying home with the tots into my middle age. I would have sacrificed my life for a man who didn't value me enough to say goodbye before he, sooner or later, would have disappeared, like he just did, without a word."

"That's what I'm talking about, Susan. There's got to be a happy medium. I refuse to believe a career and love are impossible for a woman in postwar America. I love my guy. I really do. But see, that's why we girls have to stick together, so we don't let each other give up our dreams for someone else's. Speaking of which, before I forget, what on earth did you call me about?"

"I'm feeling strange about this guy I'm dating," Susan told her. "And I'm worried this thing with Stanley is gonna take too much of your time.

You're a busy woman. I thought it was inconsiderate of me to impose on you like that."

"I'm not shy about saying no when I have to, Susan. The truth is, I'm easily bored. What's that you said about your new boyfriend?"

"I'm not sure. Maybe my emotions are running away with me because of Stanley. I wanted to hear from Adam a lot, but he's beginning to bother me. After the way Stanley treated me, I'm having trouble trusting Adam's intentions."

"I know what you mean, Susan. Men can be difficult. Their physical needs sometimes take priority over everything else. I suppose mine do too. I'm the last person you should be asking for relationship advice, but I'll do the best I can."

"I feel like I want to back off with Adam."

"Sounds okay to me. Just don't do anything you'll regret, Susan. You never know. Maybe Adam really is the man for you, and you're just getting cold feet because of Stanley. I'd hate to see you miss a chance at happiness because of what the last man did to you."

"Just talking to you has been a great help, Alice. Adam called me this morning and precipitated this wave of anxiety. That's why I called you. Instead of feeling happy like I usually do when he calls, I felt sick to my stomach. Maybe my mind is playing tricks on me. Gosh, Alice, am I crazy, or is this whole situation warping my brain?"

"I wish I could tell you what to do, Susan, but trust your instincts. Women are such easy prey. By the way, what is the name of the town Adam's parents live in?"

---

Alice awoke in the middle of the night and couldn't get back to sleep. It was pitch black outside and looked really cold. She was, uncharacteristically, alone this weekend. She rolled out of bed with socks and a sweatshirt on and looked through the blinds. There were six inches of snow on the fire escape from the last storm. All was quiet and still. Nothing was coming down at the moment. She got the broom out of the kitchen closet and put the coffee on to brew. It didn't take long before it was ready for her to put the basket in and turn down the gas. She went back to the bedroom and swept a comfortable-sized area of snow off the fire escape. She poured herself a cup of coffee, wrapped herself as heavily as possible in winter gear, crawled out the window with a pillow to sit on, and began to sip from the cup.

She was still cold but at peace with the world.

She looked out over the rooftops of the tenements and private houses that her Southern Italian neighbors lived in. Everyone was still asleep. She could barely make out the sliver of the moon glowing through the cloud cover. No stars were visible. In the summer, she often sought relief from the heat out here. No one she knew or had even heard of did this when there was snow on the ground. Every sane person was inside, eyes closed, warmed by the steam heat from their radiators, with the laundry hanging on clotheslines strung across their kitchens to dry.

Alice loved sitting cross-legged, gazing at her beloved neighborhood. The cold was beginning to get to her. Maybe this wasn't such a great idea after all. She tried not to shiver. She pulled the coat tighter around herself. She was cold and alone. Good grief, could she not spend a single night without Jim? He was ruining her. She needed him—especially in the winter, for heat—but that was not entirely true. He was not just a warm body. She would have to either get rid of him or convince him to move here and live with her in the sweetness of her little Bronx neighborhood. She'd have to think about it later when she was warmer.

It occurred to her to call her mother, her aunt, and her cousin Fran for lunch. If she didn't force herself to make the call, it would never happen. She missed them. The weekly downtown lunches with her cousin had become fewer and farther between.

She gathered herself together, got up, and went inside, fastening the window shut, and got under the covers with her coat and hat still on.

---

Alice and the three other surviving members of her family huddled in a pizza place in Queens. The storefront's window was fogged over except for some finger drawing of hearts and initials, made by romantically inclined customers. The tasty flat Italian delicacy, topped with mozzarella cheese, tomato sauce, and running with olive oil, had only recently risen to its great popularity in America. There were debates about what made it taste so much better here in New York than anywhere else. Most people thought it was the oil.

"This stuff is great," Cousin Fran mumbled around a hot mouthful that singed the roof of her mouth. "Alice, what a great idea. I was missing you too. Winter is so long. Ya think this is the beginning of another Ice Age?"

"No, I don't, Fran. It's just that we forget how cold and long winter can be."

"True," Aunt Betsy agreed. "I don't mean to

be suspicious, young niece, but to what do we owe this pleasure?"

"Can't a girl miss her family?" Alice asked her aunt. "Sheesh. I was sitting around, freezing my backside off on my fire escape in the middle of the night, cold and alone, unable to sleep, and thinking affectionately of the three of you, and about my dad and Phil, and I decided to do something about it. So, here we are. Relax. What could I possibly want from any of you, besides love?"

"That's so sweet, dear, but don't kid a kidder. Something's up with you," Aunt Betsy replied. "There's no rush. We can wait you out. There's plenty of pizza left, and I plan on having a cup of coffee afterward."

"So, Alice," Rose asked her daughter, "what's new in your life? Are you still in love with Jim? How're things at school?"

"Yes, Jim and I are still stupid for each other. He's really fixed up his place in Manhattan. It's the entire tenth floor of one of those industrial buildings near Broadway. He's the only private tenant. It's within walking distance of where he builds most of his stage sets. It's like a friggin' country estate, with a terrace and a barbecue, and potted plants for goodness' sake. One of the backers for *Auntie Mame*, the show he's working on, owns the building. On occasion, Jim comes up to the Bronx and stays in my guest room. His favorite time is in summer when the Italian families grow tomatoes in their yards, and the old men play bocce ball after church. If it's freezing, though, I sometimes stay over at his place."

"What was that thing you said about a guest room, Alice?" Fran blurted.

Alice kicked her cousin under the table.

"Thanks so very much for pointing that out, Frannie," Alice replied. "I was trying to be respectful of our mothers."

"Sorry, cuz," Fran said. "How're things at your office? Did you find a replacement for that cute boy you used to torture?"

"Yes, we did, a charming young girl. Funny you should mention Eddie. I just had lunch with him last week. He was in town from Cambridge, visiting his father and his friends. Eddie's mother died since I saw him last. From smoking. There is something else interesting going on. It would break the monotony of the season. This is strictly confidential. Please do not talk about it with your friends. Lives may well be at stake."

"My sister-in-law said you had something on your mind besides missing us," Rose told her daughter. "Alice, my baby, you are not going to risk your life on another job for that law firm you work for, are you? My God, I'm just barely getting over the murder of your two friends, that customs officer and the nice Japanese gentleman you told us about. With all due respect for your desire to help others, can't your bosses find someone else to handle the violent cases? You were always such a delicate creature when you were little."

"Rose," Betsy interjected. "You have got to be kidding. Alice was never what you would call delicate. Meaning no disrespect to you, Alice darling, but you were never what I would describe as 'delicate.' You and your brother, Phil, ran roughshod over the neighborhood like a pair of sailors. When you got older, you scared all the eligible young men away with your behavior, if you'll forgive me saying so. It took a man with a gun, literally—a police officer, Andrew—to win your hand in matrimony, and he didn't even last a year. Rose, what planet have you been living on? This is not a shrinking violet."

Rose responded defensively, "I just worry about her, that's all."

"C'mon now, Mom." Alice tried to reassure her mother. "I would not take on anything remotely dangerous without the company of strong men at my side. I'm not always a hundred percent successful at getting my friends to help me in time, but I'm working on changing my ways. Really, I am. Gimme a break here."

"Try harder, Alice," Rose told her. "You are,

after all, about to become a lawyer. Then you can hire an investigator of your own to do the dirty work."

"Fat chance," Fran mumbled over another mouthful.

Alice ignored her cousin and, this time, withheld kicking her.

"Well, Alice," Aunt Betsy chimed in. "What was it you wanted to say when we interrupted you?"

"Perhaps I was overly dramatic, saying lives might be at stake. When will I ever learn to keep my mouth shut? You may remember, I tripped an escaping purse snatcher on Jerome Avenue last summer. It was written up in the *Post*. Please, Mom, don't give me a hard time. I told you about it. I showed you the article my friend Franklin composed. It was no big deal. It was a total accident. I was coming out of the butcher shop with lamb chops, minding my own business, and this young man just happened to run past me clutching a woman's purse. Somehow I knew it was not his. A woman was running after him screaming that he had taken it from her. That was a clue. What was I supposed to do? I just naturally stuck my foot out, and he tripped. Gravity did the rest. I retrieved the purse and gave it back to the woman. You would have done the same thing in my place. Right, Fran?"

"Yeah, sure, Alice. If you say so," Fran

answered her.

Fran quickly withdrew her legs from her cousin's kicking range.

Alice's mother clasped her chest. "I would not have done any such thing. Why do these things always happen to you?"

"I don't know, Ma. Just luck, I guess. So, anyway, the girl takes me out for a cup of coffee to thank me, and we say we're going to stay in touch, but we never do. That was until we ran into each other outside my building. She filled me in on her social life. She tells me her boyfriend has disappeared, just suddenly stopped coming around and stopped calling. A couple of weeks ago, we ran into each other again. She said, out of the blue, he called her and told her he'd been captured by a gang of con artists in Manhattan. So, she asked me if I would help him. What could I say?"

"You could say no!" Rose remarked. "N.O. You've heard of it. Crooks? When will you learn? It's like you go looking for trouble. It's so hard to keep up with you."

"So, what are you gonna do, Alice?" Cousin Fran was actually interested.

"Well, I'm not sure. At first perusal, I came up with the crazy idea that I could put a gang of my own together and, maybe, pull a con on the con artists."

Aunt Betsy offered her take on the idea. "That sounds incredibly dangerous, Alice, and stupid, and if you think of anything we can do to help you, dear, please keep it to yourself. I'm not on any heart medicines, yet, and I'd like to keep it that way."

"I agree with that thought, Betsy," Rose added. "Of course, it's dangerous. Are you kidding? This is Alice White, almost-lawyer. We do not want to get mixed up in one of her fakakta schemes! That's a Jewish expression. I think it means insane, mixed up, crazy. My God. We could all end up in prison, or worse. You and Fran and Alice and I could be cellmates, or roommates in a hospital room, beaten within an inch of our lives."

"C'mon, Ma," Alice said. "I would never let you get that close to the action. Give me some credit here, will you?"

Fran asked, "Seriously, Alice. You're asking us to trust you? What are you, a used car salesman?"

"I don't know. Maybe I am. Let me think about it, and I'll get back to you. You know I wouldn't ask you to do anything dangerous. I'd only involve you in the far periphery, I promise. Only if it's as safe as can be, and only if I think you'll have fun doing it."

"Alice," her mother pleaded, "please be careful. I was hoping you could think about starting a nice quiet law practice, drawing up wills, maybe helping older people with their taxes. Then you could marry your nice young man and settle down. It's not too late to give me some grandchildren."

"Like that'll ever happen." Fran couldn't resist putting forth one last opinion.

"Seriously, Ma?" Alice asked.

# CHAPTER 12

## ON ADVICE OF COUNSEL

The clack and rhythm of Underwood, Royal, and Remington keys slapping paper against roller, punctuated by the end-of-line bells, provided the background music of the law firm on Nassau Street. Legal briefs, research notes, and client statements being formalized to pay for it all calmed Alice's nerves as she entered the safety and warmth of the storefront offices in this unsavory section of Manhattan. The lettering stenciled on the front window, BRYCE, ADAMS, AND EATON, ATTORNEYS AT LAW, was somewhat obscured by black iron security bars. Maybe someday Alice's name would be added to the list.

Brenda Fox, the telephone operator and chief cook and bottle-washer of the practice, raised her eyebrows and smiled at Alice when she saw her.

# The Con Case

Brenda was listening to a call over her headset and could not speak.

Alice strode past the switchboard and approached her friend Laura McDonald, who sat on guard duty at a desk outside the office door of the firm's only criminal defense attorney, Clarence Eaton.

"You look like a woman on a mission," Laura said to her coworker. "What's going on?"

"I AM on a mission, Laura. A diabolical plan has hatched in my brain about how to free a young man trapped in the service of a ruthless predatory gang boss. I want to run it by the partners before I get myself into serious trouble. You know, just business as usual."

"My heavens, Alice, no wonder Clarence enjoys working with you so much. You remind him of him. You are always charging into the fray without a care in the world for the consequences . . . or your personal safety. Leaping before you look. Damn the torpedoes, full speed ahead. Please, try to be careful. I'm becoming quite fond of you, you know. What happened to your plans for a peaceful practice drawing up last wills and testaments when you graduate? What happened to the safety of estate planning?"

"As far as I can tell, Laura, estates pretty

much plan themselves. Did I say I wanted quiet? I must have been temporarily insane."

"If I recall, at the time, you were depressed about losing your neighbor, the customs inspector."

"I guess I've recovered since then. But don't you worry, I carry a weapon. I need Clarence's counsel about what not to do so I don't destroy a case before I make it."

"He's very good at that, Alice. He learned the hard way, made plenty of mistakes. I watched him."

"I could either speak to him alone or with the other partners in the conference room, but I'd like it to be today. Strike while the iron is hot, so to speak. A young man's freedom, and possibly his life, hang in the balance. You've got to believe me, Laura, I didn't go looking for this. It just fell into my lap."

"It's clear to me, Alice, that your lap goes places it ought not to. Nevertheless, I will advise my boss to make time for you."

"Thank you. Please let me know when's a good time for him."

"Sure, Alice. He has some work to do on a plea for an old Irish gent who broke into a house and removed its valuables to feed his grandchildren. Needless to say, he's not getting paid by his countryman, who has nothing left after the goods were taken back by the police. The good news is that the judge is from Ireland also, and the owner of said goods has a sweet tooth for box seats at Yankee Stadium."

Alice bought baloney sandwiches on lengths of Italian bread spread with mustard and lidded cardboard cups of coffee. She took them into the conference room. Edith and Laura McDonald unburdened their friend and distributed the sandwiches and coffee to their bosses.

Clarence Eaton drew one last puff on the Chesterfield dangling from his mouth, expelled it in a series of well-formed smoke rings, and stubbed out the butt in an ashtray. Everyone was fascinated by the quirks of their new litigator.

Finally, Eaton asked, "I hear you're up to no good again, Alice. I'd guess from the news that you've recovered from the death of our late client, and you're ready to move on. I'm sorry for your loss. Though, I'm happy to hear you're back in action. It was a pity what happened, but bear in mind that Inspector Applewood waited until the very last second to seek our assistance. The labor boss, Menken, is awaiting execution on death row, up the river, in Sing Sing. Care to attend on the widow's behalf?"

"No, sir. No, thank you. That's the stuff nightmares are made of. I was shaken. I've recovered."

"Alice. In here, it's 'Clarence.' In court, you can call me mister or sir, and I'll call you Miss. I hear a young man is having difficulty extricating himself from a difficult situation. Please tell us what you plan to do about it. I do hope you took this lunch out of petty cash."

"No, I did not, but, now that you mention it, I'd be happy to. Thank you. Clarence, what can I say? It may be a lost cause, just like the last one. It's another pitiful gentleman who may, once again, not be able to pay us, at least not out front. If we succeed, however, his girlfriend and I plan to take it out of his hide. He got himself into this mess and badly hurt my friend in the process. He's a cad, Clarence. If he skips out on our fee, the firm can deduct whatever seems fair from my salary."

"Alice, for heaven's sake," Jack Bryce broke in. "It's true if we all engaged in this kind of thing, we'd go broke, and some of us would probably die in the process. But you're bringing in clients with these shenanigans, and you have your own personal newspaperman. I forget his name."

"Franklin Jones."

"Yeah, Franklin Jones, syndicated columnist for the *New York Post*. Maybe we should put him on our payroll. I've never met him, but I'm sure he's as infatuated with you as we are. However, I must ask, purely out of curiosity, if this kind of thing will escalate when you become a lawyer, maybe our partner? It doesn't matter to me. I value your enthusiasm, and we're doing well by it as a firm. So, please, keep your money and tell us what we can do to help."

Alice spoke of the maiden, Susan Atkins, the relationship she'd once had with Stanley Kramer, and the trap he had walked into, laid by employees of the criminal mastermind, Michael Pope, confidence man extraordinaire. She also reported on the stark reality of Sarah Truman's murder in Stanley's apartment—throat slashed, under dubious circumstances, all incriminating Stanley in the commission of the crime.

"My God, Alice. You are a magnet for disaster. How do you intend to prove his innocence?" Eaton asked her.

"I figure the truth will reveal itself in the process of extricating him from the clutches of his new master. Maybe the kid did it, but I'm convinced he did not. I have a clever idea of how to distract his boss while our man escapes. We'll deal with the murder in court if we have to, right, Clarence?"

"If you say so, Alice. I'll be glad to help. Let's hear the rest."

"The other day, I saw an article about horse

racing in the Post," Alice said. "I have an acquaintance who's a jockey, name of Billy Smith. I rang him up, and we discussed the ways a con artist works his victims. There are real estate deals where they sell swampland as if it were waterfront property for development. There's fake art, phony investments, and, of course, switching costume jewelry for the real thing. I asked him if he could come up with a horse-racing con."

"Billy Smith?" Clarence spoke. "You know him? I recollect he was one hell of a rider before the war. He broke horses for show-people in Southern California in the 1940s until he was drafted into the Pacific. He's one of racing's greats. I didn't know he was still riding. You sure you want to get him involved, Alice?"

"This is his idea, Clarence. Me, I need the distraction while I study for finals. You understand?"

"Indubitably, my dear," Clarence replied. "I do remember my own law school experience, made all the more difficult by my need to support myself with night labor, which severely limited my study time. I too found preparing for exams tedious in the extreme."

"On further consideration," Alice told the room, "and in consultation with Billy, I came up with the bright idea of impersonating a rich lady he knows who owns a stable in Ocala, Florida. Billy knows the perfect filly and is friends with the heiress who owns her. I would never have guessed it, but Billy turns out to be one devious little bugger. As a bonus, if the owner agrees to all this, Billy will ride for her and us. The horse is a three-year-old named Wyldfire, with a Y in wild. I ran it by my bulky friend Antonio, who characteristically thinks I'm out of my mind, but agreed, under duress, to pretend to be the horse's groom so he can stay close and protect me. I feel confident that our former client, my current boyfriend, Jim Peters, will agree to play my trainer. This is all, of course, pending your approval and that of the owner herself, Sylvia Green. Green and White. It sounds like a good name for a law firm. My friends are hoping you'll discourage me. What do you say?"

"Alice White, Investigator," Rich Adams announced. He was newly wed to the office temp he'd been fooling around with in the stationery closet. "I suppose you gotta break a few eggs to make an omelet. I don't know. I'm a little sleep-deprived, so don't go by me, but, please, Alice, if things go wrong, stop before you get hurt. I would never forgive myself if you got hurt doing something I agreed to. I don't mind wasting a little money as long as we don't lose you in the process. Are we all okay with this?"

"Fine with me," Jack said.

"Me too," Clarence said. "How do you plan to proceed?"

"For starters, I gotta ask the lady's permission to borrow her horse. Billy has set up a meeting. If she agrees, the race will be here at Jamaica Race Course in Queens, opening day in April."

"What owner would agree to do this?" Laura McDonald asked.

"Billy says she is a pip, that she will love the idea as long as we follow her trainer's plan for Wyldfire's race. He says, if he agrees to ride her prize horse, she'll go along. There's nothing illegal about me setting up someone, as long as we don't tamper with the race itself."

Bryce said, "I'm glad someone knows what they're doing. What could go wrong?"

"I'll ignore that remark. I'm planning to entertain this gangster, Michael Pope, and some other big shots in racing to plant the seeds of Pope's demise in opulent surroundings. Miss Green has a mansion in Queens. Billy is confident she will lend it to us."

"Truly amazing," Rich marveled. "Truly amazing."

"It should be relatively safe for my friends and family to help out at the dinner party, don't you think?"

Rich Adams perked up, "Relatively safe, Alice? Don't tell them that. Whatever you want to say about your antics, you've given us enough cocktail party conversation to last a lifetime. I, for one, am behind you a hundred percent."

Clarence spoke before Alice could ask him. "I'll take Stanley on as a client providing you promise me you won't let this stop you from applying yourself diligently to your studies for graduation from law school, preferably with honors, and to pass the Bar when it is all over."

"Thank you, Clarence. I'll do my best."

"Don't thank me, Alice," said Eaton. "When we're in practice together, I'll find a way for you to pay me back."

"Deal," she said.

"I'll contact the district attorney," Clarence said, "to see what he has on Pope. Even if Stanley did murder that girl, the DA could be a real help with his sentencing."

He added, "I'm glad I joined this firm, ladies and gentlemen. Keep me posted, Alice, so I can bail you out if you get into trouble. Once again, I'm happy you've enlisted the aid of your big friend, Vargas. I'd hate to think of you out there without protection. If this is going to cost the firm money, I request that you keep receipts for taxes."

Alice needed to meet Stanley face-to-face. She had to hear all this from the horse's mouth, or, as Susan would put it, from "the horse's backside." She needed to have eyes on him to gauge the veracity of his story. Despite Susan's ill will toward him, she did not want him to lose his life or freedom if she could help it. If, as Susan suspected, he was being watched by Michael Pope, she would have to find a place somewhere downtown.

In the back office of the garage at ACE Rentals, on West End Avenue, Alice conferred with Antonio.

This garage was the scene of Alice's intervention in the armed robbery that came close to ending her life and the lives of Pete Marcus, the owner, and Antonio. It had sealed a bond between the three of them that nothing could break. Pete no longer accepted payment from Alice or her firm for the use of his cars. Antonio and his crew of security thugs were permanently at Alice's beck and call.

She had no idea where she'd gotten the nerve to hit that drug-addled gunman in the head with a wrench and knock him out, almost killing him. Ever since that day, Antonio had assumed the responsibility of gently, but forcefully, impressing Alice with her true nature. She was aware that her inclination to risk her life and limb to protect others was growing dangerously under his tutelage. To complicate matters, she had struggled with an animal attraction to him ever since they first laid eyes on each other. After Alice had hit the gunman with the wrench, Vargas had used the pocketknife Alice slipped him to cut his and his men's hands free. When she looked up from the body of their would-be executioner lying unconscious on the floor, her eyes glazed with fear, there was Antonio, standing entirely too close. She looked directly into the bruiser's eyes. He was tall, big, and good-looking. Her forehead dampened just thinking about it. Thank heavens he'd married Maria and took the pressure off. Her life was complicated enough handling her feelings for Jim.

"So." Alice shook herself out of her customary initial trance when she was around Antonio. "What I want to do, Antonio, is to free this kid, Stanley Kramer, from the clutches of the con man, prove him innocent of the murder of the young girl, and, if possible, beat the living stuffing out of the man holding him against his will, Michael Pope. How hard could that be? I also have a police detective who's about to marry my pregnant neighbor. You remember Elaine Applewood, Harry's widow. The only chink in the plan is that Andrew Bennett, the cop, doesn't like me very much. He thinks I'm a danger to myself and others. Can you imagine? He puts up with me for Elaine's sake, but he told her he thinks I'm 'reckless and impulsive.' He hardly knows me. It usually takes people more time to figure that out about me, but he is a detective, after all. In any case, I need to meet up with Stanley in a secure location."

"I'm way ahead of you, Alice. I thought of the perfect public place for you to meet Stanley and ask your questions."

# CHAPTER 13

## TWO LIONS

It was a busy afternoon at the 42nd Street branch of the New York Public Library. College and high school students from the five boroughs and beyond walked between the lions on either side of the entrance steps. They were there to finish papers started during the Christmas–New Year break or to get in out of the cold to read. Alice passed between the imposing lions and entered the building well ahead of her rendezvous. A black woolen cap was stretched down practically over her eyes, making her look like the attractive tomboy she was. She wore a long dark blue man's coat off a Salvation Army rack, collar up. In her left hand, she clasped a briefcase she had borrowed from one of the lawyers in her office to complete her disguise as, possibly, a college professor.

Stanley asked his driver to stay with the car while he ducked into the library for something to read himself to sleep. He told the chauffeur he'd be twenty minutes, a half hour tops.

Alice was set up at the end of a long table in the main reading room, with pads and pencils in front of her. She had already scouted an ideal location deep within the shelves of books to meet with the desperate young man. For appearances' sake, she made some notes on a book she had found about the American Revolution. She kept the cap on, and her coat hung over the back of her chair as agreed. Stanley spotted her. When Alice saw his look of recognition, she took her pad and a pencil and headed back into the stacks to the table and chairs she had found earlier. Stanley followed her in and sat down.

In a whisper, Alice said, "Hello, Mr. Kramer. It's nice to meet you. I'm Alice White." She reached her hand out, and they shook.

"Thanks for taking the time to meet me," Stanley said quietly. "I don't think there's much you can do. I did this to myself. I made a mess of my life."

"It's good that you understand that, Mr. Kramer. However, it does not mean we can't get you out of your trouble. If we do, please do not forget the people you've hurt along the way," she told him, "and figure out a way to make it right. I may or may not be able to help you."

"I don't know if I'll ever be able to fix what I did to Susan and my friends."

Alice told him, "I'm just saying, if you get the chance, you'd better try. Why don't you tell me your story, and we'll go from there."

"Okay, Miss White. I'll do the best I can. I don't have much time before my driver comes looking for me."

"I'll help you make it brief, then. Susan told me about Sarah Truman."

Stanley was upset by the mention of the dead girl's name.

"Is there anything you can tell me about her?" Alice shook him out of his daze with her tone. "Do you have any idea who might have actually killed her?"

Stanley answered, "I was instructed to take her out that night, but not by Mr. Pope himself. One of his other employees told me to pick Sarah up and show her a good time. I don't remember anything much about Sarah herself or what happened after we arrived at my place. I was a little drunk, so I took some bennies, amphetamines, the pills truck drivers use to stay awake on the road. I keep them in a drawer in the kitchen. That's all I remember. The next morning I woke up. That's never happened to me before with bennies. Maybe I was overfatigued, and they had the reverse effect. Anyway, I came to in the morning fully dressed, sitting in the easy chair next to my bed. My shirt was soaked in blood. Sarah was laid out naked on the bed with her throat cut. A bloody knife was on the floor next to me. I don't want to hurt Susan any more than I already have, so please don't tell her the details."

"Believe me, Stanley. It wouldn't be any worse than what she's already imagined. You really messed her over."

Tears dripped from Stanley's eyes. He wiped them away with his sleeve.

"You know, Stanley, it would have been easy to substitute knockout pills for the bennies."

"I suppose."

"I'm going to assume that's what happened, but we'll need proof."

"There isn't any proof."

"We'll see about that. If we find out you did it, I have a boss who is willing to represent you. I'll bet your blood-soaked clothing and the murder weapon have not been destroyed. Keep your eyes and ears open. I'll try my best, but don't get your hopes up. You don't know me. My friends and family think I'm crazy. They may have something there, but that's exactly what it's going to take to get you out of this. I will find out what I can about Miss Truman, if that's even her real name. There's a reluctant police officer who doesn't know it yet, but he's gonna help me."

"I can't thank you enough, Miss White."

"Don't thank me yet. You treated Susan like dog doodie. You should be forever ashamed, but now is not the time to punish yourself. She may never give you the chance to apologize, anyway."

"I must warn you, Miss White. This man Pope is dangerous. Please watch yourself. I don't mind getting hurt myself. I deserve it. But I do not want Susan, or you, to get hurt trying to get me out of this. I've done enough damage to other people already."

"I'll keep that in mind. I've had some luck with impossible situations, but it's been just that, luck. Now go. And don't forget to check a book out."

---

Michael Pope lay back on the weight bench once again. He pressed the bar off its cradle and brought it down to his chest, then pressed it up and away. The forty-five-pound black metal plates on either end rose slowly and smoothly. Leonard Sabrinkoff stood over his head, spotting for him, ready to grab the bar at the slightest falter, lest it drop and crush Pope's windpipe.

After his mandatory ten repetitions, he held the weight at arm's length and complained, "Okay, okay, Len, get it off me."

Lenny lifted the bar out of his employer's hands and returned it to the stand.

Pope rolled to his left and took a puff off his smoke and a swallow of beer.

"Ah. The life of a gentleman athlete," Pope announced. "Now that that's over, I will say, Len, that I appreciate you getting me moving in the morning, even though I give you a hard time."

"It's my pleasure," Lenny told him.

"It looks like it's freezing outside, Lenny. The windows are frosted. Must be below zero."

"Yeah, it's pretty cold out there. I watched your staff getting off the elevator, and they looked uncomfortably chilled."

"I'm expecting my new protégé this morning, Len. You'll like him. The girls turned his brain to mush when they snatched him off the street. Then they cut his hair, got him a manicure, dressed him, and bought him enough jewelry to sink a ship. He looks just like a cheap whore, but don't tell him I said that. He thinks he's hot stuff, moving up in the world. He doesn't know he's a dime-a-dozen phony on his way to nowhere."

"Another naïve kid loses his soul to dreams of glamour and wealth," Lenny offered.

"That's what we do, Len. We sell people the dream of wealth in exchange for their souls. Young Stanley is fully locked and loaded. I've taken steps to dispel any ideas he may have of escaping. You remember that young girl who threatened to go to the police about me."

"You mean Sarah? She is a thing of beauty, which makes my mouth water. I love the way she looks. Maybe someday you can lend her to me. What say you?"

"I hate to tell you, Len, but she is no longer available. I tried to reason with her, but she wouldn't listen. To make matters worse, she picked up a needle and a spoon again and refused to let me send her back to treatment. She went through it before. They are the most brutal rehabilitation facility on the planet, and they're right here in New York City. They have nearly a one hundred percent success rate. They're expensive, but they're the only ones who've ever consistently got me results. She said she'd rather die than go back there, and she got her wish, if you get my drift."

"Really?" Lenny asked cautiously. "Does her disappearance have something to do with the new guy?"

"Yes, it does. He was her date the night she disappeared. Something must have gone wrong. Maybe he did something to her."

"Geez, boss. Remind me not to get on your bad side."

"When I want someone locked in, I make sure it's done right. I'm putting him on the wife of the furrier Nadine's been working. It turns out the kid is a natural. He's handsome, well built, and much younger than the wife. He'll have a good time knocking the lady's stockings off. Luckily he came to me with reasonable table manners. He's been training with Catherine, and she says he's ready to rock. I don't think she wants to give him up, but she's gonna have to. This wife assignment will help him get over Miss Truman."

"Geez, boss. You don't think it was a little too much for him?"

"He'll be fine. I suspect that under his boyish charm flows the blood of a selfish, arrogant little predator. I know how to pick 'em. He walked away from his family and his girlfriend without a second thought. He's ruthless and self-centered in the extreme. My kind of guy."

"What kind of play do you have in mind for the fur guy?"

"I'm waiting for inspiration. I'm tired of the stock market. Real estate scams are getting old. Fine art, forget about it. Drugs and guns are out of the question with this man. He thinks he's too good for them. I've done all of it to death, anyway. I'm waiting for something to pique my imagination. Got any ideas?"

"Me? No. Ideas are definitely not my thing. I get your people into physical shape and leave the business end to you, maestro. I don't have the nerve for your line of work. I'm a, what do you call it, support troop."

"Lenny, don't say that. You have plenty of nerve, believe me. Everybody needs a shot of excitement once in a while. It puts zip in your step. It heightens your appetite. Food tastes better when I'm taking chances. There's always the possibility that things will go wrong. Danger is an aphrodisiac."

"But I'm not cut out for that kind of thing. Walking down the street in New York is dangerous enough for me."

"Anytime you want to play with the big boys, Len, let me know. I can always find something for you to do."

"Don't you have trouble sleeping at night, boss, worrying about everything that can go wrong?"

"Leonard, I have an escape plan. I sleep like a

baby."

"Escape plan? Please don't tell me anything about it. I do not want to know. Everybody knows I'm your trainer. I most certainly do not want to give you a reason to have to kill me."

"My God, Lenny. What kind of man do you think I am?"

"You're a businessman, Mr. Pope. I wouldn't take it personally, believe me."

"This is why I keep you around, pal. You know who I am, and you don't hate me for it. You're not afraid to die. I trust you. Now tell me what you really think about what happened to the girl, Sarah."

"Sarah, who?"

"Good answer, Lenny. You make me laugh."

"So, what about the furrier?"

"I'll come up with something. I'm letting him marinate. He's having the time of his life wining, dining, and bedding my gorgeous creation, Nadine. At his own expense, of course."

"Lucky fellow."

"Yes, he is. And I have it on good authority that his wife is not averse to a little something on the side, herself. So I decided to launch my newest protégé, Mr. Kramer, on her, for his maiden voyage. It'll shake him out of the despair he's in over his nasty predicament. He's gonna help me preempt any ugliness Mrs. Schumann might cause about her husband's plaything or the forthcoming trip to the cleaners I plan to take him on. A woman like her is too smart not to smell that he's involved with another woman. I don't want to have to worry about her blowing a gasket and ruining our plans over something so easy to anticipate."

On cue, the double doors from the kitchen swung open, and Stanley entered the exercise area. A scantily clad maid removed his winter coat and took his hat.

"We were just talking about you, Stanley," Pope told him. "Meet Leonard Sabrinkoff, my personal trainer."

The new recruit wore gray slacks and a bulky black sweater. His face was cleanly shaven. Pope could smell Chanel on him. He'd used too much. He even smelled like a whore. He noted the heavy gold bracelet on Stanley's wrist and a Rolex on the other. The gaudiness of the little pissant's ensemble aroused Pope's contempt. The kid was gonna pay for all this expensive junk with his hide. He might be suffering about his captivity now, but he hadn't begun to experience the pain of his situation. Leonard took it all in and kept his mouth shut. *Poor naïve shmuck,* he thought.

The new employee shook Lenny's

outstretched hand. "Nice to meet you, Mr. Sabrinkoff."

"You too," Lenny told him. "You can call me Len since we both work for the same man."

"I guess we do. I was wondering why you called me here, Mr. Pope. Do you have something for me to do?"

"That's the spirit, Stanley. I'm setting up a very wealthy man named Abraham Schumann for one of my many business deals. Precisely what deal eludes me at the moment. He's been spending quite a lot of time around town and between the sheets with a woman I've provided him. I want you to see to his neglected wife so, when this is over, she will not be quite so inclined to make hunting me down her life's work. Do you follow? I'm trusting you with a delicate matter. One slip and you could cost me hundreds of thousands of dollars, not to mention pain and suffering. Some of that money I have already spent on you and Mr. Schumann both, so give his wife your complete attention."

Stanley perceived the threat in Pope's words. He was swept with despair and fear at the memory of Sarah Truman lying lifeless, naked, in a pool of her own blood.

"Certainly, Mr. Pope. I am grateful for everything you've done for me, and I will do the best

I can with Mrs. Schumann."

From somewhere deep in his mind, the faint hope arose that the bizarre, and possibly incompetent, Alice White might be able to pull off his miraculous escape from this horrible circumstance. He stiffened his back and told his boss, "I won't disappoint you."

"Good, Stanley. See to it that you do not."

Stanley faced his employer with a fixed smile. Already he hated the man. He had never been much good at deception, but with practice, he thought, he would become an expert. He knew if anything went wrong with Alice White's meddling, he would suffer for it. So, also, would his parents, and maybe even Susan Atkins if Pope got hold of her. He'd better do this right.

# CHAPTER 14

## ON THE RANGE

Antonio parked in front of Alice's apartment building. Pontiac made one of the few automobiles that comfortably accommodated his size. The heater ran full blast while he scanned the paper spread across the steering wheel. It was a cold, clear Saturday morning. High ridges of blackened snow were plowed along the famous Bronx boulevard's outer lanes. He waited patiently.

If he did not owe her his life, he would never have tolerated this behavior. Her resistance to training with her Browning .380 automatic would have infuriated him coming from anyone else, but he had a weakness for her, so he chose to be amused. He adamantly refused to admit any physical attraction to her. No matter how pretty or smart, no woman had that kind of power over him—besides his wife, Maria, that was.

Antonio chanced upon a story in the paper about a man whose wife had interrupted an episode of marital intimacy to send him out onto the fire escape to chase after her cat. The streetlight below drew a crowd, which, to his extreme consternation, applauded—the story only served to demonstrate that a man who surrenders to a woman is subject to complete humiliation at a moment's notice. One woman was enough for a lifetime.

A knock on the passenger window called Vargas's attention to the lovely Miss Alice White standing in the cold. He kept his reaction to a minimum and leaned sideways to crank the window down.

"Antonio. It's so nice of you to wait for me. You really didn't have to." Alice blinked innocently. "You have to admit I'm closer to being on time than usual. I even made sandwiches and a thermos of coffee for lunch." She opened the rear door and placed an oversized canvas bag on the floor. Then she jumped in the front and raised her window. Antonio held his tongue and made a U-turn across the central lanes of the Concourse, hoping not to be stopped by the police for the completely illegal maneuver, and proceeded north toward Yonkers.

Alice visualized breaking down the Browning, cleaning and oiling it, and reassembling it. It had been a while since she'd done so. She didn't want to mess up or they'd be there all day.

Forty minutes later, they arrived at Coyne Park Gun Range. Antonio parked but left the motor running so they could talk.

"Alice, I see smoke coming out of your ears from worrying about something. What?"

"I am worried about a lot of things, Antonio," she said. "I keep trying to empty my mind, but it just fills back up. It's hard. A lot is going on in there. There's work, school, this thing with the college boy in Manhattan. I got a man on the hook I don't know what to do with. I got important things happening in my head."

"You think thinking about any of them is going to help? It just makes things worse. Focus on what's in front of you right now, and the rest will take care of itself. That's what I do in a fight. I know it's hard, but it gets easier. You want to be here to protect your friends, and yourself, not distracted by problems in the past or the future."

"Antonio, I'll try. You are wise beyond your years."

"I'm not going to have many more years if I keep dealing with you, Alice. Now unpack your gear, and let's get started."

"Antonio, I can't help think how much you

remind me of your friend Jotaro. I don't mean to bring back painful memories. I really don't. As long as I brought him up, though, I'll ask, do you miss him?"

"Jotaro Sarisoto? Yes. I miss him every day. Don't tell Maria. She thinks I'm moody enough as it is. I miss him very much. We went through a lot together."

"I should not have brought him up. It's just, I think of him when you talk about staying in the moment. It's very Zen, just like him. I'm sorry. It makes me sad too. I liked him. He was a good man, and he made me feel safe."

"Don't apologize, Alice. Your words are a welcome relief in my separation from him. Every once in a while, I need to hear his name from somebody besides myself. You did me a favor. He was a beautiful man. He had a heart of gold. He was a fighter like I've never known. We saved each other's lives in prison. It's true, he drank too much, but he carried the weight of a Japanese warrior, forced by an emperor to break his code. Hirohito called, and he had no choice but to go. He did his duty, but he watched American prisoners be tortured and did nothing to stop it. It broke him. He came to America after the war to make amends. He wanted to die here. He was supposed to die here. He did die here. It's all good, Alice."

Antonio touched the tip of his pinkie to the

corner of his eye. Alice obliged him by looking out her window.

Neither of them showed any inclination to leave the heat of the car.

Antonio said to her, "This man you are about to attack is cruel and dangerous, is he not?"

Alice turned back to look at him. "Yes, Antonio, he is."

He continued, "People like him make believe they are someone else and ruin the lives of their marks. Nothing is out of bounds. Wives, sons, daughters, parents. In the chaos, they take fortunes from them. Sometimes more than their victims can afford. They do not care. Worse than that, they leave these people looking like fools. There is nothing more dangerous than a fool with nothing to lose. They get angry and seek revenge. They want payback—like, for instance, the life of the thief and his fellow conspirators. We are here at this range to work on your shooting because you do not want to get caught in the middle with just a powder puff and a smile to fight him off when things go wrong. Make no mistake. They will go wrong, and you can bet on it. For the hundredth time, I remind you, do not carry your gun in your purse or leave it lying around. If you are wearing a dress, you might want to consider getting a leg holster. Strap it up high on your leg, above the knee, with a spare magazine. I can find one for you and help you put it on if you want." Antonio smirked.

"Okay, okay. Don't get carried away, wise guy. I don't particularly appreciate where this is going. After all, I'm very close to becoming a barrister, a litigator. I do not want my picture on the front page of a newspaper at a cocktail party, fumbling under my dress for a pistol. I'll stick to some rig under my arm or behind my back. Okay?"

"Yes, sure. I was just having a little fun with you, killer lady."

Antonio turned off the engine, and they got out of the car. Alice grabbed her bag from the back. She caught up with Antonio as he was entering the wooden shed they had been assigned. Smoke billowed from a black metal stovepipe sticking through the roof. Inside, a fire blazed in a cast-iron potbelly stove.

There was a gun bench to the left of the firing position facing down a long alley with a head-and-torso paper target halfway down it, suspended from a rope. Antonio had told her repeatedly that her best chance for survival at close range was a head shot. Farther away, center mass, the chest or upper stomach.

"Okay," Antonio told her. "Lay out your cloth on the bench and show me what you remember."

"I will, Antonio, but I have a question first. This guy, Pope, is mostly a thief, but he's probably also a murderer. I'm not just gonna go in there and blow him away."

"Alice. You know in your heart he killed the young woman. The boy did not do this thing, and you will prove it. That man cut her throat, let her bleed to death, to make a point to the boy, and also, I am certain, to punish her for something she must have done to him. Maybe she deserved it. It doesn't matter. This tells you who he is. That doesn't mean you should execute him or whoever he sent to kill the girl. Just remember what they are willing to do when they are backed in a corner. I told you, I'm not too fond of con artists. It's all fun and games until something goes wrong. Then they're not just harmless playactors stealing from their prey. Their pride is hurt. It is not just money. It's about power, and the most power there is in this world is the power to take a life. That's how this man, Pope, gets his crew together, like the kid, Stanley. He recruited him and set him up for murder in only a few weeks. He butchered a woman to accomplish his ends. What kind of a man does such a thing?"

"A savage beast, I guess."

"Exactly. That is what we are dealing with here, Alice. Hope for the best, but prepare for the worst. You are not going to carry out a sentence. You hand him over to the law if he doesn't force you to kill him. Let justice take its course if you can but be ready. Do you understand? Practice makes perfect."

Alice said, "I understand. I need to prepare for the worst. So, why are we standing here, talking? Let's get started."

---

The Sunshine Health Club was on Madison Avenue, the most famous advertising street in New York City, possibly in the world. Stanley wore a bright yellow polo shirt with an SHC logo, consisting of the cartoonish drawing of a sun, a barbell, and the caricature of a pretty girl on a blanket at the beach, embroidered on the left chest. He was pushing a cart full of oversized powder blue terrycloth towels, and likewise adorned with the club logo. He knocked on the door of the ladies' locker room. Getting no response from twittering naked women, he wheeled the cart in and began transferring towels to the shelves.

It was after dinner on a weekday. Very few members availed themselves of the facilities at this hour. Stanley was told that this was when Vivian Schumann afforded herself the luxury of a nightly steam. Pope's people had obtained temporary employment for him as a masseur and all-around staff member. They also sent a pretty young accomplice to assist Stanley under the guise of being a prospective member. She entered the locker room through the same door Stanley had, stripped herself naked while he watched, and wrapped herself in a towel from his cart. Stanley had thought, under the circumstances, that he would never again find the sight of a naked woman stimulating. He was so wrong. This woman, her shape, her moves, could make a marble statue stand up and take notice. Michael Pope really knew how to pick them. She was beautiful and she knew it. She smiled conspiratorially at Stanley, all business, and proceeded into the steam room like an assassin.

Mrs. Schumann sat on a bench, wrapped in a towel, trying to read a wilting newspaper in the steam. The young attractive girl joined her. She nodded at Vivian as she entered, unselfconsciously removed her towel, and used it as a cushion on the bench. She closed her eyes and sat in peaceful silence. The older woman could not help but stare.

The young woman opened her eyes. "I'm sorry to impose on you," she said. "I should at least introduce myself. I'm Marcia Newman. I've been thinking of joining this club. They insisted I have a steam and a massage to help me decide."

"Well, hello," Vivian replied. "It's very nice to

meet you. My name is Vivian."

"Pleased to meet you, Vivian," the girl said. "You know, there is a handsome young man in the locker room, putting towels on the shelves, waiting to rub me down. I would consider it a favor if you would take him off my hands. I'm not really in the mood to be rubbed on."

"Why thank you very much. That sounds delightful. I don't mind if I do. I could use a little heavy pressure."

Vivian got up to leave and told her companion, "I hope we meet again."

When she entered the locker room, Stanley acted surprised by the sight of her and averted his gaze.

"Please don't be embarrassed on my account," she told him and turned him around by his shoulders to face her. "The young woman in the steam room gave me her massage as a gift."

Considering she had given him permission, Stanley looked her up and down admiringly.

She told him, "If you don't mind, I'd like it now. Just lead the way."

"Certainly," he replied. "I'll take you down the hall. It will be my pleasure to give you a massage.

# CHAPTER 15

## AT THE POST

Franklin Jones moved his considerable girth briskly along the snow-covered sidewalk, leaving Cleary's Irish Pub in his wake. The proprietor had served him as thick a corned beef sandwich as New York City had to offer, on rye bread, with mustard … and a pickle. He'd had a few too many shots of Irish whiskey and chased them with black coffee. He was headed back to his longtime employer, the *New York Post*. Founded in 1801 by Alexander Hamilton, the newspaper now occupied a fourteen-story building in Manhattan's financial district, between Church Street and Broadway.

The reporter moved his three hundred pounds with a grace most men half his size and age did not possess. Still, he took great care not to slip. A broken hip or arm, he knew, would ruin his day, maybe his entire year. He was Alice's favorite member of the fourth estate, funny, charming, intelligent. The *Post* was his family. His dependability and the popularity of his column had earned him a certain freedom in subject matter. His articles detailing Alice White's adventures not only improved the bottom line of the law firm Alice worked for, but hopefully also increased the circulation of the paper.

Franklin was currently on a weeklong rant about the despicable working conditions in the garment district. Alice was feeding him tidbits about Susan Atkins's mother's miserable circumstance as a sewing machine operator working oppressive hours at low pay in a firetrap of a factory.

Franklin disappeared through a service door into the bowels of the paper.

Alice simultaneously entered through the *Post*'s main entrance. As she approached the tenth-floor newsroom, she braced for the dense cloud of cigarette smoke, the noise of man and machine, the sheer chaos amidst a sea of scarred oak desks covered with typewriters, overflowing ashtrays, and stacks of files and loose papers. She identified Franklin's desk by its huge swivel chair, empty now except for the gaudy red velvet cushion Franklin claimed he'd stolen from the house of ill repute where he lost his virginity as a boy. No one believed that story.

Alice scanned the vast room and spotted him

in his overcoat and hat, moving through the obstacle course toward his seat. He caught sight of her, gave her a wink, and waved her to meet him at the cushion without slowing his pace. When they converged, he pulled out his chair for her to sit on, twirled his coat and hat, like a matador, onto a cluttered wooden coat-tree, and perched his ample bottom on the edge of his desk. He put a cigarette in his mouth and lit it with his desk model Ronson.

"How very nice to see you, my dear," he shouted. "To what do I owe the pleasure?"

"You look about to start work, Franklin. I don't want to interrupt you."

"Nonsense," he replied. "I assure you, the article I was about to type is firmly embedded in my cranium. You may proceed."

"Franklin, I think you're a genius, writing a daily column as you do. I'm not nearly literate enough to pull that off. I don't have half the rhetorical skill set you do."

"I disagree, Miss White. You're about to become a lawyer, for goodness' sake, and cash has a way of sharpening your verbal ability. You'll do just fine."

"Thank you for the vote of confidence. I don't want to waste your time, so I'll get to my mission. I'm about to embark on yet another dangerous undertaking. Can we agree to our usual deal? I pump you for everything you have or can get me on the subject of my investigation, and when it's over, you get an exclusive."

"I love doing business with you, Alice. You have turned a dreary winter day as a hack reporter into one of potentially cutting-edge journalism."

"You are far from being a hack reporter, my friend. If I had anything to say about it, you would have won a Pulitzer for the story you wrote about my caper on the docks last year, and I've been following your series on the sweatshops of the garment district. It may change the world."

"Flattery will get you everywhere. There's a private office they keep for me one floor up. Follow me."

They took the stairs.

When they were seated in relative quiet directly above the newsroom, Jones pulled two glass tumblers and a bottle of Scotch out of the lone desk's bottom drawer and poured them each a drink. This was a windowless space the size of a closet, two chairs, a desk, a typewriter, a chipped crockery coffee cup full of pens and pencils. It had been secured somehow for Franklin's exclusive use, but he generously lent it out to colleagues under the tremendous pressure of a deadline or other emergency.

Alice suppressed her unease at her friend's increasing intake of booze over recent years. It was none of her business. Life was short at best. He would probably outlive her, especially if she persisted in butting into other people's business the way she was doing right now.

"Franklin, this is about a gang of con artists in Manhattan, headed by a man named Michael Pope, who have recruited and trapped a young man into their ranks. He was dating that girl, my friend whose mother works in the garment industry. Actually, you wrote about the girl herself when I retrieved her purse from the thief last summer, outside the butcher shop. She's that Susan Atkins. Remember?"

"Ah, yes, I remember."

"Well, her boyfriend, a premed student at St. John's, disappeared some weeks ago. Then, out of the blue, he contacts her and tells her he's in trouble. Whatever his reasons, he called her, and, amazingly, she didn't hang up on him. Then she comes to me. She is mightily angry with him, but she's inclined to do what she can to save him if only to punish him later."

Franklin listened. "Sounds like something I would do. I can be pretty inconsiderate when it comes to women myself. What's the boyfriend's name?"

"Stanley Kramer. The boss, as I said, is Michael Pope. I met the young man at the 42nd Street library to make sure he was legit and to go over his story."

Franklin did not take notes.

"Alice, dear, you should consider a career in journalism."

"You do the reporting, Franklin. I'll do the snooping. I will never catch up with you, but I agree, this mad-dog instinct does serve me well. Stanley is a good-looking young man. If I was twenty years younger and unattached, and he had a drop of decency in him, I might have given him a run myself. His selfishness and poor judgement have turned her from a wallflower into a battle-hardened veteran. She doesn't know whether to kill him or kiss him."

"I have that very same effect on women, Alice. Maybe someday I'll meet him, and we can compare notes."

"Not funny, Franklin. He really hurt her. Do you want the name of the gang's current mark?"

"I am sorry, Alice. I spend too much time alone at a typewriter. I beg your pardon for my insensitivity. Of course, I want the name."

"Apology accepted. The man's name is Abraham Schumann. Ring a bell?"

"He's in the fur trade. Mink, ermine, fox. He has strong ties to the Russian mob, which is where he obtains much of his merchandise. He's got a showroom on Fifth Avenue. Excellent quality; expensive coats, stoles, and jackets. Outwardly a reputable dealer, but who knows when you're dealing with Russian gangsters? They can be extremely vindictive when crossed. Schumann himself runs a classy operation. He is also known in society circles for the occasional, discreet affair."

"You think he's liable to get violent when he discovers he's been played?"

"I'm not sure, but I wouldn't count on him lying down for it. Pope has to know who he's dealing with. He must be planning to retire someplace far away under an assumed name. I would bet everything I have or will ever make on it. You know, Alice, if you wait, your man, Kramer, can probably just walk away."

"I don't think so, Franklin. It sounds like Pope may have already framed him for murder to ensure his loyalty. I have to prove it."

"I know something about Mr. Michael Pope. He is as slippery as an eel. The vice squad has been trying to shut him down, the straight shooters anyway, but suspected victims have been unwilling to cooperate with their efforts. It mystifies me why he would pick a dangerous man like Schumann to scam.

Opportunity is the dumbest reason in the world, but I sense Mr. Pope has not been entirely happy with his life, and this play may be the expression of a death wish. I'm sure Mr. Pope had no trouble depositing a pretty lady into Mr. Schumann's path. It's almost too obvious. That's what I would do. Pope has him shadowed for a while and arranges for his girl to run into Abraham at one of his haunts, at a party, at the symphony, wherever."

"I'm afraid the boy, Stanley, may die in the aftermath, Franklin."

"If the part about the murder is true, it confirms what I've heard about how ruthless Pope is. You'll need to prove Pope did it or had it done. I suspect, Alice, that you already have a plan to take control of the Schumann scenario. I can't wait to hear what it is. I need another shot of Scotch. You?"

"No thanks, Franklin, but you go ahead."

Franklin poured a generous helping into his glass and returned the bottle to the desk.

"You are correct, as usual. I have given some thought as to how to work Pope," Alice went on. "I do have an idea."

"Do tell."

"It requires influencing Pope to use horse racing as a medium to bilk Schumann. I'm in the process of putting it together."

"I take it you've enlisted the aid of your friend, Antonio, and your neighborhood Italian hoodlums."

"In the end, you will leave them out of your story, right?"

"Alice, you think I'm nuts? Please. I would not have survived this long in my business if I didn't exercise a modicum of discretion. I do not wish to be visited in the night and have my suit, or my face, messed up."

"Good, Franklin. You can't blame a girl for worrying about details like that."

"No. Of course not."

"I haven't spoken to my Italian friends yet, but I will. They may be able to help me move Pope in the right direction. You'll get a kick out of the fact that I've come up with a way to use my boyfriend and my surviving family."

"Alice, you are a treasure. Please don't stop conducting these outrageous interventions. If I get a Pulitzer, I'll give you a cut."

"Deal, Franklin."

"I certainly do not wish to see you hurt, my dear. For heaven's sake, be careful."

"You're making me nervous, Franklin."

"That is my intention. You're just getting nervous now, Alice? I've been nervous ever since I met you. You have no fear, at least none that seems to stop you. Someone has to stand up to wrongdoing in the world. I use my typewriter. You, dear girl, put your life on the line. If it weren't for people like us, the underdogs would be trampled. I admire you more than you know. Please forgive me, but I will always worry about your safety."

"Gee, Franklin, don't you think I've tried to change my ways? I want to blame taking chances on my brother, Phil, or my friend, Antonio, but Philip is gone, and I met Antonio precisely in the midst of risking my life. I didn't set out to save him and his men. They were perfect strangers. I was returning my rental on a Friday night. Minding my own business. I didn't mean to be brave. I wanted to run away when I realized a robbery was in progress. I couldn't force my feet to move out of there. I hit the crazed slimeball trying to take their money in the head with a wrench, hard enough to kill him. Who does such a thing? Not a proper lady, that's for sure."

"Alice, please. You may not be what I would call a proper lady, but you are a lady, nonetheless. You have to accept the fact that you are a beautiful woman—true, a little wacko, but with a good heart and unusual nerve."

"If you say so, Franklin. I'm not gonna argue, although I don't feel that way most of the time. On rare occasion, maybe I do, but in the middle of an operation like the one I am beginning, I get terrified. I just don't let it stop me. I have physical strength, I suppose. I run in the summer. Why, in fact, not long ago, I karate-kicked and almost destroyed an offensive washing machine in my basement, which threatened to quit on me in mid-cycle. Also, I am becoming quite proficient with my automatic, which at this moment is pressing uncomfortably into the small of my back."

Franklin raised his eyebrows and looked alarmed. "I have to talk to the owner of this paper about frisking people when they enter the premises. You just walked in here with a gun? No one stopped you? We're sometimes not very popular, on the street, for our editorial opinions."

"I didn't mean to upset you, Franklin. I just wanted you to know that I travel prepared."

"I'm happy for you, Alice. It's good to know you are armed, but, nevertheless, I'd like better security here at the paper. That aside, I'll see what else I can find out for you. Please keep me informed of your progress."

"I will. Now that that's done, let me ask you, Franklin, how're things going since you broke up with the lovely Cindy Pinsky?"

"That beautiful little girl broke my heart, betraying me with her secret other boyfriend from the

Dockworkers' Union. She played me for a fool, which I am, let's face it, Alice. An old fool dating a mere child. But she's lucky she didn't do time in prison for aiding and abetting them in the murders they committed. The big boss, Alfred Menken, is sitting, at this very moment, on death row at Sing Sing, impatiently awaiting execution in the same electric chair they used for Julius and Ethel Rosenberg. I won't lie. I still ache for Cindy."

"How's it going with Janette Monroe, Franklin?"

"Comme ci, comme sa, Alice. If I were twenty years younger, my dear, you would be in serious trouble." He raised and lowered his eyebrows like Groucho Marx. "My eyes haven't aged a bit. Let me know if you and your young man break up. I can still cut a pretty good rug on the dance floor."

Alice flushed. "No doubt, Franklin, no doubt. I bet you'd be an adventure," she told him flirtatiously, envisioning being trapped naked beneath his tremendous weight. She would have to take a pass on the experience, yet she was genuinely fond of him. Her brief friendship with the duplicitous Miss Pinsky made her aware of just how debilitated Franklin was by his uncontrolled alcohol intake. Much as she loved the newspaperman, she had no wish to become a middle-aged man's nursemaid. She wasn't completely unsympathetic to Cindy's plight as a hopeful actress struggling to survive. Nevertheless, Cindy's betrayal of Franklin placed her beyond forgiveness in Alice's mind. Maybe at some point, she would introduce Franklin to Elaine Applewood's betrothed, Detective Andy Bennett. Andrew made no secret of the fact that he attended meetings in church basements to stay sober.

# CHAPTER 16

## FUNERAL

Johnny Santangelo was born in Naples, Italy in 1934. After the Second World War, Uncle Roberto, Roberto Cavuto, sponsored Johnny's family to move to the Bronx, New York City, in America. Uncle Roberto had done well in the New World, establishing a funeral business a block down the hill from the Concourse, in the southern Italian enclave on Wilbert Avenue. All the neighborhood families used Cavuto's services when—natural or unnatural—tragic circumstances warranted it. It was a favorite story among the neighborhood children and some of their parents that Cavuto used his embalming table for late-night surgery on thugs caught in the cross fire of a regional dispute. No one, except a select few who had awakened on the table to the smell of formaldehyde, knew for sure.

The young boy, Johnny, had caught a bullet

center chest when it blew through the front window of Mochio's Pool Hall. The bullet was meant for the fellow he was shooting eight ball with. Bystanders could only watch with sadness as the blood poured from Johnny's torn heart, out the bullet hole, soaking his T-shirt and pants. They had seen this kind of damage before. Nobody rushed to call an ambulance or the police, 'cause they knew it would be over in less than a minute, and nothing could stop it. When someone did make a call, it was to Johnny's uncle Roberto to notify him of his nephew's death and arrange for the body to be prepared for burial.

Roberto worked quietly on Johnny's body, now laid out on his infamous embalming table. He washed it with care and used a few coarse stitches to close the fatal shot's entrance and exit wounds to prevent further leakage of fluid. He inserted a large bore needle in the antecubital fossa, inside the elbow, and instilled formaldehyde and other solvents used for embalming. Finally, he dressed the boy's body in the suit his mother had provided.

When it was done, Roberto washed his hands, removed his apron, and adjourned to the kitchen for a glass of the wine he regularly fermented. He stored the wine in a large glass jug in a cabinet up over the sink where his grandchildren could not reach it. He pushed through the doors into his kitchen. When he saw he had company, he pulled his hunched shoulders back and straightened his spine. The sight of his two old friends Frankie Amato, "Windows," as he was called, and Enzo Trusgnich, seated at the kitchen table saddened him. They had known him most of his life and had partaken of his joys and his sorrows. They were calm but serious, already sipping the wine Roberto's devoted wife, Tina, had poured for them. Tina had withdrawn, in her private grief, to the living quarters to vacuum and straighten up.

Enzo Trusgnich exuded silent power. Now a southern Italian crime boss in the Bronx, he had emigrated from the Bay of Naples. His face was a study in frozen muscle from years of operating under incomprehensible pressure. A man of few words, he mostly blinked, nodded, or tightened his lips to communicate assent or displeasure. Most men dreaded the seldom-heard rasp of his metallic voice, which almost exactly replicated the sound of a coarse file on the edge of a sheet of metal. He seemed unable to bend his ramrod spine, appearing ever ready to spring into terrible action. Only these close friends and, of course, his grandchildren were not afraid in his presence.

Frankie "Windows" Amato, skinny, deceptively frail-looking, an old Italian with the strength of an ox and the nerve of a high-wire walker, was mostly retired from his life as underboss, capo bastion, second-in-command to Enzo. As a young immigrant also from the Bay of Naples, he'd found freedom in using his childhood acrobatic skills, scrambling over rooftops and up and down the fire escapes of Little Italy in Manhattan. He was the master of height and balance. Now in his seventies, he offered his services as a humble window washer, surreptitiously casing Bronx apartments for the small band of second-story men he commanded. The perennial hand-rolled cigarette dangling from his lips was unlit out of respect for the departed.

"Sorry about your loss," Frankie told Roberto. "We thought we'd drop by and pay our respects."

"Yeah, tanks," was Roberto's grim response. "It's a crying shame. The kid's mother is holding together pretty well. She got used to this kind of thing in the old country. The kid's father isn't talking, but he'll be here for the funeral. Nice of you two to come."

"Ah, Roberto," Trusgnich rasped. "It's a sad thing, but it comes with the territory. I know the kid was learning English, gonna make something of himself. He wasn't supposed to die. I guess you know that. You can rest easy. The strunz who shot him is already dead, if you'll forgive my butting into your business."

"Nonsense. My business is your business and the other way around."

"Good. The least I could do for you, my old friend. The guy Johnny was playing pool with owed the shooter money and refused to pay up. Now he's gonna pay the shooter's family what he owed and make it right with Johnny's parents, and, out of respect, with you, of course. I put a scare into him, but I let him live, so take whatever he gives you in restitution, okay?" Trusgnich pressed his lips together in an impression of a grin and tilted his head sympathetically.

Roberto could see tears in Trusgnich's eyes that would not spill. He spoke up. "Of course, I will. Thank you. You saved me the trouble of doing it myself, or the grieving father, God forbid, and maybe botching the job and landing one of us in prison. I would have done the same for you. The father too. I'll let him know when I see him at the funeral."

"I know you both would." A whisper.

"There is a God in heaven," Roberto resumed. "I suppose this is His idea of justice. The extra cash will pay for the best coffin I have, which I was gonna use anyway. You fellas in the mood for some pasta?" Roberto asked his guests.

"Yeah, sure," Frankie responded, his impish grin revealing the several spaces in his dental layout and the irrepressible sparkle of his eyes. It lightened Roberto's heart.

Roberto filled a pot with water and lit the stove. He threw in a large pinch of salt and grabbed a fistful of pasta from the tin can he kept it in.

"You fellas might enjoy hearing about the latest trouble our girlfriend, Alice White, up the hill, is planning to get herself into. She called me with her condolences. It sounds like she's fixin' to try and do damage to a con man who stole her friend's maybe future husband. It's a chance for a little distraction from this sadness. After all, the injured party is a Catholic girl, even if she's not Italian. Alice could use our help. She's got more guts than common sense. I'm impressed she's lived this long. She's going against a nasty guy, Michael Pope. I know him. He's dangerous, more dangerous than she thinks, maybe."

Frankie said, "I remember Pope. He's a horrible guy, but he's never crossed our path … until now. I knew this day would come. He's not against doing murder to conduct his business if he has to. Wait'll he meets Alice. She will be a real pain in his backside. He is definitely gonna want to kill her when he figures out what she's up to. She better be carrying that auto strapped to her back. Let's try not to let her out of our sight."

"What can we do for her? I owe her after what happened to the customs man," Enzo whispered.

"She needs to steer Pope to a horse," Roberto answered. "We can do that."

# CHAPTER 17

## BACHELORETTE

Alice put the coffee on to perk and fell back asleep. Minutes later, the intense smell of fresh coffee made it up her nose and she got up and took a few long strides to her kitchen. When the coffee was finished brewing, she turned the burner off and poured herself a cup. She liked the pinball-machine layout of her apartment. A few steps in any direction, and she pretty much covered the whole place. She would miss it if she decided to take Jim up on his offer and move to Manhattan to live with him in his palatial digs. In the winters, she'd gotten her exercise just pacing from one end of this so-called apartment to the other. If Jim were here now, they'd be passing each other sideways and bumping into walls.

Alice took a swallow of coffee and turned on the shower. She waited patiently for the water to heat up and got in. This was her daily vacation, standing under hot water, carefree and warm despite the winter waiting outside. A sad substitute for a real vacation. A life of independence required certain sacrifices.

Walking briskly, careful not to slide down the Concourse on her behind, Alice approached Jimmy, the newsie, in his green wooden shed at the top of the subway stairs. He was bundled like an Eskimo. The flaps of his lumberjack's hat were down. A fur-fringed hood extended from the collar of his coat, over his head. He pulled his right mitten off with his teeth to receive Alice's dime and handed her the latest edition of her crossword magazine.

Finally, he managed to speak without his teeth chattering. "Hi, Miss White. Freezing, ain't it?"

She moved her scarf down to answer him. "Yes, it is, Jimmy. Cheer up. It'll soon be even colder."

Alice glanced up at the overcast sky. "Could it be any darker out at this hour in the morning?" It appeared positively polar. She slid her scarf back over her nose.

"Have a nice ride downtown," Jimmy told her. She nodded her head up and down and took the stairs underground to the station.

She found a seat on the southbound D train, unwrapped her face, put her gloves in her pockets, and began working the first puzzle.

Just as the train pulled into Bleecker Street, she looked up, noticed the signs, and shot out the doors before they closed.

Alice wedged herself into the tiny office she refused to vacate, despite her bosses' objections. When she was seated behind her desk, her assistant, Megan, stuck her head in the open door.

"Miss White, you want coffee?"

"Yes. Thank you." The sight of the young girl made her long for Eddie. She envisioned him skidding to a stop in front of that very same doorway at her arrival every day. Her merciless flirtation with him had largely fueled his enthusiasm. He was a young, innocent high school student. There must have been a law against what she was doing, but it was a welcome distraction from the drudgery of long days of office work and nights at law school. She was finally grateful for the flood of returning service members who had taken her job at Strawbridge and Clothier in New Jersey because it had led to her employment here as a secretary and, eventually, to her enrollment in law school. If not for those brave souls, she would still be working retail or, by this time, married with children, on tranquilizers and booze.

There was a stack of file folders on her desk to

be read through and managed. As a secretary, she assisted Edith Burrows with paperwork on the noncriminal cases of her original bosses, Rich Adams and Jack Bryce. Secretarial work on criminal matters was the exclusive purview of Laura McDonald, who was, after all, Clarence Eaton's longtime private secretary. The files in front of Alice concerned real estate issues, lawsuit depositions, taxes, and wills. She could not wait to be done with law school and begin working alongside Eaton. Long after everyone else knew she would, she had decided on practicing criminal law, most likely for the defense, but who knew what kind of a deal she might be offered by the district attorney's office.

She flipped open the first file, read at least one paragraph, then seamlessly picked up the phone and dialed her increasingly pregnant Bronx neighbor, Elaine Applewood, who had temporarily returned to work herself. Elaine's husband, Harry, a U.S. customs inspector, had been shot to death this past year when he had gotten caught up in a labor boss's smuggling operation at the docks of the Port of New York and New Jersey. Elaine, pregnant with Harry's baby, was now miraculously engaged to one of the police detectives who had worked on Harry's case, Andrew Bennett.

"Hello, Elaine. It's me, Alice."

"Hi, Alice. Aren't you supposed to be at work?

How nice to hear from you."

"I AM at work, Elaine, but all work and no play makes Alice a dull girl. I opened one file, and I'm waiting for my assistant to bring me coffee. I'm sort of working. I called you because I'm gonna need law enforcement advice about people I'm dealing with in Manhattan. I know Andrew isn't particularly thrilled by the mention of my name."

"Don't worry about him. His bark is worse than his bite, Alice. What a coincidence, he's picking me up for lunch. I'll let him know you need to talk to him, and I'll tell him to be nice. How's your interborough romance going?"

"It's going all right, I guess. These winter temperatures aren't helping me hold on to my independence up there in the Bronx. There's an expansive residence waiting for me in Manhattan any night I want it, equipped with a man who, I suppose, I adore, and who, I guess, adores me. He's playing me like a Stradivarius. I am going to become a lawyer!" she said emphatically. "He knows I'll need privacy to study for the Bar, and he's prepared to give it to me. I can stay at my present firm, in a much larger office, or I can take a job with the district attorney's office if they will have me. I've got a feeling that's when I will have to decide where to live."

"Alice, what's to decide? I'm telling you, a job and marriage are not impossible to do together. Look at me." Elaine burst into sobs, then stopped. "So sorry about that. As I was saying, I am good at my job, and they're giving me time off when the baby is born. Andy's a perfect gentleman about all of this, and it's not even his child. You and I are two very fortunate women. Let's try not to blow it by overthinking."

"Right, Elaine. Absolutely. I've been spending too much time alone. It's so good talking to you. We gotta meet for lunch sometime soon. Meanwhile, I better get back to work before they fire me and make my decision about living with Jim even easier. Please do ask Andrew to call me, and thank you for telling him to be nice to me. I promise you I will do my level best not to upset him."

---

"An extra-dry martini, please," the regal Sylvia Green ordered the waiter."In fact, forget the vermouth and the olive and pour some gin over rocks, with a twist of lemon. Do you have cheese?"

"Yes mam. Swiss, Roquefort, cheddar."

"Cheddar will be fine."

The waiter wore a white apron which covered black slacks from waist to knees. A hand-knotted bow tie was affixed to his shirt collar. From years of serving customers at the center of the civilized world, 42nd Street, he estimated the lady's net worth to be easily in the millions. Diamond necklace, pearl earrings, rings on her fingers, with the notable exception of the left fourth, and a full-length mink coat draped carelessly over the back of her chair. She might as well wear a sign. "Divorced, rich. Available. Apply within." She was of medium height, blond, about forty, nails freshly polished—a knockout by any standard. Even a man who preferred men, like himself, had to suck back his saliva at the sight of her.

Her companion was equally attractive, in possession of dark piercing eyes, but, obviously, with vastly lesser resources. What were they even doing together? The poor one had black hair, no jewelry, a ratty cloth coat—likely off the rack of some secondhand store—and unpolished nails. Nothing a full makeover and a couple of million bucks in her bank account couldn't fix. The princess and the pauper. He would not want to encounter either of them in a dark alley.

"Miss?" he spoke to the less fortunate of the two.

"Yes." She caught his look of disdain, the tilt of his nose in the air, and smiled in amusement. "A 'wet martini for me, please. Three olives."

"Very well. If that is all, I will be back." He

followed his nose away from the table.

Alice addressed her guest, "Sylvia, I can't thank you enough for meeting me."

"Not at all, my dear. We girls have to stick together. Billy Smith is my favorite jockey of all time. Any friend of his is a friend of mine. I understand you're dealing with a bully. I've been married three times, so I'm an expert. I'd be delighted to help you take one down."

"I'm afraid it's an awful lot to ask, Sylvia. I want to borrow your name, your horse, and your trainer."

A tumbler of gin over ice and a martini appeared on the table between them with a generous platter of cheese and crackers.

The waiter said, "Just give me a glance, and I will return instantly."

"Thank you," Alice told him. "When we're done, I'll take the check." She tried to use sarcasm sparingly, but in this case, it was irresistible. She batted her lashes at him. He looked like he had smelled a fish that had gone bad and withdrew.

"Cheers." Alice raised her glass and took a sip.

She said, "Billy told me you've been training a three-year-old filly in Florida."

"Yes, I have, and she's fast as hell."

"Billy suggested we take advantage of her running on opening day at Jamaica, with your permission."

"That's exactly what I had in mind, anyway."

"But I want to impersonate you."

"How exciting. I'll send you to my hairdresser and lend you some of my jewelry and a mink. I'll even lend you my home near the track to put on a dinner for investors before the race. What fun."

"Are you serious, Sylvia? My God, that's extremely generous of you. My friends told me you'd think my plan was daffy. I was dreading this meeting."

"It would be my pleasure, Alice. I AM the bored heiress you may have read about. I look at you and see myself as a working woman. If you want to know the truth, I'm a bit jealous, but not enough to take a regular job. I notice you're not wearing a wedding ring."

"Yes, well, I tried that once. It lasted less than a year. He was a cop. He didn't exactly leave me rich. We had amazing physical chemistry, but, fully dressed, we both carried too much baggage."

"Me too, Alice. We are very much alike, except for the diamonds and the hair, but that never mattered much to me—though, I must say, it clearly matters to our waiter."

The women laughed and clinked glasses. Sylvia said, "Here's to the beginning of a beautiful friendship."

Alice smiled and said,. "The damage we could do together boggles the imagination. The world may not survive this."

"I hope not."

Alice took a sip of her drink. "Tell me about your horse and what it's like to own a stable. I have a boyfriend who agreed to pretend to be your trainer, as long as your actual trainer is there to tell him what to do. Jim builds sets for Broadway shows. I also have a large Hispanic protector, Antonio Vargas. He works in security. He said he wants to be a groom so he can keep an eye on me."

"When I tell you about the care and training of thoroughbreds, you'll understand why they're better than men. For one thing, they learn."

"Very funny." Alice laughed.

"My prize is named Wyldfire. As you know, she's three years old. I've been training her in Ocala, Florida, far from prying eyes. She's been clocked at five-eighths of a mile in fifty-nine and two-fifths seconds and can run three-quarters of a mile in one eleven and three-fifths. You have no way of knowing this, but that is fast. Billy would be the perfect rider for Wyldfire. He has instinct and guts. I'd be honored to have him. It would be a dream come true."

"That was what he was hoping you'd say. If anything goes wrong, Sylvia, I don't want you hurt," Alice said. "I'm not sure how to protect you. You wouldn't consider taking a vacation, would you?"

"Would you hide out if you were me, Alice?"

"Never. Not after all the work you put into getting Wyldfire ready for this race."

"Exactly. I'll get a wig and a gigantic pair of fake bosoms. I've always wondered what a big chest would look like on me. Now I'll have a chance to find out. I'll also get costume jewelry and a gaudy outfit to go with them. I can't wait. I've been planning this race for three years. I intend to be right there at the finish line."

"You can't blame me for worrying about your safety," Alice said.

"Oh, I understand all right, Alice, but no guts, no glory."

"This guy Pope fancies himself a real ladies' man, Sylvia, so with your diamonds and my new blond hair, I'm not gonna have any trouble charming his socks off."

"Seriously, Alice, flirt with him all you want. I

don't mind getting a reputation as a floozy. I've been entirely too well behaved the last few years. My ex-husbands wore me out. Besides, I'm getting what I want, which is to run Wyldfire in a high-stakes race. It's an extra treat to be part of hurting your Mr. Pope."

"If you are going to stick around, Sylvia, I insist you let our firm pay for your wig and boobs. It's the least we can do. Please don't say no."

"All right, Alice. This is going to add a whole new chapter to my memoirs."

# CHAPTER 18

## BAGS

Vincent Bagalucci had been a fixer in Little Italy from childhood. He was just a baby when his family emigrated from the old country. No one paid the slightest attention to his age. It was the force of his intention and his attitude that separated him from his contemporaries. The men on the street joked that Vinnie was buying and selling rattles from his crib. If he didn't have the rattle you wanted, he could find it for you by the end of the day. The old guys loved him. He made them laugh. He wasn't knee-high to a grasshopper before he was stealing cars—sitting on telephone books, using blocks of two-by-fours tied to his feet to operate the pedals—picking pockets, and redistributing the milkman's deliveries for profit. Sometimes he needed to be gently straightened out, sent to return wallets or other items to widows and mental defectives he had relieved of them. But he was a "good boy," pronounced in that special, deep-throated Italian voice that promised severe consequences if not heeded. He was careful always to respond to the council of his dark-eyed elders.

Vinnie's introduction to thoroughbred horse racing came at Aqueduct Racetrack, into which he frequently snuck from the age of five. He loved the smell of the horses and the shine of their coats. He was crazy about the little goats that sometimes shared stalls with the "nervous nags," as he heard some of the jumpier horses referred to. No one gave the little kid much notice because their interest was in the animals and the size of their purses.

"So, Mr. Jacobson, how're they running for ya?" Vinnie often asked his favorite handicapper, and Jacobson would fill him in. The child was an attentive listener, and Jacobson enjoyed having someone to lay the wisdom of a lifetime on. Thus, Vinnie's calling as a handicapper and bookie was established. He would slip past the guards to place bets for neighborhood working men when the track was open. He became the brain on short legs. People asked for betting advice. He knew the odds. He followed the stables and the jockeys and gossiped with grooms and trainers. He fed himself out of the buckets of carrots sitting on the ground for horse treats while he hung around the track attending to business and visiting interesting characters in the world of racing.

Michael Pope insisted on the best of everything. That included more than just wine and women. He loved the excitement of horse racing and wanted only the most educated counsel on how to take advantage of it at the betting window. It was inevitable that he would hook up with the most well-known bookie in New York, Vinnie Bags, handicapper to the rich and famous. Not only did Vinnie steer him reliably to the winners, but the wiry Italian provided refreshing company during the increasing irritability of Michael Pope's existence.

"Vinnie, Vinnie, I don't know what to do for entertainment anymore."

They sat in Pope's sunken living room, high atop an exclusive property on the Upper East Side of Manhattan. The view of the skyline through the wall of windows was breathtaking. Beautiful, very young women in extremely short black skirts and open-necked blouses served them coffee and donuts. Vinnie squirmed in their presence. He could never get used to this.

"Well, Mr. Pope, I should think entertainment would not be a problem for a man such as yourself. I mean, look around you, would'ja, please. *Madonna mia*. Look at these women coming and going with the coffee. I think you got the imagination to figure out something to do to relieve the tension. Why don't you take one or two of them on an ocean cruise to a beach somewhere, with all due respect? No offense. I know I would. Get a little tan—dancing, moonlight, music. Whatdya say? Don't it sound good? If you're lookin' for someone to keep you company or carry your luggage, I'm your boy."

"Been there, done that, Vinnie. A thousand times. I know my life looks good to you, but you should have my worries. The women, the cars, they don't begin to make life easy for me. These people I employ are completely dependent on me for food, clothing, housing. I even help out some of their parents. It's a lot of pressure."

"Mr. Pope. I wouldn't dare make you angry with the truth about these people who work for you, but you need them depending on you, so they'll do what you tell them to do. Take the girls, for instance. They're more gorgeous than any women I have ever seen, let alone been with. It doesn't take a genius to know they would never do some of the things I'm sure you ask them to do unless they were afraid of what you would do if they didn't."

"You're right, Vinnie. You may be only a bookie, but you're a brilliant man."

"Seeing as you brought up my intellect, Mr. Pope, I have something for you."

"Tell me you finally found a horse, Vinnie."

"First guess, Mr. P. I got a horse. I think you're gonna love her."

---

"Would you mind terribly if we just went down to city hall and had a justice of the peace marry us?" Elaine asked her fiancé at lunch. "This late in my pregnancy, a church wedding would be ridiculous in the extreme."

"No problem by me," Bennett said. "Whatever's good for you."

"You are so understanding, Andy. I don't want to deprive you of a celebration, but, considering the way I look, a white wedding gown? Really? They'd laugh so hard no one would be able to hear the ceremony. I love you, sweetheart, and I don't find that the least bit disloyal to Harry or his child. You are incredibly understanding and generous to me and Harry too."

Speaking her late husband's name caught in her throat. Harry Applewood, United States Customs Inspector, killed by Alfred Menken. She had no intention of taking the State of New York up on its invitation to witness Menken's execution. Why should she? It would be a horrible spectacle. She read in a magazine that the subject being electrocuted jerked with the surge of current through their body, and their clothing smoked and sometimes even caught on fire before they died. Why would she ever subject herself to something like that? It would not give her any satisfaction. It would not bring Harry back.

"Elaine." Andy Bennett returned her to the present. "I was lost from the first time I saw you at the Davis's' house. I was ashamed of being attracted to another man's wife, but it happened. There wasn't a thing I could do about it."

"I should hope you were ashamed," Elaine teased him.

Andy blushed. "Seriously, I owe it to Harry to be a good father to his kid. I'm happy you agreed to marry me and let me help you raise the child. I don't care about where we have the ceremony, as long as we have it and, I guess, that it's legal too."

"Okay, then. It's settled," she said. "I do want a party afterward for our friends and us. I'll make the arrangements. There's a catering place around here somewhere. Champagne for our guests. Club soda for you and me. Speaking of which, it's almost time for your meeting."

"Right. Thanks, honey. I gotta get there early. It's my turn to make the coffee. I appreciate you encouraging me to go to meetings. I don't think I could stay sober without them. I'll walk you back to work first."

"You go, Andy. I'll make it back to work on my own, but before you leave, there's something I want to ask you."

"Whatever it is, Elaine, the answer is yes, I'll do it."

"I don't think you're going to be entirely happy about it, but please, hear me out before you get upset."

"Uh oh, Elaine." Andy rolled his eyes. "I'm getting an awful feeling this is not about us."

"You're absolutely right. So you can relax, right?"

"No, I cannot. This is about your crazy neighbor, correct? Just spill it. I'll survive."

"Alice asked me to talk to you about her latest, uh, project."

"I figured it had something to do with her. My intuition has sharpened since I stopped drinking. Nice of you to warn me. I know you're trying to be careful about my blood pressure. I'm afraid to ask, but what might her so-called project be?"

"Well, a girlfriend of hers has lost her beau to a gang of con artists in Manhattan. He wants out, but they won't let him go."

"It's never easy with Alice White. What, pray tell, could I possibly do to help? If the guy feels that way, he should just walk away, but I've got a feeling it's not that simple. Tell me."

"Andrew. You are so patient about this, and I love you for it. She at least tried with Harry. It's not her fault he waited so long to ask for help."

"Yeah, okay. I'm not on the vice squad, you know."

"I do know, but as a New York City police detective, maybe you could give Alice a little encouragement, can't you?"

"What makes you think I would want to encourage her, Elaine? For heaven's sake. She may be cute, even adorable, but she's also very dangerous, especially if she's thinking of going up against a gang of con artists. Confidence scams are very tricky. They're based on creating illusions, so there's no telling who's actually involved and what they're really up to until they've done their damage. That's why I would like to stay as far away from Alice's so-called 'project' as humanly possible, and away from vice in particular, but that's not going to happen. I just want you to know from the bottom of my heart, and I mean this with all due respect for your friend, SHE'S NUTS!"

"Sweetie." Elaine batted her lashes. "Thank

you so much for doing this."

"You're welcome. Okay. I'll call her. Gee, Elaine, you know, this is a threat to my sobriety. Just the mention of her name causes me anxiety. It may not be enough to make me drink, but the thought of her loose somewhere in the world at the very least makes me thirsty. I surrender. Give me her number. Elaine, you know, you girls do not fight fair."

"Yes, dear, we are aware."

---

"Dinner is served," the butler announced. He wore a black bow tie that his wife had knotted according to the diagram she'd cut out of the Sunday supplement as if anyone in the sticks would ever need a bow tie. It took several tries to get the ends even. If there was ever a next time, they were using a clip-on. The butler's protuberant abdomen was draped in a freshly brushed tuxedo, rented for his debut—hopefully only ever this one—performance. His demeanor and posture spoke, falsely, of generations in service to wealth. He had no history of domestic service to anyone except his wife, which he thought was more like slavery. Therefore, he'd studied for the part by watching a good many Charlie Chan movies end to end. They were being aired in a tribute to the late Earl Derr Biggers, whose imagination was sparked when he visited Hawaii and discovered an uncannily gifted Chinese detective on the "HPD," the Honolulu Police Department, which serves not just Honolulu, but all of the islands in the Hawaiian chain. Murder had broken out in the British colony at Lahaina, an old whaling village on Maui. More times than not, at least in the Charlie Chan books and in the movies, "The butler did it!" There was invariably a speaking part for the guilty servant, which always included the immortal words, which Milton had often dreamed of reciting on the stage while installing pipe on his real job as a plumber: "Dinner is served." In place of cash, that was Milton Davis's payment for this gig.

The guests assumed the butler's burn-scarred lower face to be a combat injury sustained in the last world war. In reality, it was the result of a boiler explosion in his early career as a plumber. He was as close to the Broadway stage as he would ever get, he thought, unless Jim got them front-row seats to a production he was building sets for.

The guests had met their lovely hostess, "Sylvia Green," as she moved around the spacious living room to chat and to see that their drinks were kept full and that they got enough hors d'oeuvres. A string quartet of young musicians played softly off in a corner. They were students from the band at Alice's high school in another, less affluent Queens neighborhood. They were there for the food and glamour, but mostly because they had been in love with Alice White ever since she spoke in their auditorium on Career Day. The girls wanted to be like her. The boys just wanted to stare at her.

The house was a mile from the racetrack in Jamaica, Queens, still within New York City's limits.

The black-and-white outfit of the stout maid distributing canapés was a welcome departure from her usual nurse's uniform. On hearing her husband's so-often-rehearsed announcement, she quickly forced the few remaining hors d'oeuvres from her tray on resistant guests and withdrew to the kitchen.

"Are you having a good time?" Alice White's mother, Rose, asked her new friend Ellen Davis, when the kitchen doors had swung shut behind her.

"Yes, Rose, I honestly am. It's so much fun playing make-believe with the horse people. How's dinner coming along?"

Alice's Aunt Betsy looked up from stirring thick soup in a large pot. "Just fine, Ellen. I made minestrone, a favorite in our neighborhood. Vegetables, noodles, beans, onions, carrots, and tomatoes. Isn't it exciting to be in on one of Alice's exploits?"

The "cook's assistant," Cousin Frannie, Betsy's daughter, laughed. "If my friends at work could see me now, with my whole family pretending to be the kitchen staff in a mansion, they would split a gut."

Alice's mother said, "Who would ever have dreamed, when Alice lost her job at the department store in New Jersey, that she would become a sleuth? I must admit, my heart's been beating a little faster these last few weeks, thinking that we're gonna pull the wool over some bad man's eyes. I hope this works out, and she actually manages to remove the young man, Stanley, from captivity in the gang. It's too bad he's spoken for by Alice's friend, because, Frannie, he sounds like someone who would be very interested in you. It's time you found a man to settle down with and gave me some grandchildren in my old age, for goodness' sake."

Fran blushed. "Really, Mom? You pick now to talk about my reproductive organs? Alice and I are on the leading edge of the women's revolution in America. We're not gonna trade in our freedom for domestic slavery. Things were much simpler when you were our age. When we marry, it has to be a partnership. We are not marrying just to have children and cook and clean."

"That's easy for you to say," her mother responded. "Just how much of a partner can a pregnant woman be to a husband who works all day long to bring home the bacon? You don't have to love him. That can come later."

Fran said, "You mean I can have an affair after I marry a man and have his kids? Maybe marriage isn't such a bad idea after all. I'll get back to you on that."

Rose interrupted her sister-in-law and niece's exchange. "Please, let's you and your daughter not have this discussion at this particular moment. The so-called butler just announced dinner. We have a roast to finish, potatoes to mash, a mess of green beans to steam, and a ton of salad to put together. Maybe we can leave the problem of Fran's future marriage and pregnancy to another time and place. Do you think?"

"Right you are, Rose. I'm sorry I got carried away," Betsy apologized. "The potatoes are peeled, the beans are ready to steam, the roast is in the oven, and the salad just needs dressing. Stay calm. We've done this a million times, except for a lot fewer people."

"Sylvia Green" ducked into the kitchen for a quick check. She took a sniff, looked around at her kitchen staff, and told them, "It smells delicious in here. You people are doing a magnificent job. I must call the agency and tell them what a good job you did. I'm impressed you've kept it together. I can't thank you enough."

"Never mind about us, Alice," Rose told her daughter. "How is it going with your guests?"

"Well," Alice started. "This guy, Michael Pope, is having a very nice time. My friends from the Bronx make up most of the crowd. Some of them are gorgeous ladies, although, I must say, even with all of them fawning all over him, he's been leering uncomfortably at me. I suppose he thinks I'm playing hard to get. It's just, he gives me the creeps. As instructed, everyone is discouraging him from believing that my horse, Wyldfire, has any chance of winning her race. They're telling him I'm a rich fruitcake who has no clue what she's doing with a racehorse. They say they're here for the free food and drinks. Your work as my staff is paying off big, and I owe you all very much. Hopefully, we'll meet when this is all over for me to express my gratitude, that is after Mr. Pope has been dealt with. Thank you again. This race better go how we planned. Jamaica Race Course opens in April. That's only a few months away. I don't know if I can stand the suspense."

"Oh, Alice," her mother spoke. "Everything will go just fine. You'll see."

Alice perked up. "Meanwhile, dinner is actually served, so get moving with the minestrone…please."

# CHAPTER 19

## VICE COP

Sidney Shapiro was an unremarkable American foot soldier in Europe during World War II. He did not charge a machine gun nest, nor risk his life to rescue comrades from certain deaths. He got along by doing as little as possible, by taking as few chances of dying as possible. He counted himself lucky, at the end of every day, that he had at least survived. On leave, he did what every self-respecting GI did. He descended upon young women of all descriptions, any girl with a pulse. He drank whatever he could find when his company entered a new town. He fired his rifle in battle several times, but his eyes were closed, and he wasn't sure if he had hit anything because he was trying mostly not to get shot himself. He almost succeeded in surviving his entire military career without distinction, having no ambition beyond continuing to breathe. Near the end of the war, however, he was forced to rise to an occasion he had hoped to avoid, and thus, reluctantly, became a war hero. He never talked about it at parties, not even to impress the girls. When it was over, he tried not to think about it, like so many men who'd been through unpleasant experiences in the war. He left the fame and glory to Audie Murphy.

"I need to take a dump," Sidney unceremoniously told the sergeant he was traveling with, on foot, across the French countryside. They had stopped at a farm for a rest.

"Be my guest. Just don't do it anywhere near me."

Sidney walked around behind the barn, unzipped, and squatted. He could never go to the bathroom without reading, so he took the oft-read letter from home out of his helmet.

"My precious Sidney. Your father is asleep, snoring merrily along, as usual, rattling the windows, waking the neighbors, making the neighborhood dogs bark. It's keeping me from falling asleep, but somehow I find the sound comforting. Something normal in a time of unrest in the world. It reminded me of you, over there, fighting for our precious democracy. I hope you are feeling well. Your sister told me to give you her love and prayers next time I wrote, so consider yourself sloppy-kissed on both cheeks, the way she does to annoy you. And don't wipe it off either. She wants you safely home so she can do it in person. She's okay herself. No man will ever be good enough for my daughter. I don't know what I did to deserve no grandchildren from either of you. In the morning, I'm making matzah ball soup. I'll save some in a jar for when you get home..."

A tear fell from Sidney's eye every time he read it. This time was no different.

His emotion was cut short by a German-accented voice around the other side of the barn, yelling, "Your hands UP!"

Sidney stuffed the letter back in his helmet and put it on his head. He aborted his effort to evacuate, zipped up, and pulled the automatic from its holster. He slid the safety off for the first time in the whole friggin' war. He pulled the slide back and made sure there was one in the chamber. Two, three, four. His pulse slowed.

It was over in less than a minute. Imagine a couple of German soldiers stumbling onto them by chance. The fancier-dressed of the two must have been some high-ranking officer from all the fuss the army made afterward. Sidney's comrades were down on their knees, their hands laced behind their heads, waiting to be executed. Sidney had no choice but to blow the two Germans away, one bullet each, like in a John Wayne movie. He could hardly have missed at that range: *Blam, blam*. Medal of Honor, usually awarded posthumously. It was, he supposed, typical of his life. He wanted to move out, find another farm to rest at, and forget it ever happened, but they wouldn't let him.

Why, when he came home to America and went to work for the NYPD and why when he was given his pick of any department in the police because he was a war hero, had he picked vice, he would never know. But one thing he did know was that he now considered vice to be the rotten underbelly of law enforcement. To be fair, many men and women on the force just loved it. Prostitution, drugs, pornography, alcohol, the illegal trafficking in guns and drugs, were not the glamorous specialty they were considered to be by many members of the vice squad. On returning to New York City, Sidney had kissed the pavement, having to be repeatedly dragged to his feet by family and friends. A decorated combat veteran, no less! That was a laugh! Somehow he'd gravitated the police academy instead of medical school, which his parents expected him to. He honestly had no idea what he wanted from his life. He must have just bought the hero crap. What was he thinking? Vice sounded like a good idea at the time.

"Yes, Andy, I know Michael Pope," he told his friend Detective Andrew Bennett, who was seated in his office at Vice Squad headquarters. "He's a smooth operator, basically a big-time pickpocket, and mean to the bone. No one seems to want to press charges against him because he works his marks long and hard before he takes them down. He does his best to compromise them in some large way before the sting. Nothing's ever been proved against him. He wines 'em, dines 'em, and puts them with some of the most beautiful women on the planet. Let me tell you. He's aware of my interest in him and his business. He comes in here, to this very office we are sitting in, with as sleek a piece of feminine pulchritude as I ever laid eyes on. And, let me tell you, I been all over the world. He brings her in here 'cause he knows I'm not married and that I have a sweet tooth for the fairer sex—the nerve on this guy. But, however, as you are aware, I might as well go into the bathroom and flush myself down the toilet as take him up on an offer like that. Let me tell you, I have nightmares about having my picture taken with her in a sleazy hotel room. How much fun I could've had with her, and how close I came to destroying my life in a minute of madness. He's smooth, all right. So, my friend, what's all this about?"

"Sid," Bennett said, "I don't know if you heard the news about my partner, Scott Gerard."

"I heard he died."

"He ate his gun."

"I know, man. I was being polite."

"Right. You might also have heard that he was dirty."

"I might've heard something like that."

"Well, believe it, because he was. He never got over the death of his wife and went downhill from there. I, myself, had bad trouble with the bottle. You might've heard that too. I don't know how it happened, but I ended up drinking on the job, to be honest with you. I found the meetings and stopped just before Gerard took himself out. In the end, he took up where I left off. He got more and more miserable, more and more drunk, even on the job, and shot himself with an astronomical blood alcohol level. It was a crying shame."

"Gee, Andy. I'm sorry for your loss."

"Now to what that has to do with Pope. Scott and I were working on our last case together. A young kid, the bookkeeper for the Dockworkers' Union, was shot and killed one night, a few days after an altercation with a customs inspector who was in on their smuggling operation. The inspector was being forced, by the union boss, to turn a blind eye to certain cargo: guns. It turns out the boss ordered the hit to punish the kid for skimming from him and to frame the customs guy who was threatening to stop playing ball. They ended up killing the customs guy too. The union boss is on death row at Sing Sing, waiting to have a seat on 'Old Sparky.' Before the customs man died, I followed him north from the city to a house where his wife was hidden to keep her safe from the union. It was a conjugal visit, if you get my drift."

"Very romantic."

"I'm telling you this whole 'who-shot-John' story for a reason. I was parked outside the whole time. Later, I went back to speak to the wife and get her to tell me what was going on with her husband, our prime suspect, because this idea of him as a cold-blooded murderer didn't add up, not for me or Scott. He was a war hero, like you. He landed troops for the navy at Salerno during the invasion. A straight-up guy until he got squeezed by this boss."

"Too bad he was clipped."

"Yes, it is. But I haven't told you the thing I'm most ashamed about. She was a married woman, his wife. I was a cop, a drunk. I couldn't take my eyes off her. I fell all over myself, making sure I didn't step out of line, took her somewhere public to talk so I wouldn't be alone with her. I thought she felt something for me too. It turns out she did. But, at the time, it was all wrong. We both knew that."

"Very noble of you."

"Finally, the customs guy gets killed on the labor boss's order, but not before he got her pregnant, probably the night I followed him. I asked her if I could help raise the kid."

"These things happen, Andy. You're confessing to the wrong guy. I just told you, I almost sold my soul for a roll in the hay with one of Pope's women."

"Yeah. Well, we're getting married. I want you to come."

"Sure. I'd be honored. Don't look at me to judge you. Life is short and strange, at best."

"Elaine's neighbor in the Bronx was sort of helpful to Elaine and her late husband, if only for moral support because Elaine's husband died anyway. Mind you, this woman, Alice White, is beautiful, I admit, but nuts."

"She's pretty?"

"Extremely, Sid, yes, very attractive, but believe me, my friend, you do not want to go near her in that way. She is extremely dangerous and, I suspect, armed, and she's got a boyfriend and a very large Spanish protector. That's what it takes to keep her alive. A small army. Her name is Alice White. No matter. They have no control over her whatsoever. She calls the shots, and they do the best they can to keep up with her."

"Go on."

"This woman, White, has a girlfriend whose I

guess fiancé is trapped in Pope's gang. The boyfriend wants out. My bride-to-be insisted I help, against my better judgment. Anything you can do would be greatly appreciated."

"Women are the bane of our existence, Andy. I always say that, but it's true. Can't live with 'em, can't live without 'em. I'm not telling you anything you don't already know."

"I hear you, Sid. So what are we gonna do? To make matters worse, it looks like Pope set the kid up to take the fall for the murder of a young woman. The victim's name is Sarah Truman. It sounds like the boy might have been drugged. He woke up soaked in her blood with her dead body stretched out on the bed, and the murder weapon on the floor. Pope sent cleaners to make it all go away. God only knows if that was her real name even."

"Give me time, Andy. It just so happens I have someone I can tap on this. We trade favors. He tells me what I need to know in exchange for I let him live. Vice isn't as bad as I let on. I guess I just like to complain. It sounds like this Pope has overstepped his place in the animal kingdom once again. Maybe this time, I can nail him. Pope didn't count on this kid having friends, like your fiancée's crazy neighbor, what's her name, Alice White. Too bad she's got a boyfriend, but it's just as well. She sounds like the kind of trouble I don't need. I'll see what I can do for you. Thanks for the entertaining story of your recent life. Consider us caught up. Next time we can meet for coffee, and you can take my confession."

---

The Waldorf Astoria opened in 1893 on Fifth Avenue near 34th Street. It was demolished in 1929 to make room for the Empire State Building, and opened again in 1931 between 49th and 50th on Park Avenue in Midtown Manhattan.

Abraham Schumann booked a suite, with his date, as Mr. And Mrs. Samuel and Ethel Morganthal. She didn't look like an Ethel, but he owed such delicacy to his wife, Vivian, the only woman he'd ever really loved, with whom he had a bargain that he intended to honor. Vivian was aware that her husband was currently involved with someone else.

Abraham stepped out of the shower.

"Helen Parker" removed a luxurious terry cloth towel from the bathroom rack and began to dry him off.

"Abraham, sweetheart, I feel I can trust you with some of the more unpleasant details of my past. I was not treated well as a child."

"Helen, please, don't feel you have to tell me anything you might regret. You have opened an old man's heart in a way I thought no longer possible. What I do know about you is more than enough."

"If you say so."

"Good. You know I would do anything for you."

"There might be something you can do, Abraham. I've always wanted to get involved with horse racing. I've often thought it would be fun to invest in a thoroughbred. The animals themselves are beautiful, they smell good too, and the male ones remind me of you . . . sometimes, if you know what I mean."

"Helen, please. I never met a woman with such an appetite for physical engagement. You keep talking like that, you're going to have to deal with me again."

"So it interests you too? I don't mind having to calm you down."

"Yes, please do, Helen, before I explode."

She whispered in his ear, "Afterwards, I want to tell you about this horse I have in mind."

The hook was set.

Across town, the mark's wife, Vivian, lay completely exposed on a table while Nadine's counterpart, Stanley Kramer, rubbed her down … thoroughly, from head to toe with massage oil. She was lying facedown, and the things he had already done to her with his hands had released months, if not years, of pent-up tension and frustration. He was well trained. It's a good thing the walls of the room were soundproof for the cries of relief she had just expelled. Her head was turned to one side. She was as flaccid as overcooked spaghetti. He was rubbing her from her neck, down her spine, to the small of her back.

The groaning had ceased, and she uttered, "I owe you so much, Stanley. I will have to take a scorching, very long shower to come back to earth. Bless you, young man. I'll figure out some way to reward you."

"Mrs. Schumann," he responded. "Your response to my attentions was reward enough."

"Never, young man. Give me time, and I'll come up with something you need. You have a special talent. Guard it with your life."

# CHAPTER 20

## WINDOWS

"Frankie, how nice to see you back," Alice told the wiry old man she hadn't seen in months.

Frankie the window washer, aka "Frankie Windows," aka Frankie Amato, stood in front of her open door in his trademark gray suede vest and skullcap, with the string from his tobacco pouch hanging out of his breast pocket. She missed him. Her windows were opaque with city grime, not that it mattered because, on most days, they were so completely fogged by the frigid air outside and steam heat inside that it would have made little difference to her visibility if they were clean. He widened his picket-fence grin at her, exposing spaces where teeth used to be. It never failed to elicit a broad smile of affection back from Alice.

"Aren't you gonna invite me in?"

"Yes. Please, come in, Frankie."

She held the door open. When he was inside, she closed and double-locked it behind her. The precaution was a habit of most people born and raised in the city.

"Are you here to talk or are you here to wash my windows?" Alice asked him playfully. Now that I know who you really are, Frankie, I can't believe you would still be here to wash the windows. When it got warmer, I was going to find myself a new window washer. The last time you did my windows, you almost gave me a heart attack, jumping off the fire escape onto the bathroom windowsill to show me how the burglars got in. I have never left the bathroom window unlatched again. Then you saved me from bleeding to death when I got shot, and for that, I am eternally grateful. How have you been?"

"I have been good, Alice. It's nice to see you too. I'm not giving up washing windows. I need the exercise. I'm in my seventies. It keeps me in shape. I'm not goin' down without a fight." His squeaky voice reflected a lifetime of tobacco use.

"If you say so. I'm thrilled to have you back," she told him. "They left me to die on the floor of my neighbor's apartment. It's hard for me not to have new respect and gratitude for you, following me there, putting a tourniquet on my arm. It seems like years since it happened, but it's only been a few months."

"You're a woman after my own heart, Alice. I was happy for the chance to help you out. Someone has to keep an eye on you. The more of us, the better. I'm not saying you're reckless. You might be, that's what it sometimes takes to stay alive, but, I have to say, you were in a dangerous situation, and you weren't careful enough. I hope you have smartened up since then. You're as pigheaded as I was when I was your age. You were all set to die. Good thing I learned about them tourniquets when I was a kid. It's too bad about the customs guy croaking. My friend Enzo respected him for standing up to that union boss and for what he did in the war. But I'm glad you stayed alive. If you were a man, you'd be me."

"That is high praise, Frankie. Thank you again for what you did." Alice rolled her sleeve up to show him the scar. "It's still red, but it's clean, and it's all closed up."

"Nice job, Roberto did," the skinny older man observed. "Now, to work. I'm gonna fill the bucket and get started on cleaning up your view."

She followed him into the kitchen, like the little girl she was in his august presence. He got the bucket out of the broom closet, put it into the deeper half of her double sink, and poured a splotch of ammonia into it, then soap powder, then water to fill it halfway. The smell of ammonia permeated the apartment. The familiar odor reassured Alice that everything was as it should be despite the chaos and uncertainty of the world she lived in.

Alice rolled her sleeve down and buttoned the cuff. "Why do you really keep washing windows, Frankie?"

"My life got too aggravating doing the other thing, and my bones got too brittle. I didn't want to sit home and play with my grandkids and get old. I decided to use the climbing I did when I was a kid in Manhattan, you know, Little Italy, running up fire escapes and jumping across alleys from roof to roof. So I wash people's windows. It keeps me busy. Puts a little change in my pocket."

He left out the part about sending his men to rob selected clients.

"This way, I get to check on you. It's a nice neighborhood you live in compared to the ones down south of here. You're not my only customer, but I cut down since you seen me last. So, how are things with you? You still with your boyfriend? Roberto told me about this business with the con guy in Manhattan. Pope's a mean one. You sure know how to pick 'em."

"Gee, Frankie, it's nice of you to keep tabs on my goings-on. I guess I provide you and your friends with comic relief, huh? Yes, I am getting ready to make a run at this man. He recruited a girl I know's boyfriend and won't let him go. I'm masquerading as some society dame with a stable of racehorses. If they didn't have our boy framed for a murder, I'd break him out of there, and that would be that. I entertained the bad guy at a dinner party in a borrowed mansion in Queens to convince him I don't know what I'm doing. Misdirection is his preferred method of operation, so I thought I'd give him a taste of his own medicine. My plumber friend and his wife came down from up the Hudson River to be my butler and maid. They were hysterical. My family was the kitchen staff. Your buddy from down the hill has been looking over my shoulder. I am a pain in the neck, I know."

"No, you aren't, Alice. Let us do what we can to help you. You can never have too many friends. You're keeping us young. Please do us a favor, though, and don't take so many chances. I know, with you, that's easier said than done."

"So, Frankie, not to change the subject from my erratic behavior, but where have you been these months since you saved my life?"

"Uh, Alice." The thin old man seemed embarrassed. "I had some business down in Miami Beach. I'm retired, I know, but I have to put in an appearance once in a while. Otherwise, I really would die a' boredom. One of my boys drove me. Too bad I didn't get to sit in the sun in one of them beach chairs, you know, with a cold drink in my hand. I coulda got a tan in the winter, like some rich guy. Anyway, someone needed a little straightening out. You're a woman of the world. You understand such things. Sometimes you have to let people see you face-to-face to convince them you're serious. While you're at it, you might as well make some physical contact to be sure they understand that you mean what you're saying. These old hands aren't as tough as they used to be. Probably break a few knuckles if I tried anything like that. That's where Tony, my driver, came in. He did double duty. It's all taken care of now, except the guy needs a few weeks to heal. It makes it difficult for him to be taken seriously when he can't walk or breathe. Some people are just a little hard of hearing. Capisce?"

"Frankie, I love you like a brother . . . or an uncle. I shouldn't have asked. I'm sorry. That's more than I needed to know, but I do understand the philosophy behind it. I thought you said you were done with that life forever."

"I did. I am really, Alice. That's why I had Tony drive me down. I only went as an observer. I guess I still look scary to some people. Not to you, though. You think I'm an old pussycat."

"I don't know, Frankie. In a different light, I can see myself being terrified of you, though I'd rather have you as a friend."

"You need some help with this guy, this con

artist? Tony and me could visit him if you want."

"I'll keep you and Tony in mind if Plan A doesn't work. The guy's name you already know, Michael Pope."

"Yeah, I heard of him. He's one a' dem high-end grifters. Not much of a threat to my friends and me, but now he's gone and stepped on your toes. It's the biggest problem in his line of work. You never know who you're messing with. I can tell by your face this guy's gonna wish he was in another business. Am I right?"

"I get bored too, Frankie. It's not enough that I'm trying to study for my law school examinations so I can graduate in the spring. I can't keep from sticking my nose in other people's business. It didn't work out so well last time, did it? But I wasn't looking for this. What kind of a lawyer do you think I'll be?"

"You kiddin', Alice? You're gonna be a killer. I dealt with plenty of shysters in my time. That's not who you are. You're smart and fair. Me and my friends can be your consultants, you know. We can help you out with resistant witnesses, things like that."

"My God, Frankie. I appreciate your enthusiasm, but I'm going to try something a little more refined in my practice. I would only use your help in the most extreme circumstances, only if they attack me. And I do not want to insult my good friend and protector, Antonio Vargas, and neither do I want to get a reputation as an arm breaker. It doesn't go over well with judges. That's why, instead of just having your guy, Tony, take care of Pope, I decided to pull a con on the con artist. Get it? It's more dignified."

"I don't do 'dignified' too well, Alice. But I respect you for trying."

"You never know, Frankie. Maybe I can show you something about being subtle, or at least give you a laugh while I'm trying. My jockey friend, Billy Smith, is helping me set this guy up using a lightning-fast three-year-old filly named Wyldfire. Pope thinks she's gonna lose. She's running opening day in Queens, at fourteen to one against her. She's gonna beat the pants off the even-money favorite, Fortunate Princess. Don't tell anyone."

"This is gonna be fun, Alice, to see this guy's face when he knows he's done. I hope somebody told you there are no guarantees in horse racing."

"Yeah, Frankie, I've heard that. Billy warned me a million times. But I feel lucky, and, you know, I'm not going to stop until I do what I said I would do, and the young boy is free and cleared of the murder they framed him for."

"Good luck with that. You're as crazy as I ever

was. Now I'm gonna climb outside in the cold and clear away the incinerator ash and dirt from the window so you can see out over your piece of the city. After that, I'm going down the hill to visit my friend Roberto and laugh with him about your horse race. Don't be surprised if you see us around the track between now and race day, pretty girl. Like I said, you're keeping us young."

# CHAPTER 21

## ABOUT ADAM

Adam and Susan walked over to a sandwich shop when her shift was over.

Susan had received the news from Alice that no family named Murphy existed on record as ever having lived in the town in Indiana Adam said he was from. Furthermore, no such person as Adam Murphy was enrolled as a student at Columbia University.

Her worst nightmare was realized: Adam had been sent to her by Stanley's new employer, and she had fallen for his attentions. She was such an easy target. It confirmed that Stanley was in a terrible situation if his boss was willing to take this trouble with her, to force him to cooperate.

She told Alice she was breaking up with Adam.

Alice said, "Be careful. If you need any help, let me know."

Susan and Adam were served their Coca-Colas and awaited their sandwiches.

"Adam, you're a sweet guy. I've thought a lot about us, and I feel funny dating you on the rebound, so soon after my heart was broken."

"Susan, please, give us a chance. I've been preoccupied with school. After my finals in the spring, I'll be able to give you my full attention."

Adam was upset at Susan's sudden change of heart.

She became even more distressed. This wasn't going like she'd hoped it would. She did not want to aggravate this man, but she wanted to get as far away from him as possible.

"It isn't anything to do with you, Adam," she told him. "Believe me; I'm not looking for your full attention. I have worries of my own, things I have to do, and places I want to go. I wasn't planning on being a waitress for the rest of my life like some of the women who work with me. I don't feel the same as when we first met. I'm still fond of you, truly I am, but I feel less romantically inclined toward you, more like a sister than anything else. You're a good-looking guy. I don't want to keep you from having fun with other girls."

She listened to herself speak. To her ears, it sounded less like breaking up and more like pleading for her life.

Adam wondered what had prompted this change of heart. He listened.

"There's no one else, Adam, if that's what you think. I did have a boyfriend, but he's gone forever. I'm probably gonna die an old maid, and I think that's not such a bad thing."

Adam finally said, "Would you mind if I stay in touch with you, Susan?" In her panic, his words rang with threat. He acted deflated, but he was clearly scrambling to maintain a hold on her. "We could still meet for coffee once in a while," he told her. "Right?"

"Sure, Adam, whatever you say."

---

"Hello, Alice," Susan spoke into the telephone. "Do you have a few moments?"

"Sure, Susan. I need a break. You're doing me a favor. How did it go with Adam?"

"Not as well as I hoped it would. I realize what an idiot I was to fall for him. Oh, Alice, it's time for me to grow up and learn to stand on my own two feet. If I ever see Stanley Kramer again, I'm gonna make him pay for what he has put me through. This is all his fault."

"Perhaps I'm not an entirely good influence on you," Alice told her.

"On the contrary, Alice. You are exactly who I needed to get me to take control of my life. Keeping house for my parents and being used as an object by men is no way for me to live. These people can do without my services. I've just been hiding behind them. Things are changing for women, and I intend to take advantage of that. The first move I have made toward that end is to fire Adam Murphy as my boyfriend, much to his chagrin. I was scared to death when I did it."

"Good for you, Susan. I've been thinking, when I finally start practicing law, I'd like you to consider giving up your glamorous job as a waitress and coming to work for me."

"Really, Alice? What an idea. I was actually considering moving out of New York. I figured I could always get work in a diner someplace else. Maybe I'd become a career waitress, you know, like one of those women with tobacco-stained fingers and a raspy voice I work with now. 'How ya doin', hon? Can I get ya a cawffee and a danish?' Even if Stanley does manage to escape, I'm not sure I want to spend another minute with him. He needs a woman who's willing to build her life based entirely on his selfish needs. I want to find out who I am and what I want out of life. I might take you up on your offer, Alice. Wouldn't it be a laugh if I ended up going to law school, too?"

"I've created a monster. I'm so proud of myself," Alice told her. "I gotta get back to the books if I'm going to finish what I started and be in any position to hire you."

---

Formica is a laminated composite invented by Daniel O'Conor and Herbert Faber at Westinghouse Electric Corporation in 1912. Manny Harrison used his white prescription bench made of the material to count pills, prepare exotic ointments, and melt chunks of white chocolate in a metal cup over a Bunsen burner to pour into suppository molds. It was early morning, a time before most people were out and around on the streets of the Bronx. Manny stood behind the elevated bench at the back of his drugstore, writing out a merchandise order for his wholesale jobber. From this height, he could occasionally glance over his tiny retail empire.

He scratched his scalp through the greased

and combed-over black hair that covered it, pondering the stock he needed to replace. He trusted no one else to do this job. His white pharmaceutical tunic's top button was casually undone, giving him the rakish charm that neighborhood women found very appealing. They evinced little respect for the ring on his left fourth finger as they wantonly flirted with him by turns.

He looked up and saw Lou Morris standing at the counter.

"Hiya, Manny. Whatdya know?" the usually nattily dressed advertising executive asked him. Today he was heavily bundled. The bags under his eyes told the story of another night of smoking, drinking, and carousing with his girlfriend of the month. A notorious playboy, often divorced, he lived in the apartment building above the store. The building had been completed the previous year. It had reintroduced this area of the Bronx to its prewar splendor by installing a doorman, a uniformed thug on duty twenty-four hours a day at the lobby entrance. All the doormen along the four-mile stretch of the Grand Concourse had been drafted into military service, and Concourse residents had become used to opening their own doors and maintaining their own security these past fifteen years. Now they were buzzed into their lobbies by family members, or they used their keys.

"Hey, Lou. Whatdya say?" Manny gave his customary response. He welcomed a break from the drudgery of compiling a merchandise order.

Manny stepped down from the bench and moved to the glass counter near the cash register to serve his friend.

"I don't say much." Lou concluded their morning ritual. Lou wore a fur-lined Alaskan hunting cap with the flaps down over his ears. This for the short run from the building's front entrance, maybe thirty yards. Lou was not born to tolerate the cold of a northeast winter. He was meant to reside in the tropics—South Florida, to be precise—but his employment was here on Madison Avenue in icy New York City. The collar of his long cashmere overcoat was raised and held closely against his neck by several wraps of colorful scarf. Ever a fashion statement was Lou Morris. He looked to be suffering in the cold. Anyplace but this corner of the Bronx, he would have looked like a homeless person.

"A pair of dromedaries, if you please." His daily quota. "I'd buy a carton, but then I'd miss our morning visit, Manny. If you weren't open seven days a week, I don't know how I'd survive. You sure you don't want to come downtown and work at my company? C'mon, Manny. They'd love you down there. You're funny, hard-working, talented, and, let's face it. You are a magnet for beautiful women. I see the way they look at you."

"Lou, for heaven's sake, I'm a happily married man. My lovely wife more than satisfies my needs, which, by the way, are not that many. She is a good mother to our kids and a wonderful cook. She is also, I might add, a much sought-after bookkeeper. She helped start a lot of businesses all over the Bronx. After a year or so, they typically give her a bonus and fire her 'cause they can't afford to keep her on. I enjoy hearing about your work, Lou, but I would not trade it for the life I have. It's too rich for my blood."

"Gee, Manny, you've got it all wrong. I'm the one who's jealous of you. I tried marriage more than once, but I couldn't make it work. I would come home from a day's labor ready to party, and my wives would have a list of things for me to do. The kids would be squawking; dinner would be late. The pretty ladies at work, the secretaries, and the artists, they understand me. It's hard to keep my hands off 'em. I just wasn't cut out for a one-woman lifestyle. I'd rather pay alimony and child support. It's a shallow life, Manny, but somebody's got to live it. So, my friend, it's another frigid, overcast morning in the Bronx. What're you up to in your cozy little pharmacy?"

"The usual, Lou. It's nice of you to ask. I got my coffee and a buttered roll up there on my bench, and I'm making up an order. I got the radio on low.

I'm eking out a living, but I love the work. I have no idea why. It's exhausting. The hours are long and, believe it or not, the pay is not so great. Who woulda thought when I gave up playing saxophone in my jazz band that I'd find happiness owning a drugstore in the Bronx? I love this little place, Lou, but I miss making music with my guys."

"See, Manny, that's what I'm talking about. Maybe someday you'll play music again. I'd give anything to be as happy as you are."

"Most importantly, Lou, how're the horses running for you?"

"So-so, Manny. In a few months, though, the track in Jamaica opens. There's a very fast three-year-old filly looking good for some pocket change. Her name is Fortunate Princess. She's the favorite. There's a long shot named Wyldfire running against her. Rumor has it, Wyldfire is the distraction of a bored heiress who's dabbling in thoroughbred racing, and her filly doesn't stand a chance in heck against the Princess. I'd be happy to put down a bet for you if you want. F.P. is from a long line of winners. No other horse should come near her, not even Wyldfire. If we play it right, we can leave the 'City That Never Sleeps' behind and move down to Boca Raton together. You can bring your wife and kids. I can wear my favorite hat and that white patent leather belt I like so much all year long instead of having to wrap myself up in this unholy getup that the peasants around here have to wear every winter. I will sport a perpetual coat of tan. If you join me, I'll show you the sights, and your family will live in the lap of luxury. Maybe you'll even find a jazz gig. If you don't come with me, I'll miss your company, my good buddy, but I'll leave you my muffler. Think about it."

"I'm gonna have to pass on your offer, Lou. Thanks anyway. Please remember, if there's one thing you've taught me about racing, it's that you cannot trust the nags. You DO remember all those betting slips you tore up and asked me to flush down the toilet in the back? I don't want to spoil your dream of sitting on the beach in Florida with a babe on each arm, but, as your friend, I'm telling you, leave a little something in the till in case your horse loses her way running down the track. You'll still at least be able to afford a vacation there once a year."

"Point taken, Manny. I'll try to keep one foot on the ground."

"Now you're talking, Lou. Let me know how 'fortunate' your Princess turns out to be."

"Will do, my friend. Have a good day."

With that, Lou lit up a Camel and moseyed over to the phone booth. He unwrapped his muffler, dinged a dime into the slot, and, of course, dialed his bookie. He closed the door of the booth and soon disappeared in a cloud of smoke. Manny could barely hear Lou's voice after that. He trudged back up to his prescription bench, took a sip of coffee, tore off a bite of roll with his teeth, and resumed putting together his order. He wanted to finish before the morning rush.

# CHAPTER 22

# GROUND RUSH

"*Cherie,*" Michael said to the little French girl, "I finally found a play worth making. I can break the bank or go broke trying. If I'm wrong, I'll have nothing left, except a nest egg hidden far away. I am betting absolutely everything else I own."

Her head appeared from under the covers. "Why must you take such chances, *mon amour*?"

"Because I can't stand my life as it is. I have been too careful. I didn't get what I have by being careful. I made plays that could've broken me, just like this one. My flock grew. Expenses went through the roof. I've been treading water here like I lost my nerve or something. This whole gang is like an albatross around my neck."

"My poor darling." She threw her arms around

his neck.

He angrily pulled them away from him. "Get off me. You're part of the problem. This thing at the track is exactly what I've been looking for to help me escape. It's a chance to make a fortune and take a pile of someone else's money while I'm at it. It's a shot at the brass ring."

"Oh, Monsieur Pope, in this case, I am happy for you." The girl was less than half his age.

"You should be. I want to get back my appetite for the good things in life."

"Perhaps I can help," she said.

Pope pulled back the comforter and rolled away from her, out of bed. He put on his bathrobe and looked at himself in the mirror. He grabbed his stomach with both hands. "Fat and happy. That's me."

"You are not fat, my sweet. Look at your arms. They are so powerful. You are such a man."

"That lady, the stable owner, Sylvia Green, she's some woman. I watched her at that little dinner party she threw for herself and that miserable loser of a horse. She is a looker, though. She moves with an arrogance I find hard to resist. After her horse loses, I should take pity on her and have her come over for dinner and drinks."

The time was not yet right for Sylvia Green,

he thought. She was a spoiled brat, a divorcée, but she would be broken very soon. Her filly, Wyldfire, was gonna lose big. Then the mighty Miss Green would be more accommodating. He had bumped into her deliberately at her party, to get a feel of her and smell her perfume. She didn't pull away. She noticed though. She was definitely worth pursuing. Maybe he could take the edge off her infuriating conceit. It would be interesting to try.

"Get outta here," Pope suddenly yelled at the girl.

Tears carried mascara down the youngster's cheeks. She looked like a crazy woman in a horror movie. She gathered her clothes and padded silently from the bedroom, stopping out of Pope's sight to put her skirt and blouse on and to stuff her underwear into her purse as she exited the apartment.

Pope ignored the girl's distress. When he heard the front door close behind her, he took a key from the night table and removed the Monet print from the wall. Behind it was a large secure cabinet, which he unlocked with the key. He powered up the shortwave radio inside and took out a pad and pencil.

"K-A-6-U-T, this is W-A-2-G-R-C," he sent in Morse code, using a straight telegrapher's key. "Do you copy? Over."

Through the sizzle and pop of the distance

came a signal in short and long tones: "W-A-2-G-R-C, this is K-A-6-U-T. Copy loud and clear. Over."

"How is ur weather? Over." He sent.

He wrote the words out as he listened to her response. "Nice dear. Lounging under palms on the beach. I came inside to keep our schedule. How goes it? Over."

"Better. No idea what happened to my nerve. Fear got the best of me. No more. Over."

"Good for you. Over."

"Nerve back. Minions despise me. I despise them. Join you soon. Over."

"Happy you feel better, sweetheart. Till tomorrow. Same time. Over."

"Fine. Love you. Over and out."

He shut the radio down and tore up the paper he had written on.

When the room was returned to its normal appearance, he resumed musing about the provocative Miss Green. She had gotten under his skin. He could see she was in over her head with that horse. A pampered party girl with lots of money to buy her a decent thoroughbred and a decent trainer. But even her trainer would not be able to get her horse past Fortunate Princess. Vinnie had assured him the Princess would leave Wyldfire in the dust. It was money in the bank, he said. He would escape with Schumann's bundle and clear a few million at the windows himself. He could live like a king for years on the island he had picked out, waiting for the heat to die down.

Vinnie had spread his money in $100,000 bets around the country. Pope was trusting Bags with his life. He was looking forward to watching the race in a box seat, with Vinnie at his side. Vinnie had other plans.

---

Alice was reading a magazine article about jumping out of an airplane. This case was unfolding, just like it said in the article. At first, after you exit the plane, there's a period of free fall. Then you pull the rip cord, and suddenly you jerk to a seeming stop because the chute opens and pulls you up. You hang there in space and swing back and forth for a while, enjoying the scenery and experiencing a false sense of security. Everything is peaceful and calm. There's plenty of time to adjust the lines to the parachute, to steer yourself to where you're supposed to land. But time eventually runs out, and the earth speeds up toward you. You hit it hard. It could kill you if you don't bend your knees, relax, and roll with the impact.

That's what was happening to her now. She knew ... it could kill her.

"What am I doing?" Alice asked her friend Edith Burrows. They were both crammed into Alice's little office, sipping coffee from cardboard containers.

"My final exams and my graduation from law school are only a few months away. Time is running out. Finally, I'm gonna finish what I started at the end of the war. The soldiers deserved my job, but still, I resented them. I was forced to become a lowly secretary, no offense Edith. You were there when the bosses asked me to investigate for them. Let's face it, I was expendable, If I died, they could put an ad in the paper and get another secretary to replace me. But I liked what our bosses did for a living, and I wanted to do it too, so here I am. If all goes well, I'm gonna graduate from NYU Law School, Boola, Boola. At a time like this, I cannot believe I allowed myself to get involved in this stupid caper I had to free the not-so-innocent kid, solve the murder, and get rid of the evil boss. It's not like the firm begged me to take it on. Don't ever let me do anything like this again. Promise me, Edith."

"Calm down, girl," Edith told her. "You talk like I could have stopped you. Your motives are pure. Frankly, I'm jealous. I'm not really jealous, but I do admire your guts. I'm satisfied catering to Jack

Bryce's every whim, just as long as that doesn't include the use of my body. He kept me sane when my husband died. Now I have a boyfriend. That's partially your fault. If you hadn't stayed over at my apartment the night before you drove Jack upstate to save Jim, we would never have had that conversation where we agreed not to give up on ourselves. I would have continued those sordid affairs where men took what they wanted and left me for younger, greener pastures. This is who we are, Alice. Thank God we're not all the same. The world would be a dull place. This is what you do. Try to enjoy it more, maybe even while it's happening. When you're old and toothless, you're going to be glad you took these chances to save people from horrible circumstances. Not everyone is cut out for this. You just drew the short straw."

"I love you, Edith. I'm so glad you found someone to share your life with again. Nevertheless, despite all my other responsibilities, I have become entangled in this insane endeavor, which I'm beginning to doubt will do anything to bring down this mobster and free the callow youth from his grip. I cannot believe I'm spending my time on this fool's errand. Maybe I should go in there with my Italian friends and kidnap Stanley Kramer and arrange for his and his lovely girlfriend's relocation to another state with new identities and driver's licenses. That is, if Susan ever speaks to either him or me again."

"Don't panic, Alice."

"That's easy for you to say, Edith. Where do these crazy ideas of mine come from? I wonder if I'm too emotional, too vindictive, to be effective as a lawyer. When I see an injustice being done, I start foaming at the mouth. I should take up chess, or knitting, or something, and stay off the street. People being taken advantage of, especially if they are women, are the bane of my existence. I have only one response, which is, unfortunately, that the bully must be put down like a cow at a slaughterhouse. Michael Pope is a tyrant, and I intend to be the hammer that hits him in his forehead. He has committed the ultimate crime of messing with a sister's happiness."

"God help him, Alice," Edith opined.

"No wonder I hesitate to marry Jim. If he crosses me and I kill him, it will be all too easy for the police to establish a pattern of behavior. See, Edith. I haven't been entirely asleep during my classes at NYU. They'd hunt me down and fry me in Old Sparky, upstate. It isn't safe to be around me. Perhaps when I'm elderly, it might be safe for Jim to marry me, you know, when I'm walking with a cane. Probably not. I'll still be hobbling up the Concourse to the meat market on Jerome Avenue, maybe in long pants so as not to offend the men and women along the way with my wrinkled legs. Did I mention, the prospect of getting old disturbs me?"

"Alice, don't get hysterical. You are endowed with talents you have to use to help people. Stop and smell the roses. You're a woman ahead of her time."

"I suppose that's why we fought a second world war. To defend the world against bullies. The further we get from that conflict, the more acceptable bullies are becoming, you know? Never will they be acceptable to me. That's why I want to be a lawyer. It's not about power or money. It's about my naïve belief that we can each make a difference. We can help each other out of a jam. Please understand me. I like being a girl, flashing my legs in public, having men give me the eye. That is a kind of power I like. Me and my two neighbors nearly caused an accident on the Concourse last spring. A driver got distracted. We were sitting on the sidewalk, having a conversation, minding our own business. All he saw was our crossed legs, and he lost his mind. Why is it so important for men to think they're in charge? Jim and Antonio laugh at the idea that they have any power at all over women. They're thrilled to be doing me and Maria's bidding, glad for the work. Without their ladies, life would be duller than dull, which brings me to the conclusion that we must make life hell for Michael Pope. He thinks he has control over women. That irritates the heck out of me. I saw the way he looked at me with his more-powerful-than-thou disdain. I've met men like him before. I wish I could live and let live, but that's not gonna happen. I cannot, in good conscience, allow him to remain unscathed."

"Like I said, Alice. God help him."

"Exactly, Edith. Things are coming to a head. The ground is rushing up almost faster than I can stand. Let's hope I don't get hurt when I hit it."

# CHAPTER 23

## SNITCH

"How's it, my friend?" Vice Detective Sidney Shapiro asked his man. They were at a table in the shadows at the back of a waterfront diner on Staten Island. The bulb in the wall fixture emitted a dingy, dull yellow glow, like in some B movie. It was a cold and overcast afternoon in February, and the weather matched both their moods. They nursed black coffees. Sid took a sip while his was still hot and waited for his informant to settle down. Eventually, the younger man quit fidgeting, though his eyes never stopped darting around the restaurant, looking for trouble . . . or witnesses. He looked like a trapped rat.

Sidney traveled to the borough regularly to conduct such face-to-face interviews. He needed direct observation of facial expressions and body language to gauge the relative truth of his intelligence. Nobody was perfect at it. His life and the lives of his fellow officers depended on his skill at lie detection with pond scum. He had something nasty on all of them. They were accomplished liars, skirting the truth just close enough to buy themselves another day of freedom.

"Everything's good, man," the snitch replied, starting the ball rolling with his standard bit of dissemblance. The tug-of-war had begun. "How're things with you?" Like he cared.

Back to Sid. "C'mon, man. Don't be a wiseass. I haven't even asked you a real question, and already it feels like we're in a knife fight. Take a slug of your coffee before it gets cold."

"What're you, my mother?"

Shapiro said, "I heard you were such an ugly baby that when you were born, the doctor slapped your mother."

"Very funny. I have to remember that. Okay, lawman, ask away. I'm all yours."

"Try not to forget it. Our mutual friend is attracting attention down at the squad."

"In what way, Sheriff?"

"In the way of the racetrack. He's spreading bets on a particular horse all over hell and gone. I need to know what he's up to. A girl is dead."

"Everything with him is on a need-to-know basis, and as far as he's concerned, nobody needs to know nothing. He likes to keep his people in the dark. Less chance of a double cross."

Shapiro counted blinks like Morse code and figured the kid was lying.

The kid went on, "My best advice about the track is, don't bet on the horses. They ain't exactly reliable."

Shapiro ignored the remark. "I'm asking because, when things fall apart, I don't want anyone getting hurt—especially my people, but you too. You dig?"

"Yeah, I get it. I don't know anything about the track." Two quick blinks. Three slow.

The canary saw Shapiro register the lie and followed it with some truth. "He's got a new boy, a guy named Stanley Kramer. Maybe he's using Stanley to work an angle at the track. I'll find out what I can about it, and the girl too. Honest."

"It never ceases to amaze me the kind of crap you feed me."

"Mr. Policeman, sir. I get the feeling you're about to make a move. Maybe I could help. The boss is losing it. He's angry, paranoid, depressed. He's gonna snap, and when he does, he's gonna leave us all hanging out to dry in the wind. What's your plan?"

"You think I was born yesterday, kid? This is a one-way street. You give me info. I give you nothing. I'm not gonna let you sell us out. You oughta thank me. If you think he's paranoid now, you gotta know he would cut your throat in a second if he finds out you been talking to me. I'm saving your life. Just keep a suitcase packed and your mouth shut."

"That soon, huh?"

"Maybe it is, maybe it's not. You may find this hard to believe," Shapiro told him, "but I've grown sorta fond of you over the years. Get me what I need, and maybe I put in a word for you with the department and, God forbid, arrange for you to work for us as a 'consultant' in your areas of expertise. I can't stand you consorting with that bum. Capisce?"

"A Jew talking Italian. Only in New York. Yeah, I understand, Shapiro. Appreciate your concern. I'll get back to you when I got something."

"I won't hold my breath, just don't take all year deciding."

---

Enzo Trusgnich, in his seventies, the oldest of the New York–New Jersey Italian crime bosses, sat in a straight-backed wooden chair at a table in the back room of his men's club on Arthur Avenue in the Bronx. Young men rotated sitting guard duty, inside the club's front door, with a shotgun across their laps.

*Knock, knock.*

"Yeah," came a rasp from Trusgnich's age-worn vocal cords.

The door was half-opened by the kid from up front, his shotgun dangling behind his back from the sling over his shoulder. The youngster quickly adjusted to the room's stifling heat and withheld any visible sign of discomfort.

"Good morning, Mr. T.," said the youngster, resisting his thick Italian accent as he had also been forcefully instructed. "The newspaper from Napoli just got here." He spoke in his best American English and raised the paper in his hand.

"Gimme."

Every morning the boss read the previous day's edition of *Il Mattino*, flown in from the city of his birth. The kid gave it to him and left, closing the door softly behind him. He went back to his post and collapsed in the chair in nervous fatigue. He found encountering the boss frightening. Mr. T. was like Death Himself.

"Mmm, mmm." Humming ensued as Trusgnich ran his eyes over the headlines. Periodically he sipped from the small cup of espresso, spiked with anisette, on the table. This morning, he was distracted, waiting for his lieutenant, Alfredo Bonazzi, whom he had sent for thirty minutes ago. He took a bite from a cannoli left over from last night's supper. The radiator banged a few times then settled back down. Plenty of heat was needed to support Trusgnich's subnormal body temperature. He had once traveled down to Miami with the idea of escaping the New York winter, only to return a week later, fed up with the sunshine and the surf, and too many old people. It was depressing. He had nothing against Jews per se, but these were not the kind of Jews he was used to doing business with. These Miami Jews were annoying gabbers, constantly complaining about the service in restaurants, the traffic, the weather, their bowels, for God's sake. It was like one big old-age home. They made him feel ancient and weak, and a man in his position could not afford to feel weak, ever. He'd rather freeze to death in New York.

Two knocks on the door. Bonazzi. The lieutenant didn't wait for an answer. He came in and stood in front of his employer, espresso in hand.

"Boss. Sorry I'm late. I was out getting the veal for tonight's dinner."

Alfredo put his espresso down on the table and pulled up a chair so his employer wouldn't have to bend his rigid neck up to look at him while they talked.

"Alfredo," the rasp sounded. "How nice of you to join me. Our young lady from up the Concourse is getting ready to endanger her life again. She makes me laugh. Didja do what I said?"

"Yeah, boss. It's all taken care of. I told him you appreciate his service and you won't forget. Vinnie'll be on vacation somewhere in Italy with a couple a' bodyguards when it goes down."

"I wanna be there to see the race with my friends," Trusgnich commented.

"Sure, boss. I'll get you a box and some high-power binocs so you can watch in comfort."

---

In the early morning hours, before dawn, Andy Bennett, NYPD detective, sat on a folding chair in the family room of St. Philip Neri Catholic Church on the Concourse in the Bronx. His pregnant intended, Elaine, was fast asleep in bed a block away. Bennett held a chipped cup of black coffee in one hand and a lit Chesterfield in the other. Sobriety was worth the freezing trek in the predawn darkness. There were slippery patches of ice barely visible in the moonlight, but he made it to the warmth of the church basement without incident. He was relaxed and at peace, for one of those rare times in his life. It had been a struggle to get sober and stay that way.

"I'm lucky to be here," he told the roomful of familiar faces when it was his turn to speak. "I've never been this okay with myself. It's a harder job than what I do for a living, but I'm doing what the guy that's helping me says to do, and I'm feeling better every day. That's all I have to say."

Father Jack Donovan stuck his head in the partially open back door and caught Bennett's attention with a "Psst." When he had Andy's attention, he made a duck-talking motion with his hand and mouthed "afterward" and pointed back to his office. Andy nodded up and down at him, and the priest disappeared.

In the office later, Donovan said, "Andrew, my boy, how goes the struggle against the forces of darkness?"

"You talking about me personally, Father, or my job?"

"Both, Andy. I love seeing you come to your meetings here. I never knew a man, or a woman for that matter, who came every day like you do who didn't stay sober. Some of my fellow priests could use the meetings, but I leave that up to the Lord God Almighty. Now, about your life on the streets, are you being careful?"

"Yes, sir, I am."

"We both do the same kind of work, you know. I visit with my friend, Manny, in his drugstore. He catches me up on the neighborhood gossip and points me in directions he thinks could use my attention, and God's." The priest rolled his eyes toward the ceiling, and Andy thought of Pat O'Brien in *Angels With Dirty Faces*, He shook it off.

"So, Father Jack, what's really on your mind?"

"Cut to the chase, eh, my son? A few things come to mind. For one, the church needs work. A few of the bathrooms are only good for washing hands, if you catch my drift. The toilets are unusable. Some of the lights have begun to flicker, worrying everyone about the risk of fire. I know you come into contact with all sorts of men in your line of work. I was hoping you could find someone who would help us out, for a modest fee, of course. Pardon my honesty, but we also need some structural work around the playground out back and the room the children use in the winter. The walls seem to be crumbling."

Andy chuckled, good-naturedly. "That all?"

"That's all for the work that needs doing here, yes, but I have other concerns, Andrew, about you and your soon-to-be wife. Your spiritual condition has been on my mind more than the condition of the church. I know you're not Catholic, but my door is always open if you need to talk."

"We're doing great, Father. That's what my recovery is all about. God."

"I'm pleased to hear that."

"I appreciate the offer. I'll pass it on to Elaine."

"You do that."

"I know a guy who builds stage sets for Broadway shows whose annoying girlfriend owes me a favor. I'll ask him to put a crew together to take care of the stuff that's falling apart here. I'll tell him about the electricity and the plumbing too. He may know a plumber. Thanks for your concern about my intended and me. The child, as you may have heard, is not mine. It's Elaine's late husband's and hers. I think she would welcome your concern, and she may want to consult you about her grief over Harry's death. With her stomach sticking out like it is, she wants to get married in front of a justice of the peace. It's gotta happen soon, though, Father Jack. I'll let you know in case you want to attend the ceremony unofficially."

"Do that, please, my son."

# CHAPTER 24

# AT THE TRACK

April. The weather was warming into early spring. Susan felt pretty good about herself since she'd dumped Adam Murphy. Silence from him was better than she had expected. Evidently, he had taken her rejection like a gentleman. She hoped she never saw him again. She was a free woman. Being hunted by Adam was one of the creepiest experiences she had ever had. She was glad it was over. Alice, her friend, had told her to stop thinking about Stanley and Adam and concentrate on whether or not to start working at the law firm this summer.

It was just dawn. Susan dressed for work in what she had come to think of as her brothel costume. The short plaid skirt, white blouse, and knee socks of a Catholic schoolgirl. Preparing to leave the depressing basement apartment her parents rented, she thought about Alice's offer. She could dress and act like a lady, instead of the prostitute she was forced to impersonate at her diner job.

Her parents had already left for their respective jobs. She double-locked the door to the darkened courtyard and began her trudge through the alley to the street where the bus stopped. When she reached the sidewalk, she spotted a black sedan parked at the curb. A man in a dark suit got out from behind the wheel, walked around, and opened the rear door for her. Smiling, he bowed and gestured an invitation for her to step in. She moved tentatively closer to the car, ducking down to see who might be inside. To her horror, there sat Adam Murphy, smiling menacingly. Abject fear gripped her by the throat. She turned to run. The driver was too fast for her. He wrapped his arms around her and lifted her off her feet. He pressed a damp handkerchief over her nose and mouth and held it there until she took a deep breath. Chemical fumes filled her nose and throat. As she lost consciousness, she felt herself being shoved into the outstretched arms of her ex-boyfriend, Adam Murphy.

The big day had arrived. Alice and Jim were bunked in Sylvia Green's master bedroom in the mansion near the racetrack in Jamaica. It was the house where they had held the dinner party. Sylvia was asleep in one of her own guest rooms. Alice awakened to pitch blackness. Jim was sound asleep, breathing deeply, exhausted from spending the past week with his crew repairing the Catholic church in the Bronx. Milton Davis had kindly installed new toilets and fixed faucets wherever necessary. Walls were replastered; wiring and fuse boxes were replaced upstairs and down. The Father had been right to be concerned. The place had been a fire-trap. Not so anymore.

Alice wanted to let Jim sleep so he could enjoy race day. Not a sound was coming from down the hall where the Vargases were bedded down. She took comfort from knowing that an Italian gentleman was sitting in the living room with a shotgun in his hands, on guard duty, courtesy of the acquaintance of her undertaker and window washer friends.

"Jim? Are you awake?" She couldn't help herself.

"I am now."

"I can't sleep, and it's still dark. Do you think I'm doing the right thing?"

"Alice. I will try to remain calm, but"—his

voice rose an octave—"*are you frigging kidding me?*" He might have woken Antonio and Maria, he didn't know, but they would easily fall back to sleep as he gained control of himself. He, however, was upset enough that he knew he would not be able to fall back to sleep.

Jim surrendered to the inevitable and pushed himself up to a sitting position against the headboard. He wedged a pillow behind his back, his eyes still closed.

"Seriously?" He opened his eyes, but that made no difference in the pitch blackness. He couldn't see a blessed thing. "You're asking that question now? After all you've put yourself, your friends, and your family through? You pick now to ask if you're doing the right thing? You're joking, right? Please tell me you are not serious. Lie to me and tell me you're sure everything will turn out just perfect. It'll give you practice for when you talk to the others."

"All right, okay, I'm not serious."

"What a relief, because you sounded like you meant it. Listen, Alice, I don't mind if you work off your stage fright on me, but you do not want to alienate your troops just before the big show. You want them to think, perhaps mistakenly, that you are optimistic and know what you're doing. You are their fearless leader. They're looking to you for inspiration and confidence that this dangerous game you asked them to help you play will succeed. I'm begging you, do not destroy their faith at this delicate juncture in time. As for me, I love you. I never think you completely know what you're doing anyway, but that doesn't stop me from being willing to follow you through the gates of hell if necessary. These people have risked a lot for you. They love you almost as much as I do, but none of them is above inflicting grievous bodily harm on you if you screw with them now. Get a grip on yourself. Everything is fine. Do something strenuous, like pushups, to get yourself under control; then we'll sleep a little longer, wake up refreshed, and go watch the race like civilized human beings, about to jerk a tiger by his tail."

"I don't do push-ups. Isn't there anything else I can do?"

"As a matter of fact, there is, and it'll take all your attention away from the race."

"I'm listening. I promise I'll behave myself and I won't tell the others I'm scared if you don't. So, what do you suggest I do to relieve my anxiety?"

Jim got out of bed and locked the door.

---

Jamaica Race Course opened on April 27, 1903. The

day marked the first running of the Excelsior Handicap. The Metropolitan Jockey Club of Jamaica, Queens, operated the mile-long track.

Three friends sat in a skybox overlooking the track and the throng of racing enthusiasts. The crowd beneath them held betting slips for the first race in one hand and their fourth beer of the day in the other.

The undertaker said, "These people are excited, fellas. It's been a long time since I've actually come to a track to watch a race. I couldn't resist watching our girlfriend drop the hammer on this guy."

"Yeah," the window washer chimed in. "It's like her first communion. If she pulls this off, she's gonna be a legend in the neighborhood."

A raspy voice weighed in. "So many things could go wrong. Are you kidding me? How'd we let her talk us into helping? Just 'cause she means well don't mean it's gonna happen like she says. If I had a nickel for every time things went wrong . . ."

"Come on, Enzo," the undertaker told him. "Relax. She can dream, can't she? We used to dream, remember? We always thought everything was gonna go as planned, and it did a lot of the time. If it doesn't, she'll think of some other way to get the young scungilli away from that thief."

"I guess so. We'll see," Trusgnich responded. "I don't trust the nags, never have. They're jumpier than a safecracker with an alarm going off. Can't trust 'em. They need head doctors to keep 'em running in the right direction. I say we kill the guy and take the kid back."

"That'll be our backup plan, okay? Let's sit back and enjoy the show," Frankie said. "Somebody paid good money for these seats. You never know. This could work."

"Sylvia Green" and her entourage sat in the stands, in the front row, at the finish line. In the second row, a woman with extraordinarily large breasts, a black wig, and dark sunglasses was right behind them. She wore tons of fake jewelry, a wide-brimmed straw hat, and she reeked of cheap perfume. She had a big smile on her face. Directly in front of her, Alice sat, too nervous to speak. Her face was drained of all color. Her lips were sealed tight. She'd never been in such a state before in her life and hoped never to be again. Maria Vargas had applied eye shadow and rouge to Alice's face since Alice's hands were shaking too badly to do it herself.

Antonio broke the tension. "So, Miss Green, this is Wyldfire's big day. I appreciate your confidence in us. John"—he spoke to Jim—"I do believe Miss Green has lost her ability to speak. If you have anything to say to her, now is the time. You may never get a chance like this again."

Maria told her husband, "Quit it, Antonio. It's not funny. She's a nervous wreck. She looks like she might be about to have a stroke."

Jim told them, "I'm gonna have to take her away for a rest when this is over."

Antonio asked, in a low, concerned voice, "Are you okay, Alice? I didn't mean to hurt your feelings."

Alice tried to answer, but her mouth wouldn't work, so she smiled weakly.

"Maybe I should get her a drink," Jim said.

"Alice, honey," Maria said. "Snap out of it. We're supposed to be having fun."

Alice finally said something. "I will never do anything like this again. Ever. Remind me."

"I'd love to believe that, Alice," Jim said, "but you know you will."

Alice said, "I really lost it just now, didn't I? I apologize."

Jim stood up. "Well, you're back now, that's all that counts, and I gotta go give Billy a boost up onto Wyldfire's back. I have to pretend I know what I'm doing."


Michael Pope sat alone in his box. Vinnie was

nowhere to be seen. Something was up.

Pope's luggage was packed, his Chevy gassed up. His girlfriend, Darlene, awaited his arrival on their little island in the Pacific. There was money stashed under the floorboards in the bedroom of their house there. Schumann's million-dollar investment in Wyldfire, the loser, had never made it to the betting windows. It was packed tightly enough to fit under Pope's seat on the plane. It would join the rest of his nest egg under the floor in the Pacific. The lease was terminated on the penthouse in Manhattan, and the place had been stripped of its contents. He had no idea when the heat would blow off, if ever, and he could return to New York City. His people had his betting slips on the winner, Fortunate Princess. His winnings on Fortunate Princess would cover severance pay for the troops, but most of it would be wired to an offshore account for him. He'd thought of skipping the severance pay, but it was a small enough cut. He'd still make out like a bandit, and he might want to reassemble his troops sometime in the future, you never knew. Abraham Schumann would be left with nothing to show for his money but memories of Nadine yelling, "Oh God! Oh God!" underneath him.

Moving in on this much money brought to mind Miss Sylvia Green. She was almost too good to be true. There was something off about her. She was too cheerful about spending so much cash on a losing horse. Maybe his mind was playing tricks on him. He found her with his binoculars. Cute. It'd be a shame if she was playing him. He started sweating. He blotted his face with his shirt. If something funny were going on with her, he would have to have Pete Reynolds track her down.

---

Billy Smith lay on his back on a short couch in the jockeys' room. His head was propped up on one of the armrests, a Raymond Chandler book sitting open on his chest. *The Big Sleep*. He loved Phillip Marlowe, the detective.

*Them was the days,* thought Billy. *I should have such problems as this General Sternwood. A mansion. A butler. All that money.*

Now and then, Billy reached over his head and took a sip of coffee from the cup on the table. He looked at the countdown clock on the wall. Forty minutes to post time. He closed his eyes and emptied his mind, except for his trainer's instructions—the real John Wanamaker—about the race ahead. He would be hovering, on bent knees, over the back of Wyldfire, hoping to survive the speed, trusting in God. He relied on the jockey room custodian to tell him and his fellow riders when it was exactly sixteen minutes to post time, at which moment they were supposed to get up and put on their silks and helmets. He was already wearing his riding boots, crossed at the ankles, propped on the other arm of the couch. Joe Ortega, the valet assigned to the number 3 horse in the opening race, had escorted Billy to his weigh-in and taken the saddle and padding from Billy's arms as soon as he stepped down from the scale after the clerk of scales had recorded his weight. Joe took it all out to the paddock's saddling stalls, and Billy returned to his couch and his book across the hall. At the paddock, Antonio, acting as the groom, steadied Wyldfire while Joe laid the cloth on her back and cinched the saddle down over it, leaving the number 3 displayed on the filly's haunches.

Silence in the jockey room. The anticipation of the featherweight riders—some sipping beverages, some absorbing words from a book, some staring at the ceiling, one chomping on an apple—was palpable. All of them were preparing mentally and spiritually for the sensation of a thoroughbred thundering at top speed under them. Most people had no idea of the feeling. The time could never reflect the experience of crouching over a horse's back, knees bent, backside high in the air above the saddle, suddenly released from the gate to ride a bolt of lightning a million miles down the track, in a matter of seconds, to the finish line.

In Billy's book, General Sternwood was interviewing Marlowe in the greenhouse where the wealthy old gentleman was forced to spend most of his life. He needed the warmth his body could not generate. He encouraged the detective to drink the whiskey he could no longer tolerate and smoke the cigarettes he could no longer afford to inhale. Sweating profusely, Marlowe takes off his jacket and rolls up his sleeves.

Thirty minutes to post time. Billy took another sip of coffee and looked around the room. The other jockeys were draped all over the place, on chairs, couches, the floor, relaxing as best they could.

Two sat at a card table. One whispered, "How's the wife?" barely audibly.

"She's okay. How's your new baby boy?"

"He almost took a step yesterday, man." Big smile.

There were other couches scattered around the room holding jockeys in various positions of repose. One man was on the floor with his legs propped against the wall, reading a Bible. One sat cross-legged, hands in his lap, palms up, eyes closed in prayer.

They had all been weighed in. Their mounts

were saddled and waiting for them in the paddock.

*Geez, this guy Sternwood's got his hands full with those two daughters. He's not joking that he probably shouldn't have indulged in fatherhood at his age. I have enough problems with just one kid.*

"Chaplain's here," yelled the retired jockey in charge of the room.

They stopped what they were doing, stood, and bowed their heads in silence.

The chaplain, a young man from Churchill Downs in Kentucky, spoke the words, "Heavenly Father. Bless these riders as they go out from here to do their jobs. Let them each walk away, after their races are over, under their own power, without the need of assistance, and may their horses survive without injury, whether they win or lose. We thank you, Lord, for this beautiful day and the many blessings you have given us. Amen."

A chorus of Amens sounded, and they all went back to what they were doing.

The clock ticked on.

Sixteen minutes to post time. "Time to get ready! Put your helmets and silks on!" yelled the super. The jockeys jerked to a stand and put on their colorful silks and black helmets. They grabbed whips, and as they filed out of the room, they each took the leather number corresponding to their ride from the basket at the door and clipped it to the metal loop sewn onto the right shoulder of their silks.

Moments later, the room was empty. Lockers with street clothes stood ajar. *The Big Sleep* lay facedown on the floor. Coffee cooled. A half-eaten apple sat next to the Bible on the card table.

# CHAPTER 25

## AND THEY'RE OFF

Outside, the sun was shining. The spring air was an even seventy degrees. Billy loved New York. The excitement of the city got into his blood. He would need every bit of it to beat this field, particularly the favorite, Fortunate Princess. He smiled broadly at the thought he had helped spread the rumor that his horse, Wyldfire, was not as fast as she was. The three-year-old filly was exponentially faster than anyone knew, but there was no "sure thing" in racing.

It was opening day at the track in Queens, the easternmost and the largest of the five boroughs that comprise New York City.

Owners, trainers, and jockeys prepared for the first race. Hearts pounded. Mouths dried. The race was for three-year-old fillies only.

"Riders up!" the paddock judge shouted, and seven riders stepped into the laced hands of trainers and grooms for a lift into the saddles of seven spirited horses.

Jim Peters boosted Billy onto Wyldfire's back. Peters was beyond thrilled at the chance to be part of an actual thoroughbred horse-racing event. From the visit Jim and Alice had paid to the stables in Florida, Wyldfire recognized Jim and settled down in his presence.

Billy now sat atop the number 3 horse. Everyone knew she had speed, but could she go the distance? The odds were fourteen to one against her. The educated opinion had it she was no match for Fortunate Princess. Billy eyed the even-money favorite, number 7. The Princess was known for her outstanding workouts. For him to beat the 7, he had to keep her on his outside, away from the rail, and make the length of her ride just enough longer than Wyldfire's to give Wyldfire the advantage.

Calm Bay, the number 1, was first out of the paddock to parade in front of the grandstands. She was followed by number 2, Doctor's Dandy. Number 3 was Billy himself on Wyldfire. Number 4, Crack Shot, was next. Then came the Number 5, Gracious Heart, Number 6, Free for Me, and Number 7, the favorite, Fortunate Princess. People in the stands nervously checked the horses they had put money on. None of them was as nervous as Alice White, who had crossed the line into speechless hysteria once again. The real Sylvia Green wrapped her arms lovingly around Alice's neck from the seat behind her, trying not to let her fake boobs get in the way. "It'll be all right, sweetheart. You'll see. She's my baby. I promise she won't let you down."

The horses warmed up by trotting short distances back and forth near the gate. They had ten minutes to get into position.

Assistant starters helped load the horses in the gate and close the doors behind them.

They were set.


The starter pushed his button. The bell sounded. And they were off.


They broke in a straight line.

Number 3, Wyldfire, shot out in front, with number 5, Gracious Heart, and number 6, Free for Me, running a half-length off her lead. Number 7, Fortunate Princess, got outside Wyldfire, positioned for her move. Number 5 and number 6 momentarily dropped back. Numbers 1, Calm Bay, 2, Doctor's Dandy, and 4, Crack Shot, fell back even further.

The first quarter mile was run in twenty-three and two-fifths seconds. Billy crouched over Wyldfire. He had a grin on his face, knowing that he wouldn't have to use her up because number 5 and number 6 had moved up on his outside and were holding number 7, Fortunate Princess, hostage.

The half mile was forty-seven and three-fifths seconds.

They made the turn and headed for the wire.

Number 5 dropped back. Number 6 was still there. Number 7, Fortunate Princess, was still trapped on the outside but was inching ahead. She would try and make her run down the middle of the track and beat number 6 and number 3. On 3, Billy nudged his horse, then flat-out hit her with the whip, and she responded. The wire was getting closer, and so was 7, Fortunate Princess, running alongside Wyldfire, neck and neck, down the middle of the racetrack.

Billy pulled ahead by a full length and crossed the finish line.

In the stands, Alice nearly collapsed with relief. Sylvia Green leaped over the row of seats and hugged and kissed Alice. They jumped up and down, crying for joy. Antonio and Jim's eyes darted around on high alert, looking for any immediate consequences of the upset in Michael Pope's plans.

Wyldfire pulled up on the track, turned around, and came back to the finish line. The photo and the winner were flashed on the tote board. Billy kicked his feet out of the stirrups and jumped to the ground, fists in the air. He had beaten the favorite, just like he knew he would.

The time for the six-furlong race was one minute, thirteen and two-fifths seconds.

The old Italians watched as Michael Pope shot up from his seat in a rage and hurried out of his box.

"His fuse is lit," Cavuto observed. "Now is the time of maximum danger."

"Listen up," Pope told Sebastian Lupo on the other end of the line. "There's been a change in plans. Things did not go like I was told they would. The horse lost and took my bankroll with her."

"You don't sound too good, Mr. P."

"I'm fine. Things didn't work out how my good friend Vinnie assured me they would, and he didn't show up at the track, either. He set me up. I'll deal with him later. If you hear from Nadine, tell her I'll get back to her, which I never will. There's no telling what 'Abe the babe' will get up to when he figures out she was in on the scam. She knew the risks. If he doesn't kill her, she'll do the prison time without ratting me out if she knows what's good for her. If she doesn't, she'll be looking over her shoulder for the rest of her life, and, as she knows, she'll never see me coming."

"Should we get her a lawyer if she needs one?"

"No way. I'm gonna need all the money I got to take care of myself. She's gotten a little too big for her britches. Prison will shrink her down to size. Maybe she'll get hooked on smack again. It's been waiting to jump on her back again ever since I took her off the street. I half expected it to happen when this job was over. Women like her are a dime a dozen. The rest of the gang too, not including you. I'm not sure I can trust anybody anymore."

"Whatever you say, Mr. Pope. You're the boss. Any instructions about the new guy, Stanley? Pete Reynolds has him and his girlfriend stashed away somewhere. What do you want us to do with them?"

"Tell Pete to kill them both. I got a sneaky feeling they had something to do with this race going bad. If the girl wants Stanley so much, she can have him. They can die together. That'll tie up the loose end of the late Sarah Truman. This was a gigantic screw-job, only I'm gonna have the last laugh. Vinnie better hope I never find him. And I got a feeling that woman Sylvia Green was in on this too. That dinner party at her place was part of the setup. I know that now. I've done that same thing a million times. It serves me right. She conned the con man. That might not even be her real name. Her cruddy horse ended up winning. I think she knew it would all along. It was not luck. And to think I had big plans for her. Tell Pete to find her, whoever she is, and do her too. Bury the three of them together. Poetic justice."

"Okay, Mr. Pope."

"Make the call now. I'll be in touch. Don't mess this up, Lupo."

Pope hung up, found his car in the lot, and headed for the airport.

Lupo hung up and dialed.

"Where are they keeping them?" Shapiro, the vice cop, asked him.

"I don't know for sure."

"Guess, dammit."

"352 East Thirty-Fourth, Apartment 805."

"My God, boy, good for you. You are an accomplished liar. You'll work out fine as one of us if we all live through this crap."

"I think you got some time, Detective Shapiro. They don't know who the horse lady is. They're not gonna kill anybody until they find out who she is and grab her too. It's already late in the day. You know who she is?"

"Yes, I do. I'll send someone to pick her up."

"Listen, copper. There's something I gotta tell you."

"Finally. A moment of sanity. It's about the dead girl. Sarah Truman? Spill."

"I was there. A witness, not an accessory, you understand? I'm not lying. I didn't do it. I would never cut a woman's throat. It was brutal. I would have let him kill me first."

"I knew you'd come through for me. I'm proud of you. Don't worry. I won't let you take the fall. You're too valuable to waste."

"Promise me."

"I promise, but I need a name."

"Pete Reynolds. He's been Pope's cleaner for a while. He knocked Stanley out with chloral hydrate, did the girl, left her body with Stanley in the apartment. Stanley came to, soaked in her blood, hours later. Then Pete turns around, takes me and some other guys to clean it up. They collect the evidence against Stanley and clean any trace of the murder out of the apartment. I just stood there and watched, I swear. He said he was killing two birds with one stone for Mr. Pope."

"Good boy, Wolfie. I believe you. Let's get the hostages loose."

Pope had second thoughts after talking to Wolf. He stopped at another pay phone and called Pete himself. "Find out who Sylvia Green is and scoop her up. Torture the kid Stanley if you have to, or, better yet, his girlfriend. Something tells me Miss Green, if that's even her name, knows them. After you get the three of 'em together, kill them all."

---

Alice asked Jim to drop her off at her place in the Bronx. He offered to take her to dinner, but she had no appetite. She was exhausted and elated by the day's events and felt the need to be alone. Maybe she'd be able to get some rest after all these weeks of excitement. She didn't think she was fit company and promised to lock herself in. It was dusk when he left. She planned to stay put until one of Antonio's men came by to pick her up in the morning. She wasn't going anywhere without a bodyguard. She locked both locks of her thick metal front door and engaged the chain for good measure. If anyone knocked unannounced, she would not answer but would pick up the phone and call for help.

Alice was proud of what she had accomplished today, but she was unsure if it had achieved the desired result of breaking Michael Pope's back and freeing young Stanley from Pope's grip. She still had no clue about the young woman's killing. Patience was not her strong suit. She would have to wait until the dust settled, at least overnight, to make further inquiries. For now, she had earned a quiet evening at home.

As night fell, she became jittery with post-action excitement. She could not help herself. What an amazing last couple of months it had been. She had kept up with her law school studies while carrying on this elaborate charade. She was ready for final exams, and her horse had won her race. She had a policy of not overstudying before an exam, so cracking a law book at this late date was out of the question. She would review just before the actual tests.

She was bored. She did not own a television and would not leave her apartment to watch even a single show on a neighbor's. She suddenly became ravenously hungry and checked her cabinets and refrigerator for the makings of a snack. She could taste Luigi's meatballs and spaghetti.

She checked her Browning automatic, safety off, a bullet in the chamber, and felt guilty as she slid it into the waistband of her slacks at the small of her back.

She put on the man's trench coat and the brimmed hat she favored for the rain at this time of year and unchained and unlocked the door. She took the elevator down to the basement, pulled the brim of her hat practically over her eyes, and proceeded, invisibly, out the side entrance of her building and down the half block to Luigi's.

The chef at Luigi's did not disappoint her with a perfect plate of the spaghetti and meatballs she had been fixated on. She downed it voraciously and washed it down with red wine. The meal was uneventful. She vowed to lock herself back into the safety of her apartment for the rest of the night.

As she ascended the short distance uphill, she paid strict attention to her surroundings.

She was almost at the gate to her basement entrance's small courtyard when an uneasy feeling overcame her. Her nerves and her guilt about stepping out without one of her armed friends to protect her were playing games with her mind. She pretended to drop something on the ground and bowed down to retrieve it and take a look around as a precautionary measure. Well-timed, as it turned out. While she was down there, scanning her environment, she heard the *pfft* of a silenced bullet sailing over her head into the dirty white brick of her building.

How could they have found her so fast? She was all the way up here in the Bronx, and she had only been out of her apartment for less than an hour.

She dove for the little courtyard inside the gate and threw herself on the ground while reaching back under the trench coat for the comforting grip of her automatic. She brought it around, held it with both hands, and pointed it out the open gate toward the sidewalk.

Resting her elbows on the cement pavement, she looked and listened, scanning the parked cars.

She saw movement between two cars and fired. The unsilenced bang was followed by a man's cry of pain in the darkness and the sound of him falling. Hopefully, the shot was loud enough that someone would call the police.

She heard a car door slam down the hill on Wilbert. Maybe it was one of the neighborhood mafia soldiers coming to her rescue.

The basement door burst open behind her, and a man landed on her back. He banged her forearm repeatedly on the ground until the gun dropped out of her hand. After that, everything happened so fast. A piece of cloth was stuffed into her mouth. Her wrists were tied behind her back. A sedan came down the hill and stopped at the curb. A large man emerged, left his door open, and took her by the shoulders. The man who had restrained her lifted her by the ankles. They threw her onto the back seat of the car. A man limped from the shadows, the one she had shot, and got in the front. The car reversed up the hill before the door was even closed. In the car, a hood was pulled over her head.

The soldier from Wilbert Avenue arrived to help, gun drawn, but too late. He watched as the car backed into Concourse traffic. Horns blew in protest. The car reversed direction and sped away down the Concourse. A nondescript car pulled out of its parking space at the top of the hill and tailed the first one down the Concourse at a distance, unnoticed in the heat of the moment.

# CHAPTER 26

## CAPTIVITY

Sunday morning in Stanton on the Hudson River, two hours north of New York City, it was sunny and clear. Birds chirped, and a gentle breeze blew. Spring was in the air.

The Davises were entertaining guests for breakfast in their kitchen. The pregnant widow, Elaine Applewood, and her fiancé, Andy Bennett, sat at the table covered with a red-and-white-checkered cloth. Elaine and Ellen were still in their bathrobes and slippers. Andrew and Milton wore sweaters and slacks. Sections of the *Sunday Times* were stacked on a nearby stool. The table was strewn with hard rolls, bagels, lox, white fish, cream cheese, cups of coffee, and company-style cloth napkins. Cream and sugar were in a set of matching crockery.

Elaine and Andy had arrived late the night

before for a visit and thanked their hosts for the hundredth time for their kind hospitality to Elaine during her and her late husband's ordeal.

By the nature of her profession as a nurse, Ellen was a student of human behavior, fascinated by everyone she met and everyone's lives and professions. She asked Andrew, "Tell me all about being a police detective, Andrew. How is it protecting the public from crime in the city these days?"

"Crime is thriving as always, Ellen," he answered. "I hunt down a perpetrator, lock them up, and a dozen more show up to take their place. It's a relay race designed to wear us down. Crime stops for no man . . . or woman. Speaking of which, neither does your girlfriend, Alice White, stop for any man or woman. As you know, she just pulled a fast one on a dastardly criminal in our fair city. He's what we in law enforcement call, in the wind, long gone. I suppose we owe her a debt of gratitude. Miss White has locked herself into her apartment until we can assure her safety."

Ellen exclaimed, "I'm so proud she found a use for us in her little adventure. Milton fulfilled his lifelong dream of playing a butler when Alice entertained the gangster before the big race. I, of course, was the maid. Milton became quite frisky when we were in our uniforms, didn't you, dear?"

"Who, me?"

"Him all handsome in his tuxedo, me in my black dress and white apron. It's no wonder those Hollywood people get married and divorced so often. It is positively exhilarating playing dress-up."

Andy told her, "Please don't tell me Alice involved you in all this. I do not want to know she used innocent civilians to set this guy up. Just don't talk about that part to me, okay, because it threatens my blood pressure and challenges my sanity. She lives a little too dangerously for me, Ellen, and I am a police officer, used to danger. Thank heaven, and in the interest of public safety, she has finished meddling in other people's lives for the moment and is confined to her quarters. I'm not worried about her. She's got friends in low places to protect her until this guy, Pope, is found and dealt with. Then, I believe, we can all relax and brace for her next crisis."

The telephone rang. Ellen Davis stood and plucked the receiver from the wall.

"Hello. This is Ellen," she said. "Yes, he's here. I'll put him on."

She turned to the table, "I suppose you gave them our number, Andrew. It's Sunday morning, for heaven's sake. Don't you get a day off?"

"No, Ellen. I told you. I am officially off, but crime rests for no one. I always leave a number so they can get hold of me. Sorry for the imposition."

"Nonsense, Andrew. If you go into the foyer, you can use the table phone out there. I'll hang up when you get on the line."

Andrew did as Ellen suggested. When Ellen heard him speaking, she hung the kitchen receiver back on its cradle and sat down at the table.

Milton Davis asked Elaine, "So, when are you due, young lady? If you don't mind my saying so, you look about ready to pop."

"I am, I am, please, God. Next month, Milton. I am definitely ready to pop. This is my very first baby. I had no idea nine months could last so long. It's been bittersweet with Harry gone. I don't know what I would have done without Andy by my side. I am so grateful for him. We met right here at your front door. He was so polite, so careful to make me feel safe. Harry was alive, and Andy wanted to help him. Now the detective waits on me hand and foot like I'm an invalid. He's busy enough without having to do the grocery shopping, which he does almost every day on his way back from work. He even cleans the apartment and cooks breakfast and dinner. It breaks my heart how generous he is to me."

"What a guy," Ellen said. "Only a real man can put on a kitchen apron and keep his pride. I'm happy for you. You told us you're getting married. When is that happening?"

"We don't have much time, so it's in a week. We're doing it at a justice of the peace in the Bronx. We only want a small group. That's part of the reason we came up here. We were hoping you would make the drive. Alice is gonna be my maid of honor. When it comes to Alice, Andrew is all bluster, but I think he's genuinely fond of her too. She amuses him. He's always warm to people who have been kind to me, and Alice definitely qualifies in that department."

Andy strolled back from the foyer.

"I heard that," he said. "And yes, I am sort of warm toward her, but there's bad news. It seems like your maid of honor has gone missing."

---

Alice lay on a bed on her side. The hood was gone. Her hands were still tied behind her back. She could hear the muffled sound of a man speaking on the phone through the closed door. She thought she was alone in the room. There was a lamp lit next to her on the bedside table. She could see dawn peeking through the edge of the window shade.

*Who's gonna know I'm gone?* Alice wondered. *I shoulda stayed in my apartment and ate a sandwich for supper. A lot of good it does me to think about that now.*

She wriggled on the bed, trying to free her wrists, but no give.

"Alice, is that you?" Susan's voice came from somewhere on the floor. Alice looked around but couldn't see her.

"Hey, Susan. Fancy meeting you here."

"Yes, it's me. I'm so sorry for getting you into this. They hurt me, but I wouldn't give you up. Stanley, on the other hand, told them everything. He shoulda just kept his mouth shut and let them kill me."

"Don't be too hard on him, Susan. These guys sound like they knew what they were doing."

"Alice, how can you defend him? He betrayed both of us."

"Susan, I don't know what I would have done if I was him. Blaming him is not gonna get us out of this. Sadly, this has happened to me before. It's beginning to annoy me, I'll tell you that. I stick my nose in other people's business, and they take it personally. It all comes crashing down on my head. Where is Stanley anyway?"

"Stanley and I are handcuffed back-to-back on the floor. Stanley, say something to Miss White, so she knows you're alive."

"Hello, Miss White," Stanley spoke. "I'm sorry I was such a coward. Susan has more nerve than I do. I couldn't stand to see them hurt her. I'm sorry I did this to you. Please forgive me."

"That's enough, Stanley," Susan told him. "You can shut up now. You're right. You are sorry. What a jerk I was. The dumb waitress from the Bronx falling for a college boy with big plans for himself that didn't include her. I should have guessed by how fast you left after you got what you wanted, whenever you came to see me. You used me like a Kleenex. I can't believe I allowed it. I'm sorry, Alice, but I am still so mad at him and at myself too."

"That's okay, Susan. Anger is good. We're gonna get out of here, don't you worry. Then you can take your time and slap him silly."

Stanley whispered, "Susan, I'm really sorry for what I did to you. I mean it. I didn't know how good I had it until I lost you."

"You didn't lose me, Stanley. You threw me away."

"You're right. I felt sorry for myself, and I did it without thinking. I'm not that kind of person, Susan, you've got to believe me. I really had feelings for you—have feelings for you, if you don't mind me saying so. If we ever get out of this, I want to try and make it up to you."

Susan said, "Didn't I tell you to be quiet, Stanley? They probably handcuffed us back-to-back so I wouldn't kill you."

The door opened. Pete Reynolds stepped in. "Shut your mouths, all of you, or I'll shut them for you."

Stanley recognized the voice but couldn't see him.

"Is that you, Pete? Pete Reynolds. I am so glad you're here. There must be some mistake. Please let us go?"

Pete walked around the bed Alice was lying on to confront Stanley.

"It's no mistake, Stanley. Haven't you figured it out yet? You don't matter to Mr. Pope. You never did. None of us really matter to him. We're just a means to an end. We stay alive at his pleasure. It doesn't matter anymore, so I can tell you. I swapped chlorals for your bennies that night, and then I killed the girl. When you came to and called the next morning, Mr. Pope thought it would be funny to send me back to clean up the mess I made. He's got your blood-soaked clothes and the knife with your prints stashed away in what he calls his 'blackmail file.'"

"Thanks for telling me, Pete. I can at least die with a clean conscience, about the murder anyway. But Pete, can't you let the women go? They don't know anything. They're innocent. Pope got what he wanted from me. Kill me."

"You double-crossed the boss, don't you get it? The women were in on it. It cost him big. How's he gonna run his business if he lets people do that to him? This way, people will think twice before they ever try anything like this again."

"How did I ever get into this in the first place?" Stanley asked out loud.

Pete told him, "Same as the rest of us, Stan. You bought into his bullshit story about a life of wealth and power, peppered with beautiful women and booze. The women think it's all gonna be bright lights, big city. Nothing that good comes free. I'm sorry, but I can't let any of you go. I'm gonna have to kill you, your girlfriend, and Miss 'Green-and-White' over there. Nothing personal, man. It's strictly business."

He spoke to Alice. "Once we got hold of your friends over there, you were easy to find."

"Pete," Stanley pleaded. "We work for the same man. Doesn't that count for anything? I'm begging you. Just let us go?"

"Can't do it, kid. You seem like a good enough guy, but I got my future to think about. Pope is out of town now, but he'll be back, and I don't want to spend the rest of my life running from him. When he comes back, there'll be hell to pay if I don't do what he told me. Relax. It's not time yet."

Pete turned and left the room, closing the door behind him.

"Well, Susan. I don't want to upset you," Alice spoke as quietly as she could, "but, in my mind, things just took a turn for the worse. It doesn't look too good for us. At least we'll die knowing Stanley didn't kill Sarah Truman. That's something. Too bad no one knows we're here. Try taking a nap."

"Alice, you are crazy. How can any of us sleep at a time like this?"

Before Alice could answer, the window began a slow, scraping ascent on its tracks. She felt a gust of spring air hit her in the face. She watched as a large leg stuck out from under the shade, clad in black denim. There was a motorcycle boot at the end, reaching for contact with the floor.

"What took you so long?" Alice exclaimed, as quietly as her excitement and relief would allow. "It's about time."

Antonio appeared and put his index finger to his lips, commanding silence. "Don't be wise, Alice," he whispered back at her. "What's the matter?" he went on. "You couldn't dial the phone for some company when you got hungry? You're going to drive me crazy, Alice. The guy I had watching you was alone and couldn't take those guys on without risking your life. So he did the next best thing. He tailed you here."

"I'm sorry, Antonio. I'll do better next time."

"The police are outside. They found out where this place is all by themselves and gave me five minutes to get you out before they bust in."

"Antonio, meet my friend, Susan Atkins. The guy she's with is her former boyfriend, Stanley Kramer. He's in the doghouse right now for getting us all into this mess. If she doesn't kill him, he's looking at a world of pain the next time they're alone together."

"Stanley, what are you doing?" Susan asked her ex-boyfriend.

"I'm opening the handcuffs. Being with a gang of con artists was not entirely a waste of time. I spent a whole day learning how to pick pockets. I took the key when they were snapping the cuffs on us."

Antonio grabbed Alice by both shoulders and held his face close to hers. She thought he would take advantage of her hands being tied behind her back and kiss her, on the mouth, she guessed. She didn't care. She would leave that part out of the story when she told Jim. Her stomach fluttered. Instead, Antonio flipped her onto her front and cut her loose. Embarrassed at her untoward thoughts, she turned over and rubbed her wrists to give herself time for the humiliation to pass.

"Enough chatter." Vargas kept his voice low. "Let us get the hell out of here before they come back to kill you, or the cops kick in the door, and all hell breaks loose."

# CHAPTER 27

## FREEDOM

Abraham sat up in his pajama bottoms, skimming the *Wall Street Journal*. He reached for the champagne flute on the bedside table and took a sip. The Waldorf Astoria was one of his favorite hotels, and he'd been around the world a time or two. This was the nicest suite at the Waldorf. He was more at ease in this moment than he had been in many years. He was excited to be here with her.

Earlier, they had dined at another of his favorite places, the Stork Club. Afterward, a romantic carriage drive through Central Park. During the ride, he'd handed her a black velvet box with a diamond bracelet in it. While working the clasp, he looked at her smiling face and kissed her passionately on the lips. She glowed with a love for him she had never felt for any other man. They were the happiest either of them had ever been, anywhere, at any time.

Now, she came out of the bathroom, barefoot, clad in a practically transparent nightgown and, of course, the diamond bracelet, which she thought about never taking off again. Stunning. Exciting. Her curves, visible through the material, were a thing of particular sweetness to him. His heart was full.

"My dear," he told her, "you look amazing. I don't know what I was looking for all these years, but no one compares with you."

"Darling," she purred seductively. "I think we both gained a certain amount of wisdom in our travels. It's time we showed each other what we learned."

She flicked off the ceiling light. He got out of bed to face her. She put her arms straight up in the air. He lifted the gown over her head and dropped it on the floor. He took her in with his eyes, then lifted her into his arms and placed her on the bed.

She undid the string of his pajamas.

"Vivian," he said, "I haven't been a perfect husband to you. I intend to make that up, starting tonight."


Afterward, they shared a cigarette. She leaned forward from the headboard and draped his free arm up over her shoulders.

"That was fairly explosive, dear," she told her estranged husband. "Holy smokes. If I'd have known it was gonna be this good, I would have seduced you a long time ago."

He responded, "Gee, baby. We didn't know what we were missing. I may never have to go to the gym again. You are more exciting than you have ever been. I intend never to take you for granted again."

"Abraham. I want you to do something for her."

"For who? Do you mean Miss Nadine Byrkowski, also known as Helen Parker? What did you have in mind?"

"I do not want her returning to the street. You not pressing charges is not enough. She unintentionally helped save our marriage."

He said, "When I talked to her with that vice detective, Shapiro, she said she intended to work as a personal trainer, maybe for professional athletes, but it sounded like a pipe dream."

"Have you forgiven her?"

"She hurt my pride, Vivian, but you have helped me rise above that. I guess I have forgiven her, but I will never forgive her boss."

"I don't expect you to. I've never seen you take

something like what he did to you lying down. There doesn't seem to be any way to get at him."

"Don't you worry your pretty little head about that."

"I see," she said with a look of understanding. Abraham was not a man to be fooled with. She respected him and knew enough to stay out of his business.

"Okay then," she said. "We'll speak no more about it. So then, why don't you send Nadine to school to learn her trade? See if you can hook her up with one of your sports friends."

"If that's what you really think, sweetheart. You know, you're a very generous woman. Speaking of forgiveness, what about the boy, Stanley Kramer, Mr. Pope sent to appease you?"

"Did that make you jealous, Abraham?"

"Maybe. I suppose it did, a little, even though he's just a young punk."

"Good, I'm glad. It'll give you something to think about."

"You know," Abraham said, "his girlfriend is the one who got that nutty woman to set Pope up? But, he still got away with our money."

"She is not nutty, Abraham. Alice White is just a little eccentric. There was an article about her in the *Post*. She's going to be a lawyer."

"Yes, I saw that. The guy who wrote it, Franklin Jones, must have a crush on her a mile deep. Let's say she's high-strung then. What do you think we ought to do about the boy, Stanley, Viv?"

"You haven't called me Viv in years. I like it. It makes me want to cry."

She kissed him on the cheek. A tear leaked out of her eye.

"Just let me rest a few more minutes, Viv. What was Stanley doing before he worked for Pope?"

"Premed."

"Is he smart enough to be a doctor?"

"Yes, very. I talked to him. He's just incredibly naïve about women and life in general. What are you thinking, Abraham?"

"You talked to him when you were with the police?"

"Yes, and before, when we first met at my club."

"Where was he going to school before Pope recruited him?"

"St. John's, in Queens, why?"

"If he sticks with it at St. John's, and his grades are reasonably good, I can get him into

Harvard Med. I have an old classmate, a neurosurgeon at NYU, who's got pull there. I'll cover his tuition, but he has to work for his books and living expenses. You know what they say. Idle hands are the devil's workshop. That'll keep him out of trouble."

"How very generous of you, my husband. I promise I won't ask you any more questions about what you plan to do about his former boss."

"That's smart of you, Vivian. I always gave you credit for common sense. One thing I will ask of you, dear. Please do not unpack your bags. Tomorrow we leave for Russia. I've made arrangements for us to stay in my absolute favorite accommodations in the world, the recently opened Hotel Ukraine on the Moskva River. I have some fur trading business to attend to while we're there. You can help me pick out sable and ermine for them to ship back to me here in New York. I won't lie to you. I have another, darker matter to attend to with some extremely rough men, which I intend to handle alone. It won't take but a few hours. After that, I'm all yours for as long as you want to stay and enjoy the caviar, the vodka, and the spacious bed in our hotel suite."

"Enough about beds, Abraham. If we're going to leave America tomorrow, we'll have to get some solid sleep tonight. You've had your rest, so let's get cranking."

She kissed him once again, tenderly, on the

mouth.

He kissed her back and conceded, "Work all day, work all night."

---

"How's my favorite patient?" Cavuto asked Alice when she appeared at the door of his funeral home.

"Healing well, thank you."

"Come in, please."

She did.

"I want to say again how sorry I am about the loss of your nephew, Mr. C. He was a good kid, Johnny was. I liked him. It's unfortunate."

"Thank you for saying so, Miss White. You're a very thoughtful woman. I appreciate that about you. We were close, my nephew and me."

"Please tell the rest of your family I send my regrets."

"I will, certainly."

"I'm also here to express my gratitude for your help with the Michael Pope affair. Without you and your friends, I would never have convinced him to bet on the wrong horse."

"There's no problem, young lady, that together we cannot solve. You're a precious friend. What other beautiful woman would we have to play bocce for in the summer if you didn't sit up there on that iron fence?"

"You're making me blush, Mr. C. I suppose I'm going to have to accept the fact that I need help from other people if I want to keep doing what I do."

"You are correct, my dear. You will need help from time to time. We all do. Trust is not an easy thing to give another. So many people let us down. There's not many you can rely on. But, in the little time we've known each other, it has become clear that you are one of us. Just remember the old Italian saying: 'Friends are nice, but always carry a gun . . . in case your friends get delayed in New Jersey.' You know what I mean."

"I'll remember, Mr. Cavuto. I do carry a gun. In fact, it's on me right now in the small of my back. That's a hilarious saying, though. I have to remember to tell it to my friend Antonio."

"Alice, call me Roberto. I have a feeling you're gonna barge in here with your troubles from time to time. I don't want it to be awkward for you. And, I think you'll find my wife, Tina, to be a good listener and a trustworthy adviser if I ever get stuck in

New Jersey and you need help right away. You should make friends with her. She's saved my mozzarella more than once."

"Gee, uh, Roberto, thank you. I'm honored."

"It comes at a price."

"I understand, Roberto. I will come running if you call me."

"You are indeed fast on the uptake. It may never happen, but I will count on you if I need your help, counselor."

"Counselor. I like the sound of that. You have already cleaned up a gunshot wound in my arm on your embalming table, and now you and your friends have helped me out in an impossible situation. The young man is exonerated and may be reunited with his fair maiden if she will have him."

"Ha. That is the question, is it not? I would not trade places with that young fellow for all the world. He's in for some serious pain, especially if he loves her, which I suspect he does. Young men are so easily distracted. I doubt he will ever be so distracted again."

"I think Susan is still hurt and angry, but yet, at least, sort of open-minded. He owes her his freedom, which I do not envy him, either. We found out who killed the girl they framed him for murdering. They have him in custody."

"Excellent. Speaking of Mr. Pope, I wonder where he has gone. The police are looking for him to arrest him. He took money from the furrier, Abraham Schumann, who must be conducting his own search."

"I wonder how much of his life Pope has spent running," Alice asked.

"Guy like him? A lot, but he keeps coming back for more. He's like a bad penny."

She observed, "Pope played this guy Schumann for a fool. Schumann doesn't seem like a man I would want to cross, even by accident. You ask me, Stanley Kramer is lucky to be alive."

"Another old saying," Cavuto said. "'He who laughs last . . .'"

"I know, '. . . laughs best.' I don't feel sorry for Michael Pope, if that's what you mean," she replied. "In the end, I have no doubt; he will get what is coming to him."

"Don't be so sure, Alice White. Life is not a fairy tale. If the man is well hidden and planned long enough in advance, he could be safe for years. It's not true that there's no place to hide. Even so, watch the papers."

"You and your friends are enjoying this, aren't you?"

"We're immigrants, Alice. No one handed us

nothing. We were grateful to be here in America, and we did what we had to do to provide for our families. We make no excuses. Life is not always pretty."

"I think I understand."

"I think you do too. Mind your business, and don't worry about people getting what they deserve. Sometimes they never do—I mean, get what they deserve. You'll be a happier attorney if you keep that in mind. Meanwhile, try some of my latest batch of wine," Roberto offered.

"I'd love some. I'm not too fond of the threat of Pope still being out there, Roberto. Ever since I was taken, I haven't felt completely safe. There's a guy who walked me down here waiting for me outside."

"I understand. Keep taking precautions. No matter what I said, I have a feeling things will work out sooner than you think. Stay awake and keep your gun loaded and attached to your body like your friend told you. Even on the subway, have someone with you and at the entrances to your building, until we hear Pope's been taken care of. Not like you did when you went out to eat! Go back to your studies. Make us proud. What are your intentions with that man you been keeping company with?"

"God, Roberto, you're standing in for my late father. I don't know, Roberto, maybe I'll throw him back in the river?"

"You love him?"

"Yes."

"There you go. But you cannot use the Catholic church because you have both been divorced."

"Who said anything about marriage?"

"Right you are. It's none of my business. I got carried away, being your father. Drink up."

Roberto clinked his tumbler of wine to hers. "Salute," he said.

---

"Hello," Susan answered the phone.

Listening.

"Yes, Stanley. I know exactly how long it's been since we were handcuffed together in that dreadful room."

More listening.

Alice was standing beside Susan. She had stopped by for a visit. She had her hand on Susan's shoulder, smiling at the restraint her friend was displaying.

"I am not going to meet you someplace private. You want to meet, we're gonna do it in public, someplace with witnesses. What do you want with me anyway, Stanley? You've got places to go and things to do. Why would you want to spend time with a peasant like me? You've got to clean up the mess you made when you dumped all your friends and your family members for a life of wealth and power. After everything that's happened, you can understand how I might have trouble trusting you."

She listened some more. "I tell you what. Get us a booth at Jan's ice cream parlor on Fordham Road. Don't even think about coming here to pick me up. I'll meet you there in two hours, maybe. If I'm not there," she said, "start without me." She hung up.

Alice laughed out loud. "That gives us plenty of time to get you ready," Alice told Susan. "Step into my office"—she motioned toward the bathroom—"We'll start with your hair and makeup."

Stanley hung his phone up. He was in physical pain from the exchange. It was the best he could expect, he supposed, considering how badly he had treated her. He was grateful she even agreed to meet him—maybe—and didn't just hang up the phone when she heard his voice. He had never seen this side of her. He had completely ignored the damage he did to her pride, just disappearing the way he had. He deserved whatever he got, including nothing at all. Go ruin some other woman's life, she should say. He'd never thought of Susan as assertive, but by mistreating her, he had created a monster, a monster that had just verbally abused him as he had never been abused before. At least one of them no longer felt sorry for him. This was a different woman, dangerous, capable of inflicting great pain. Endless humiliation awaited him if he pursued her. He owed her more respect than he had ever shown her and, God help him, perversely, the beating he had just received made him want her more than he ever had.

It was warm out with the season change, but there was no spring in Stanley's step.

He entered Jan's through the massive glass door at the front and sat down alone in a dark burgundy-colored leather booth, as far back as he could find. A popular Bronx meeting place near Fordham Road, Jan's was famous for its "Kitchen Sink," loaded with as much ice cream as could fit in the tub it was served in. They also served hamburgers and a limited variety of sandwiches. There were already a fair number of people scattered throughout the establishment, more of an audience than he cared for.

He sat self-consciously alone for some time after the appointed hour, fighting the urge to flee and the aura of impending doom as best he could. He had to face the guilty reality that this was nothing compared to the pain the lonely, defenseless young woman had experienced at his hands. She no longer seemed quite so defenseless.

How could he have been so blind? After he had unlocked the handcuffs that bound them together, he had taken a good look at her. Despite her hair being messed up and the fact that she was boiling over with resentment at him, she was a beautiful woman and a better person than he deserved. Why had he not seen that before his infantile urges almost cost them their lives?

While he was musing over his many defects, Susan arrived at the entrance. He saw her. She pushed open the heavy glass door and walked in. She was wearing a simple blue denim jacket, but he could see she looked amazing even at this distance. He twitched uneasily at the sight of her. She was made up like he had never seen her before. As she walked toward him, she opened the jacket partway, like a runway model, revealing the most feminine outfit he had ever seen her wear. He was stunned. She was more beautiful than any woman in Michael Pope's employ.

He tried to pull himself together, but his legs felt like Jell-O, and his mouth had gone dry. He rose in a sudden jerky movement, banging his thigh into the table and almost overturning it. His face caught fire, turning beet red, as he grabbed the edge of the table to prevent it from crashing to the floor. He regrouped and tried to get control of his breathing.

None of this was lost on Susan. She tried not to laugh, maintaining a sphinxlike expression. She paused to twist the knife of what she and Alice had accomplished into his gut, then continued toward the table. She gave him no chance to take her jacket, sliding it off her shoulders herself to reveal a mind-shattering, yet tasteful, ensemble that Alice had put together. Alice had convinced her to get over her self-consciousness. She wore a short black skirt with nylon stockings and a white cotton blouse, buttons tastefully, but revealingly undone at the top. A small gold cross on a delicate chain lay against Susan's exposed chest. She threw her jacket into the opposite end of the booth from where Stanley stood and slid in after it, giving Stanley a good look at the shortness of the skirt and the intoxicating seams of her stockings. Half the patrons were falling out of their booths staring at her. She sat facing him, her lashes thickened with mascara that she had never worn in her life. Her cheeks were slightly rouged. A single pearl pierced each earlobe. Her lips were coated with red lipstick. Stanley thought this was it. He was actually going to have a stroke. His gums ached with longing for her.

Having missed his opportunity to take her jacket or offer her a hug or a handshake, he stood awkwardly at attention for a moment, then sat back down. If she had taken a baseball bat to his entire body, she could not have inflicted more physical abuse.

"Well, I'm here." Susan broke into his stunned silence.

People tried to look away and give the couple some privacy, but they could not. Twenty strangers listened intently to their every word.

"Uh, yes, Susan." Stanley had reseated himself with minimal destruction of limb or property. "It's so good to see you again. You look . . . beautiful."

"Oh, this old outfit. I never got a chance to wear it with you since we never actually went out on a date."

His face could not accommodate much more blood.

"Would you like me to order us something?"

"I'm not sure I'm staying, Stanley. What is it you wanted to say to me?"

"Uh, well, God, Susan. You look terrific." He was aware he had lost control of his mouth. He did not want to give her an excuse to get up and leave, especially with this cast of thousands listening in and staring at them like they were in the finals at

Wimbledon.

He went on, "I'm sorry for the way I treated you. I wouldn't blame you if you just got up and walked out of here. I was selfish. I didn't think about how my actions would affect anyone but myself. There's no excuse for my behavior. Please give me a chance to make it up to you."

"You're right, Stanley. There is no excuse. You made me feel ashamed of myself for ever being with you, and then, ta-da, blessedly and mightily angry at you for deserting me without a word."

Stanley thought he heard a collective groan of disapproval from the crowd. They were going to lynch him without a trial.

Susan asked him, "What makes you think I could ever forgive you or trust you again?"

He looked at her. The sight of her was killing him. His heart was breaking seeing how beautiful she was and thinking that he might never see her again, that this mob might drag him out of the restaurant and beat him to death for mistreating such a beautiful woman.

He needed to say something to save this meeting. "Susan. To think of the suffering I caused you, and what I did to my parents and friends in my selfishness, is beyond my ability to forgive myself. I don't know how, or if, you and I will ever get past this. But, I'll tell you, I'm a new man, and I desperately want to. I don't expect you to take my word for that. Please, don't send me away. Give me a chance to show you I've changed. I don't know if it's possible for me to make up for what I've done to you, but if you give me a chance, I'm willing to die trying."

He looked out at the crowd and saw that some of them were looking hopeful. He would never be able to come here for ice cream again.

"Let me take you to the zoo sometime, and maybe downtown for lunch, in daylight, so you feel safe. I won't touch you. I'm so grateful for what you and your friend, Alice, did to get me out of the mess I was in. I will never forget your generosity as long as I live. I promise if it doesn't work out between us, I'll understand and leave you alone. I'll even leave New York if you want me to, but please consider giving me a chance to show you I'm sincerely repentant, and that I would never do that to you, or any woman, ever again, as long as I live, so help me God. You have all these witnesses who will swear under oath, I'm sure, that they heard me promise you." He swept his arm at the audience, some of whom were applauding timidly.

"If you can think of anything I can do to make it right between us," he went on, "I beg you to tell me."

"Okay, okay, Stanley. Lighten up. Geez. You're breaking my heart." She raised her voice. "You can never make it right, so don't even try. You deserve to suffer. Believe me, I thought about letting you rot in that situation you got yourself into. I'm surprised Alice helped you at all. She must have had a mental lapse. I don't know what to do with you, Stanley. I've changed since you've been gone. I'm not the woman I was."

"Give him a chance," a female voice from the rabble pleaded.

"I can see that, Susan," Stanley said.

"Would you all please go back to what you were doing? We need some privacy here. Thank you for your kind attention."

Everyone in the place turned away but kept their ears open.

Susan spoke low, in almost a whisper, "I was a doormat when we were together. I suppose that was not entirely your fault. I wasn't brought up to think much of myself. Your boss, Pope, sent a boy to romance me. I'm sure now he was using me to threaten you, but while he was pretending to like me, I felt worthwhile at the lowest point in my life. When I found out he was a phony, I broke it off, but I didn't lose the confidence he had given me, and for that, I am honestly grateful. Of course, like you did, he ended up hurting me, almost killing me, in fact. Men are scum sometimes. I don't know, Stanley."

"Don't make up your mind right away, Susan. Take all the time you need. I hardly expect you to act like none of this happened."

"You know, Stanley, you may have done me a favor, dropping me like a bag of dirty laundry."

"Please, Susan. You're killing me."

"Yeah, well, maybe someday you'll get over it. As I said, you may have done me a favor. My spine seems to have grown stronger and straighter. I've been so weak, afraid to make a mistake. How much I thought I had to please you. What a moron I was. I don't feel like that anymore."

"You aren't that way, Susan, believe me."

"Call me sometime. We'll go to the zoo if you want. Meanwhile, make what peace you can with your parents and your friends. I'll be around. Enjoy your lunch."

With that, Susan grabbed her jacket, slid out of the booth, and gave him and the other patrons something to stare at as they watched the swing of her hips move toward the door.

# CHAPTER 28

## ISLAND IN THE PACIFIC

"Chester Baker" had lived on a little spread with his girlfriend, Darlene, for two weeks. It was on the island of Kauai, part of the Hawaiian chain, in the Pacific Ocean. They were far from the hustle of the government buildings, hotels, and bars of Honolulu and Waikiki Beach on Oahu. They hardly saw anyone besides each other and their one servant, Akino, but they intended to lay low as long as it took for the heat to die down. Their isolation was not entirely without benefits. They had enough groceries and alcohol laid in for a month. The view was spectacular. They were finally able to touch each other after more than a year of separation. It could have been a lot worse.

The two of them sat on the beach sipping Mai Tais made of rum, curaçao, and pineapple juice, shaded from the afternoon sun by a large banyan.

"Oh, honey," cooed his companion, "I've been waiting so long to be with you. Just the two of us on 'A little island in the Pacific and everything about it is terrific,' whiling away the time, together, with all the money in the world to enjoy it for as long as we need."

A year ago, Michael Pope and his mistress had slipped out of New York to purchase the house and the few surrounding acres of beachfront property in paradise. Darlene took up residence with their single servant and bodyguard, Akino. Akino was a three-hundred-fifty-pound Hawaiian, jack of all trades, strong as three gorillas, who lived in an outbuilding nearby. Every day he bench-pressed more than his weight in a makeshift gym he had put together long ago. These past weeks he had spotted Michael Pope at the weight bench on a few occasions, using a quarter of that weight. The weak, small, arrogant man from the mainland was, in the local language, a "haole," a derogatory term for one who is not a native Hawaiian and who did not drink half enough beer to qualify even as a "kamaʻāina," a longtime resident.

Before they left New York, they had taken the trouble to obtain amateur radio licenses and install receivers and transmitters with a thousand watts of power at both ends. They stayed in touch with brief shortwave contacts in Morse code, using telegraph keys. Pope did not even trust long transmissions, let alone telephones which could be traced and his hideout blown.

He'd left her plenty of cash to furnish the place and pay for supplies. There were now two million dollars hidden under the house, accessible only through the trapdoor under a rug in the bedroom. Now her man was here with her, safe and protected from the last person he had stolen money from and from the law. It was too bad the severance pay for his former employees had been lost in the double cross at the track. If he had won, he was not sure he wouldn't have taken that for himself, also. His consolation lay in the fact that Pete Reynolds would extract his pound of flesh from those who had betrayed him, especially the meddlesome Miss Alice White, of the Grand Concourse in the Bronx, New York. He had heard no news of her kidnapping or of her successful escape. He was cut off from everything in this God forsaken jungle he was now trapped in. Paradise the natives called it. Hardly. Vinnie Bagalucci, he figured, had vanished without a trace, but sooner or later he would be found and made to pay for his betrayal.

"Yes, Dar. Here we are. This is the life. All the sun, pineapple juice, and exotic cocktails we could ever want, living on the beach like aborigines. I suppose I could get used to this."

"Honey, you sound restless. Is mommy gonna

have to take you inside and show you how good life in retirement can be?"

"In a little while, baby. God knows there's no rush. Where do we have to go? I've only been here a few days, and already I'm losing my mind. Some things never change. I'm not used to all this quiet. I miss the sound of traffic, the smell of exhaust, the skyline. This retirement thing is harder than I thought it would be."

They sucked their drinks to the bottom of the glasses. Akino heard the sound of their empty straws gurgling and came over.

"Maw drinks, Boss Man?"

"No, Akino. We're going inside. Why don't you take these glasses away and wander out on the road for a smoke, so the sound of us rutting around doesn't disturb you? Give us an hour."

Darlene took his hand and led him toward the house.

An hour later, Chet Baker was sated, lying naked under a sheet on the huge bed in the master bedroom, hands clasped behind his head, gazing out the French doors at the bushes outside. He was loose as a goose. He smiled with satisfaction. Darlene came out of the bathroom, grinning widely.

"That was quite a workout, my big Hawaiian mon," she said. "We never made that kind of noise in the city. I trust you're feeling better. I certainly am. I knew retirement would agree with you. Beautiful beaches and barnyard behavior works every time."

"What're we having for supper?"

"Steaks on the grill. Akino got the best, and a bottle of your favorite red."

"Chester" listened without responding. He spun off the bed and slid on a pair of shorts. He'd been eating nonstop with nothing but the bedroom for entertainment, so the shorts were snug. He had had a few workouts with Akino, but it wasn't the same without Lenny to egg him on.

"Ready for more sun?" Darlene asked him.

"Not yet. I'm gonna sit out on the front porch and flip through some magazines for a while." He grabbed a couple off the chest of drawers and left the bedroom.

*It's only been a few weeks,* she thought, *and he's already bored.* What more could she do? How was she going to keep him entertained for the months, maybe even years, they would have to stay here waiting for things to cool off back home? He would lose his mind on this island, and she would lose hers with him. Other women? Maybe, but that would never satisfy his appetite for the kind of risk that had led to his recent loss at the track.

Yes, the great con artist had been hustled. The pretty girl from the Bronx, Alice White, was the bump, in pickpocketing language, the distraction. His good pal, Vincent Bagalucci, was the dip, the one who had lifted Michael's wallet. How could he not have seen it coming? How many hundreds of times had he arranged just such a setup on other people? He was losing his touch. He needed this forced vacation to get his edge back, but she was the last person he needed to hear that from. She valued her life too much.

Darlene stood and looked down at the scene of their antics, the wrinkled sheets, the stains. It took stamina and experience to carry on that long with such intensity. The exertion would have killed lesser people she thought proudly.

Trying and failing not to become desperate, she was getting worn out. She stood, with no clothes on, letting the breeze from the lanai cool and calm her. That was the nice thing about living in the middle of nowhere, far from prying eyes. They could walk around naked as jaybirds anytime, day or night.

From behind her, a huge arm wrapped around her neck and pressed against her windpipe, threatening to cut off her air supply. A large calloused hand covered her mouth to prevent her from screaming. She knew enough not to struggle.

A Russian accent spoke low into her ear, "Keep trap shut, lady. Plenty of time to scream after."

He must have been on the lanai while she and Michael were making their racket. A second man passed by them like a shadow on his way through the room to the house's interior. As he exited, Darlene spotted an automatic with a silencer hanging from the hand at his side. She did not want to listen, but that was not her choice to make. Akino, she thought, must be dead. She tried to think of something to take her mind off what was about to happen. Coconuts, palm trees, nothing gave her a moment of relief from the terrible certainty.

A few weeks. That's all they had to show for a year of separation, and before that, years of hard work. How had these men even found them? But she knew from her time with Pope that there was nothing that money could not buy, including information. She had better get her head into gear because she would not have much time to beg these men for her life.

*Pfft. Pfft.* The shots sounded clearly through the Hawaiian air. Her heart sank. Tears poured from her eyes. Terror gripped her stomach.

The shooter came back. "Mission accomplished boss," he said in an equally thick Russian accent.

The gravelly Russian voice behind her said,

"Take hand off your mouth. Scream all you want. No one to hear you now. The big man on the road is dead too."

The arm released her. She did not scream, but she sat down on the edge of the bed to keep from falling. Her whole world was gone in an instant.

She looked up at them. They were large. The second man just stood there with his pistol at his side.

The one who had grabbed her asked, "Where money, lady?"

"What money? There's nothing here. We lost everything on the mainland. That's why we came here. To think of a way to get it back."

He ignored her. "Buried, I think."

The shooter came over and put his gun to her temple.

"Under the rug you're standing on."

"That better."

The talker stepped off the rug and peeled it back from the floor. He lifted the metal ring set into a depression in the wood and heaved a trapdoor open to reveal bundles of crisp hundred-dollar bills.

"How much?"

"Two million," she said. "More or less."

"Excellent. One million for our friend,

Schumann, what your boyfriend steal from him, and one million for us tracking it down. It is good; we do not go home with empty hands. If we dared, it would not have gone well for us."

The talker continued, "What are we going to do with you? You know we outside window whole time you make love. You think you can forget us?"

"Yes," she sobbed. "Of course, I can. I'll never talk. You've got the money. You will never hear from me again. I promise."

The men looked at each other and grinned.

"I dragged body inside," the second finally spoke. "We have time before we need to go."

# CHAPTER 29

## LUIGI'S ITALIAN RESTAURANT AND BAR

The night air was that wonderful moderate temperature of spring. You could see the bar at Luigi's through the front window. Laborers and businesspeople were having a few drinks on their way home from the subway up the hill, on the Concourse. Most of them lived in the modest wood-framed houses and tenements that lined this narrow lane. The linoleum in their kitchens may have been curled at the edges from age and mopping, but they were grateful for a home to crowd children, parents, and grandparents together inside here in the New World.

It was May of 1957. The window of the bar was framed, at great expense, with black Italian marble imported by the so-called "organized" relatives, in Manhattan and on Long Island, of these hard-working immigrants. Their wealthier relatives also provided sentries who wore silk suits and sat playing music over the radio, reading paperbacks, or going over racing sheets in expensive late-model cars throughout the neighborhood. Jaguars, Mercedes-Benzes, and shiny new Cadillacs never moved from their parking spaces, engines running in winter for heat, now silent with their windows down to let the fresh air in. The glow of lit cigarettes was visible by passersby. Occasionally a ceiling light went on to better study a racing form. The young men were unimpressed by the alternate-side-of-the-street parking regulations of the Sanitation Department, who swept the streets around them without complaint.

    Alice and Jim arrived early. They stood out front for a while, holding hands, appreciating the men—and the lone neighborhood woman—seated at the bar in subdued but joyful camaraderie. The wiry bartender moved smoothly and quickly, left to right and right to left, to pick up empty glasses, take orders, pour liquor, make change for the paper money pinned under the ashtrays, and interject sage advice into ongoing conversations, which Jim and Alice could not hear through the glass.

    Inside, at the hostess podium, Alice greeted the owner's wife. "Hello, Mrs. Luigi. How nice to see you on such a lovely evening."

    "You're funny, Alice. 'Mrs. Luigi.' You know

that's not my last name, right? It makes Luigi laugh when you call me that. You are a pleasant addition to our regulars tonight, unwinding after a hard day moving cargo at the docks, driving trucks, manning factories, staffing offices. It's my job to get them home, into the arms of their waiting families, not too drunk. Maria, over there finishing her drink, you don't know her. She's a recent widow, but even she must get home to her children and her parents holding supper for her. 'Mr. Luigi' and I had a bunch of these folks, and their families, over last Sunday. As many as could make it came for veal, to celebrate the change of seasons. We've done well here in the Bronx, so we like to share our good fortune with our countrymen and women. God bless America."

Alice said, "I'd like to be as grateful as you are for this wonderful country I was born into. Sometimes I take it for granted. You make me remember how precious it is."

"I see you two got here early. The back room is all set up for you and your friends. Giuseppe is in the kitchen, going over your menu with the chef. Big party, huh. That's nice, eh. The policeman and the pregnant widow are getting married, and you are graduating law school. Wow, Alice. You're a neighborhood celebrity. Everyone knows about you knocking that robber out in the garage last year and saving the owner. You got a black mark, though, 'cause you lost the customs man, the father of the baby. He was under your protection. It discouraged new business from the neighborhood for a while, but you got hired anyway by the purse-snatch lady and saved her man. Not bad."

"Gee Mrs. L., I'm glad to know I provide food for the neighborhood gossip machine, but the 'purse-snatch lady' did not actually hire me. She and I got to be friends. It was an accident I got involved at all. News of my escapades travels fast. I'd better behave myself."

"They talk about everything in here, sometimes late into the night if we let them stay, if their families are okay with it . . . and if they promise to get home safely. It's a good way for us to spend our time. We can't stand the television. Three channels are all we get, with interference, I should add, and soap operas and the same ads over and over. 'You don't have to go to univers-ity to know what you should drink when you are 'thirs-ity!' I sing that in my head all day."

"I don't even have a television," Alice told her.

"You two still take a drink, right? You told me the detective is on the wagon, and his pregnant lady keeps him company. You want a little wine?"

"Sure," Jim said. "You know, you've been so good to Alice, and you say you don't like television.

So, how would you like to see a Broadway show sometime? I build sets for a living you know? *Mame* is the last show on Broadway I built the stage sets for. Of course I had a lot of help."

"Alice, you better keep him. Sir, you are so kind. I'll check with my husband directly and get back to you, but I would love to go. Thank you for your sweet invitation."

"It doesn't have to be at night," Jim said. "They do matinees too."

"I may divorce Luigi and marry this guy, Alice. By the way, our last name is Cantori. I'm Helena. You're a very nice man. I'm so glad Alice finally met a gentleman to bring her in here. She's a lovely girl, and I was sad seeing her always eating alone. She's too young. She's too beautiful. I hear her call you Jim. You can call me Helena."

"It's nice to meet you, Helena," Jim told her. "Alice loves your place. Now I understand why. I hope you'll be seeing me around for a very long time. Alice is slowly getting used to the idea herself. I'm extremely fond of her."

"You know, Alice," Helena said, "you are still young enough to have a child or two."

"Please, Mrs. H. C., in keeping with your new name. We're not even married. Take it easy with my reproductive organs. A lot of people have been giving me advice lately about what to do with them. Everyone, especially my mom, seems to have an opinion. Mom will be here shortly, if she takes the right train. This has been a big step in itself, bringing this man here to my private sanctuary. Besides, I think I'm entirely too selfish to have a child. It's a stretch for me even to date a man this long."

Helena raised two fingers in a V across the restaurant to the bartender, with a grip indicating the stem of a wineglass. He got the message and produced two glasses of red wine, handing one to Alice and one to Jim.

"On me," Helena told them.

"Thank you," Jim accepted. "Would you mind if we sit in a booth for a while before our guests arrive?"

"Not at all," Helena told him. "You two are a beautiful couple. It fills my heart to see you together. Come back for dinner sometime, and my husband and I will join you. Sit close to the front window with your wine. It'll be good for business."

Alice knew Luigi's Italian Restaurant and Bar, in this southern Italian enclave, would have a place in her heart for the rest of her life. The marble storefront, the busy bar, the white tablecloths, the soup spoons for twirling spaghetti, the generous wineglasses, the awkward politeness of the mobsters having dinner, guns bulging under their jackets, sometimes with other thugs, sometimes with their families. Then there was the aged Giuseppe, still waiting tables, and the stories of listening devices regularly cleared from the undersides of chairs and tables, behind paintings on the walls, inside light switches and fixtures. They found them in both the restaurant and the big banquet room where Alice entertained friends from time to time. How did the law manage to plant those things in such a well-guarded place? She often thought about what the tapes they made sounded like. Murder being plotted, sometimes at the request of important people in the city. Tapes that were so hot they needed to be erased by the cops immediately after they heard what was on them, God forbid ever to be used in court. It was insane, the intermingling of ordinary people, law enforcement, and mobsters in one place. It shook Alice's belief not in justice itself, but in the justice system. It was the stuff detective fiction was made of, yet who was she to judge? She was involved in it as much as anybody here. Frankie "Windows," Roberto Cavuto, and their silent crime boss friend, she suspected, lived somewhere near Arthur Avenue, the Bronx's Little Italy. God knew who else they'd talked to about her escapades and got to help her behind her back. She was a regular gun moll herself.

The smell of garlic, tomatoes, onions, oregano, basil, parsley, and freshly baked bread made her swoon. If she ever left this neighborhood, she would miss the sense of family, of welcome, like she'd felt growing up in Queens when her father and brother were still alive. Her dad, Fred White, died from the smoking he'd started in the army. Philip died in action in Korea. His loss was still fresh, just a few short years ago, at times too painful to bear. They had been happy together in their childhood years in Queens.

Now, here in the Bronx, she often went out on her fire escape, looking up at the sky and down on this neighborhood with its smells and sounds—the banging of pots and pans, little kids screaming in delight or crying after a spanking, barking dogs of all kinds, honking horns to get people to unblock the narrow street from their double-parked cars.

"Oh, Jim," Alice said to her boyfriend. "I love you, and I love it here too. I want to move in with you in Manhattan, but how can I possibly leave these people? If my bed and my refrigerator weren't here, I'm not sure I'd come back to visit."

"Quite so," her robust reporter friend, Franklin Jones, opined, as he glided toward their table. "I don't mean to poke my nose into a domestic interlude, but I think this neighborhood is about as charming a place as I have ever been. If I didn't spend half my life at the paper, I would move up here in a second. It's the best combination of New York City and the Italian countryside. It's only because you live here, Alice, that I ever even get to see it."

"Dear Franklin." Alice smiled. After he kissed her on the cheek, she raised her wineglass to him. "That's why I read you in the paper. You capture the people and places of this city better than anyone I know. How are you?"

Franklin slid in next to Jim. He smelled of the cigarette he had smoked on his way from the subway station.

"Just fine, Alice. How are you two faring? I'm between girlfriends, so I came alone."

The bartender halted at their booth and deposited a cocktail napkin and an almost-full pony glass in front of the reporter.

The bartender told him, "Welcome to Luigi's, Mr. Jones. I read your column every single day. The whiskey is on the owners. I'll tell them about it if I see them." He bowed and departed.

Jones raised his glass to the bartender's back and took a sip.

"Franklin," Alice exclaimed, rising from her seat. "It's such a pleasure to see you here. Let us adjourn to the banquet room."

"I'm looking forward to dinner." Franklin took his glass and napkin. "I can still taste the food from the last time I was here."

The three of them moved between tables across the restaurant to the dark corridor leading to the banquet room. It was already set up with linen and flowers. Giuseppe appeared with a water pitcher, filled their glasses, and then filled the rest around the room.

"So, Franklin, how's the newspaper treating you?" Jim asked.

"Very well," Jones answered. "The show you're working on got a stunning review from our ordinarily stingy theater critic last week. I hope you had a chance to read it."

"I won't lie," Jim told him. "I didn't see it, but I heard your paper was very generous. Miss Russell was happy, but, let's face it, she would have been happy if you had panned it. She's a unique individual, loves her work so much she'd play to an empty house. I hope I'm learning something from her."

"Yes, Rosalind Russell is a special lady. There are not many like her around. I've never met the woman. Think you can introduce me?"

"Are you kidding, Franklin? Here's my card." Jim took out his wallet and handed Franklin a business card. "Give me a ring when you're free, and I'll set it up. I only build sets, but for some reason she knows who I am."

"Be assured," Franklin said. "I will take you up on your offer very soon. So, how are you two lovebirds getting on? Any plans for cementing your relationship more than it already is? I could get a photographer up here, and a judge, in an hour, or is marriage too mundane for you of the avant-garde?"

"Alice, you answer him," Jim said. "I am not qualified to speak on this matter, Franklin. She knows what I want, and I think you do too. There's nobody in New York State that doesn't know how I feel about her."

"Uh, we're working on it, Franklin. Okay?" Alice said. "It does appear that we're already joined at the hip. This man is willing to do anything I say, which was never my intention, but I like it very much. I can't shake him off. We're both so totally independent in every other way. I'm about to begin life as an attorney, so, as they say in the business, I'll take it under advisement."

"Really, Alice?"

"Don't push it, Jim. We'll talk about it later when we're alone, and I can yell at you if things get out of hand."

Franklin drained the rest of his drink. "My ex-wife used to say things like that to me all the time."

Alice's mother and aunt arrived. Cousin Frannie trailed behind them with a date.

Alice stood and embraced her mother, Rose, and her aunt, Betsy. She kissed her cousin and waited for an introduction. Fran rolled her eyes and said, "This is my friend Peter. Pete, this is my cousin, Alice, about to be the family lawyer when she graduates NYU Law School next month."

Pete extended his hand. "Pleased to meet you, Alice. I'm Peter, and I'm crazy about your cousin."

Fran blushed and rolled her eyes again.

"I am too, Peter," Alice told him, "so watch it. Treat her good or I'll find you and hurt you. Welcome to our gathering in honor of my friend and neighbor's imminent marriage and my graduation. She ought to be here any minute now. And Pete, she's pregnant, so try not to stare. It's a long story, which I'm sure Frannie will tell you if she hasn't already. Why don't you all take a seat, and Giuseppe will bring you some wine or whatever you want to drink?"

"Oh, my precious niece," Aunt Betsy said. "I consider myself my dear departed brother's representative when I wish you all the happiness, and money, in the world as you enter your new profession." She kissed Alice on the cheek.

"I appreciate that, Aunt Betsy, especially the part about the money. I will accept your wishes as if they were from my father. Now take a load off."

Antonio and Maria Vargas entered the room.

Maria wore a lightweight parka. Antonio hugged Alice but refused to kiss her, not even on the cheek. Maria wrapped her arms around Alice, gave her a kiss, and said, "Gee, Alice, it's always so beautiful up here in the Bronx. Congratulations on graduating from law school. Here is a little something I picked out for you. I hope you don't mind. I kept the receipt so you could exchange it for something less dramatic if you want."

Maria reached into her jacket pocket and extracted a small gift-wrapped box.

Alice opened it and lifted out a pearl necklace. "How beautiful, Maria. I love it. You shouldn't have." She hugged Maria and turned around so Maria could do the catch.

Antonio and Jim shook hands.

With Antonio's assistance, Maria slipped out of her jacket. Underneath, she wore a red dress with spaghetti straps. Her ears and neck were bare. She stood still for a moment smiling at Alice, unselfconsciously adorable. It took Alice's breath away how beautiful she was. Alice grabbed her again and kissed her. "Thank you for the thoughtful present."

The Vargases sat with Alice and Jim.

Elaine Applewood showed up with her fiancé, Andy Bennett.

Elaine told them, "It's so nice of you to put on a celebration like this." She put her hands on her protruding belly and asked, "Is there a doctor in the house?"

"That close, huh?" Alice inquired.

"Yes. I expect labor to start at any moment now. I hoped we could get married first, but what the heck."

"Sit down and relax, my friend," Alice said. "You might still make it."

The law partners from Alice's firm, with their families and secretaries, arrived en masse. They had met at the office and taken the subway up together. Giuseppe slid chairs back and forth for them and made his way around to take drink orders. He wrote nothing down. Without assistance, he delivered oval dishes of celery, radishes, and other vegetables. In a short time, he had them all seated and served with drinks and antipasto. Alice made a mental note to give him a large tip.

She surveyed the crowd, her family and friends, a tableau of the last ten years of her life, beginning when she'd lost her high-paying job at the department store in New Jersey to returning servicemen and sought employment as a secretary at the firm. Now here she was graduating law school, for heaven's sake. A glance at her mentor, Antonio

Vargas, reminded her that she was capable of great violence. He would be pleased to know that her automatic was, even now, pressed into the small of her back.

Alice rose and tapped her wineglass with a butter knife.

"Okay everybody, quiet down just for a minute. We're in my favorite restaurant. We're here to celebrate Elaine and Andrew's impending marriage, to be followed by the birth of their baby. Out of respect for Elaine's late husband, Harry, and with Andrew's permission, I agreed, heaven help the baby, to be its godmother, to share with it, as he or she grows up, the wisdom of a lifetime, for whatever that's worth. We're also here to celebrate my graduation from law school next month. So raise your water glasses, and your wineglasses, and let's toast to Elaine, Andrew, the baby, and me!"

# CHAPTER 30

## BEDTIME

"C'mon, Jim," Alice shouted from inside the closed bedroom door of her apartment. She had decided to put the top of his pajamas on in private. She was not one of the boys. Where these thoughts came from, she had no idea, but she was determined to act like a lady as much as possible and at least pretend a degree of shame.

"I'm a-coming." Jim's words were distorted by the toothbrush and toothpaste in his mouth. "Hole yaw hawses." He sprayed the mirror of the medicine cabinet with white foam.

"What?"

Jim removed the brush and spit. "I said, hold your horses. I'll be right there." The sound of brushing resumed, followed by swishing, gargling, and spitting. Jim splashed water on his face, dried it, then toweled off the mirror, the sink, and the floor around the sink, where water and toothpaste had mysteriously splashed. He turned off the light and came out of the bathroom in his pajama bottoms. He opened the bedroom door, scooted into bed, and wrapped his arms around Alice.

"Another perfect night in the Bronx," he exclaimed. "Your party was a success."

Alice said, suddenly all business, "Pope and his girlfriend are dead. They were shot in Hawaii, where they were hiding out. I called Antonio, told Susan Atkins, and asked Susan to tell Stanley."

"That's good news, I guess. I didn't mean that the way it sounded."

"I know what you mean, Jim. The man was a thief and a murderer, but it's still a shock to hear that he was hunted down and killed. Jim, would you turn off the light, please?"

He unwrapped himself from around her, got out of bed, and flipped the light switch off.

"Thank you."

"You're welcome, Alice."

He settled in, hugged her again and kissed her a few times, then sat upright in the dark with his back against the headboard of the bed. Alice sat up beside him and wrapped his arm around her shoulders. They turned to look out the open window on her side of the bed. She'd lock it before she fell asleep. The venetian blinds were raised all the way. No building in the neighborhood was high enough for anyone to see in. They gazed out at the star-filled sky.

"God, Jim. It's beautiful out tonight. The clouds are gone, and the sky is lovely."

"You sure you don't need anything from the kitchen?"

"Don't you dare move. Just stay right here and hold me. Are we gonna be this happy forever?"

"Maybe, but probably not, Alice. I think, though, we can come pretty darned close if we try."

"Really? Can we?"

"When I was eight or nine years old, I used to ride my bicycle to construction sites north of the Bronx. I think I knew, even then, I wanted to build things. If it were lunchtime, I'd sit with the men and listen to them talk. For crusty old guys, they were deep thinkers. They talked about women a lot, and romance, and sex, which I could not relate to then, but which later came in handy."

"Really, Jim, like what to do in bed? You mean some of your moves are not your own?"

"It's typical of you, Alice, to focus on that part

of what I'm trying to say, but now that you ask, yes, I owe some of my moves to old Irish construction workers who traveled from their country to New York to put up buildings in America."

"So what'd they say?"

"Well, I once heard one of them say his marriage was falling apart, and he couldn't stop it. They'd lost interest in each other, like Ann and me did, and maybe you and your policeman, Andy. When they were together, they fought all the time."

"That's what I'm afraid will happen to us, Jim."

"I know, Alice. Me too. It's what ended both our first marriages."

"What'd he do?"

"He said they stopped trying so hard to put up with each other and started spending time just sitting together like we're doing now. They refused to fight, and they slowly fell back in love. He said they figured they were expecting too much from each other."

"You think we could get through that?"

"Yes, I think maybe we could. We love each other."

"It would be worth a try, Jim. Do we have to get married?"

"No, Alice, I don't think we do. I haven't run

into that many happily married people, but maybe we could live together, do you think?"

"You mean like friends?"

"Yes."

"Like Claude Rains and Humphrey Bogart at the end of *Casablanca*?"

"Which one am I, Alice?"

"Well, Bogart is prettier, so I would be him. But let's go back to that thing you said about not having to get married. Do you really mean it?"

"Yes, Alice, I do. I've given it a lot of thought and put myself in your place. There's no reason we can't compromise. Marriage is all about the future anyway. It's enough that you're willing to be with me at all. Why push it? A woman like you could have any man she wants. I thought I was gonna be alone for the rest of my life, and I was okay with that. Then you came along and ruined everything. I'd be happy any way you want me."

"Gosh, Jim. That is so sweet. I don't mean to sound so relieved, but I am. I'm willing to risk living together even though we can't promise each other that it'll work out."

"Great, Alice."

"Where shall we conduct this relationship?"

"Spoken like the lawyer you're about to

become. How about here?"

"What, here in this apartment?"

"No, not in this apartment. It's too small for a long-term relationship. I've been thinking about it. How about a larger apartment in this same building?"

"Oh, Jim! That would be wonderful!"

"Please, Alice, for heaven's sake, don't cry. This is gonna take every ounce of love we have for us not to kill each other, even just during the move itself, let alone afterward. Think about each other's dirty underwear. It is not gonna be easy."

"Jim, I have a secret. I go into a cleaning frenzy before you get here, every time you stay over. There's a pair of my underwear that's been living under the mattress for weeks. I keep forgetting to put it in the laundry. You may not be able to stand what a slob I really am."

"Alice, it takes me hours to iron a shirt the way you like it. If we only have one iron between us, you'll have to make a reservation to use it. I leave dirty dishes in the sink, but I'll try to wash them."

"You're scaring me."

"I just want you to know what you're agreeing to."

"It would be a great help if you would try not to spray water all over the bathroom walls and floor every time you wash your face. I'm not sure how you even do that. I've tried to duplicate the exact splatter pattern you create, but I can't. It's a mystery."

"I just wiped the bathroom down. I'll do my best to remember. What do you say, Alice?"

"Jim, I think I love you more than I ever loved anyone in my life. There, I said it. The fact that you would give up the luxury of your place downtown and trudge up here every night to be with me is almost more than I can bear. I'm willing to give it a try if you are. We should notify the landlord."

"We have an appointment tomorrow morning to look at an apartment on the other side of the building."

"You rascal. How'd you know I'd agree?"

"I didn't. It was wishful thinking."

"You know, Jim, I uh, uh, love you. Now that the biggest decision of my life has been made, let us slide under the covers and demonstrate the truly immoral foundation of our arrangement."

"You are a barbarian, Alice."

"I am aware."

# ACKNOWLEDGMENTS

First and foremost, I want to thank my wife, Millie Allen Hirsch, who has stood beside me through thick and thin in my years of medical practice and, now, in my years as an author of detective fiction. She has graciously accepted the emotional vicissitudes of living with a stressed-out doctor and a writer. She's also had the patience to read the final drafts of my three books and the guts to tell me when words, paragraphs, or even entire chapters must be removed and/or rewritten. I am beyond grateful for your love and support, and I send it back to you with interest.

To my fans in Kentucky and all over the United States and Canada, I send my warmest thanks for your encouragement and appetite for my writing.

To my one and only, ever, writing mentor, Rich Krevolin, professor of screenwriting at USC and UCLA, thank you for believing that I could write someday . . . in a land far away, in the distant future, when I first got serious about learning the craft. He taught me about storytelling, about developing tension, about character arc, writing and rewriting ad infinitum until I got it right, experimenting with ideas and throwing out the ones that don't work, and writing cinematically, putting my readers in the room with my characters. Thank you for your patience, for teaching me patience, and for your inspiration.

Laura Hagan-Smith, Attorney at Law, has been invaluable in helping me understand the life of a woman in both law school and practice. She reviewed the courses and the choices with me, and she's also given me legal advice about my writing. Thank you.

My extreme gratitude to my friend Frank Smothers, one of thoroughbred horse racing's greatest jockeys. I could write a whole book about you. I want to thank you for your story, your imagination, and your tolerance of my difficulties in understanding the many aspects of thoroughbred horse racing as you explained them to me. He met me for breakfast on numerous occasions to discuss his own story and details of my book's plot. The character of Billy Smith is based on him.

Frank was rejected by the military at the start of WWII because, at four foot ten inches, he was too short, and at less than 100 pounds, he weighed too little, so he was approached at the recruiting station and offered a career breaking horses and racing for the likes of Bing Crosby in Southern California. Once he became established as a jockey, he grew taller and put on enough weight to be drafted into the war in the Pacific, finishing his service in the Second World War on Okinawa.

After returning to racing and reestablishing his

career, he was again drafted, this time into the Korean conflict, during which he developed malaria. That made it difficult for him to control his weight, and he was offered a new career as the superintendent of jockey rooms all over the country, starting primarily in California, at times alternating between Northern and Southern California, and in Kentucky, including at Churchill Downs.

In his nineties, he is still in charge of the jockey room at Kentucky Downs. I have exhausted myself following him around to capture the flavor of a jockey superintendent's responsibilities during a day of racing and the experience of the jockeys themselves, which I depicted as best I could in this book. Frank's agreement was most exciting to "announce" the climactic race of my story from the perspective of a jockey on the back of a horse in the race. My heart pounds when I read that segment. Thank you, man.

# ABOUT THE AUTHOR

Marc Hirsch was born in New York City in 1945. He grew up in the Bronx on the Grand Concourse at 205th Street, in Alice White's dirty white brick building, and walked down the hill, through the southern Italian enclave, to attend the Bronx High School of Science. He entered Boston University's School of Medicine in Boston's South End, adjacent to Boston City Hospital, and graduated in 1969.

Upon graduating, Dr. Hirsch moved to San Francisco to intern at the then Pacific Presbyterian Medical Center in Pacific Heights. The view from the main operating amphitheater was of the San Francisco Bay, including the Golden Gate Bridge and the island of Alcatraz, the abandoned site of the famous maximum-security federal prison.

In November of 1969, a group of heavily

armed American Indians of All Tribes overtook Alcatraz in protest of the extensive removal of their lands over the years by the federal government and the policy of "assimilation" of their tribal cultures into mainstream American culture, which had been instituted by the federal government shortly after World War II.

Dr. Hirsch was asked to travel to Alcatraz to treat illness among the Native Americans in those first days of their occupation. He was told that he was at risk of fine, imprisonment, and loss of his medical license. Thankfully, none of those things happened.

On arrival his first day, he was greeted by Richard Oakes, the on-island leader of the occupation, and Oakes's young niece. They took him on a tour of the abandoned facility, including of the staff quarters, the dungeons beneath the prison left over from its time as a Spanish fort, and, of course, Al Capone's cell.

A medicine woman accompanied him on his rounds to approve his treatments.

In the end, the cold drove many families off Alcatraz, but thousands of acres were subsequently restored to American Indian tribes, and the policy of assimilation was officially ended.

After training, Dr. Hirsch lived for several years in a small cabin on a cliff on an island off the

British Columbia coast. He bought cartons of used detective fiction from a bookstore on a neighboring island. He discovered the works of Raymond Chandler (Philip Marlowe), Dashiell Hammett (Sam Spade, Nick and Nora Charles), and Earl Derr Biggers (Charlie Chan), which he consumed voraciously at night by kerosene lamp. It was the first nonmedical reading he had done in many years and helped develop his lifelong passion for detective fiction.

Eventually, he returned to mainstream medical practice in California, New York, and finally Kentucky, where he retired in 2011 and lives with his wife, Millie, and writes his own detective fiction. Stay tuned for more of the same.

# COMING SOON:

## The Case of the Butcher, the Bank Robber, and the Blonde: Book 4 in the Alice White Series.

Daring, some would say reckless, law firm investigator and graduating law student, Alice White, takes on a murderous gang in 1950s New York City. A butcher and retired Marine war hero has been falsely implicated in a recent bank robbery and murder and Alice feels compelled to come to his aid.

## AND

## The Case of the Little Island in the Pacific: Book 5 in the Alice White Series

After taking her New York State Bar exam Alice White is escorted by her boyfriend to a remote island off the coast of British Columbia, in the Pacific Northwest, for a much-deserved holiday. Despite her best intention to stay out of trouble, and through no fault of her own, a businessman on a yacht anchored off the coast of the tiny island they are staying on is murdered and the extravagantly expensive diamond bracelet he had bought for his wife to celebrate their wedding anniversary has gone missing. Alice is asked to take on the investigation while the authorities are being summoned.

Visit www.marchirsch.com to buy Marc's other novels.

Made in the USA
Columbia, SC
01 August 2024